Medical Meeting

Also by Mildred Walker

FIREWEED

LIGHT FROM ARCTURUS

DR. NORTON'S WIFE

THE BREWERS' BIG HORSES

UNLESS THE WIND TURNS

WINTER WHEAT

THE QUARRY

MILDRED WALKER, 1905—

Medical Meeting

New York

HARCOURT, BRACE AND COMPANY

PRINTED IN THE UNITED STATES OF AMERICA

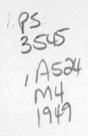
for Meg and Roger
who keep their souls from the lions

Part One

"*(With) the man who leaves the crowd and goes pioneering . . . is an idea, which is his life.*"

ROBERT HENRI

THEY had dinner at the Daltons' before going to the train. Liz hadn't wanted to come, but Hester and Carl had invited them. "We can't very well say no," Henry said. And tonight, as Liz sat in the Daltons' living room, a sense of pleasure lay beneath each simple thing: the taste of the sherry, the feeling of the slender glass stem between her fingers, even her glance around this room that had sometimes seemed to hold a threat. She moved her glass ever so slightly to catch the light from the fire, but carefully so it wouldn't spill on her new suit. Hester's Dalmatian dog came up to sniff at her shoes and skirt.

"Caesar smells the molds, I know, but he certainly makes me feel like a social outcast," Liz had complained privately to Henry. But tonight she rubbed Caesar's long black ears and forgave him.

"I wish we were going to Chicago with you," Carl Dalton said, smiling at her. "I should like to hear Henry give his paper."

"You must know the paper almost as well as Henry does," Liz said. She was fond of this quiet, gray-haired doctor who had been such a help to Henry, fonder of him because she didn't quite like Hester, his wife.

Henry called Hester "a restless female." "She loves Carl, I guess, in her own way, but she has a father complex and never should have married any doctor." Hester's father had been the eminent Dr. Ernest Murdoch of Baltimore.

Across the room Henry bent to light Hester's cigarette. She laughed at something he said and her olive-skinned face brightened.

3

"You know how I adore Henry," Hester often told Liz, and Liz pitied her because Henry wasn't too fond of her.

Hester always sat in the "throne chair" when she had guests. And Caesar always lay at her feet. If the guests were new in the house, she explained the chair, always in the same deprecatory tone that failed to deprecate. "This funny old chair was made by hand in Italy. They call it a 'Savonarola' chair. Father brought it back from one of his trips to Europe, and although it doesn't look it, it really is comfortable."

Liz often remembered how impressed she had been the first time she met Hester, that other spring when they had come here fresh from Henry's internship. Hester was a slender dark-haired woman in slacks and white shirt kneeling beside the tulip bed. When they drove up, she came across the lawn to meet them, pulling off her gloves and holding out her hand so cordially to them.

"You have my sympathy for coming way off up here. I loathe it." And then she had smiled so warmly, Liz had wondered if she had heard her rightly.

"We feel very fortunate in coming," Henry had said a little stiffly and gone across to the sanitarium to find Dr. Dalton.

"It's a good place to raise babies anyway. You might as well have half a dozen while you're here. There's little else to do," Hester had said, looking at Nancy in Liz's arms. And then Liz had followed her into this room that was as unexpected in the small town of Pomeroy as Hester Dalton herself: a decorator's room with each effect carefully planned. She changed it every couple of years. Liz glanced now at the chartreuse curtains lapping against the chocolate brown walls that flowed without any baseboard into the dark olive green sea of carpet. Oversize crimson cushions against the ivory couch made a slash of color

4

that was as abrupt as some of Hester's comments. But over by the window stood the shabby old leather chair with an ottoman in front of it. A table beside the chair was covered with medical journals and magazines and a can of tobacco. It had been there that first day. Then Hester had waved toward it and said, "Meet my husband before he comes. He is just like that chair."

And he was, Liz thought again as she talked to him. He was a big man, grown a little stout, in slightly wrinkled clothes, his clean white shirt collar frayed a little at one corner, his gray hair a little long. His eyes behind their horn-rimmed glasses were mild brown eyes, and his mouth had a patient look about it. He gave a good brand of medical care and divided his time about equally between the executive demands of the state sanitarium and the medical needs of its patients, and was as interested in ordering a better brand of tongue blade or sputum cup, and getting a better discount on them, as he was in lowering the mortality rate of his tuberculosis patients. He wasn't well, and he had no ambitions beyond staying here until his retirement. The small town, the poker games with a few cronies, the affection of his patients and their families filled his life satisfactorily even though these satisfactions of his sometimes irritated his wife. Hester had fallen in love with Carl Dalton as the promising young doctor on the private floor when she was threatened with tuberculosis as a young girl. If he was not so dramatic a figure as she had thought him, there was nothing he could do about it. And if life in this sanitarium in upstate New York was confining, she had a small income of her own so she could get away now and then both from the sanitarium and from him.

Liz had not known in the beginning how closely they would have to live with the Daltons. Henry had come as

5

assistant at the sanitarium because of some work he wanted to do. They had their own cottage across the grounds and to the back of the Women's Building, and there were times when she didn't see Hester for weeks, but still their lives were linked too closely.

"Mr. Cooper was here last night, Henry," Carl Dalton said.

"About my using the state sanitarium laboratory for research? I know, he called me about it and I told him that I wouldn't stay a week here if I couldn't carry on some investigative work. I told him that was why I came in the first place, and he backed right down." Henry felt himself growing angry and laughed a little apologetically.

"Oh, he's such a pompous old goat!" Hester said, lighting her cigarette. Hester was like that, but sometimes Henry found it a relief from Carl's conciliatory manner and Liz's worry about people's opinions.

"Well, you can see his point," Carl said. "He's worried about the taxpayers' money being used, as he says, 'for experimental purposes that aren't authorized.' You don't want to anger him, Henry. He's head of the Board, you know."

"And you knuckle under to him every time," Hester said.

When she flashed out like that at Carl, it embarrassed Henry, and yet there was some truth in it. Carl was too docile with his Board. He let them hold him up on so many projects that were to the advantage of the sanitarium. Sometimes they came around in the end, but that took so long.

Carl seemed not to hear Hester. "We'll take it up at the Board meeting and see if we can't get it smoothed over. I believe if you had told Cooper just what you were doing, taken him into your confidence a little more . . .

6

But you will have presented your work at the Chicago meeting by the time of the next Board meeting, and I can tell them how important it is."

"Oh, Carl, they're so stupid they wouldn't understand what he was doing!" Hester said. Carl pulled at his pipe without answering. Liz glanced at him uncomfortably. Henry thought Carl was used to Hester's way of sniping at him, but he looked annoyed all the same. The next time Hester was away, they must have him over. He always seemed to enjoy being there.

"They ought to be thankful the first time there's been anyone here who wasn't satisfied with complete mediocrity!" Hester stood up. "Come on, children, we must go in to dinner right away so we won't have to hurry."

Liz swallowed against the horrid trembling feeling she had.

Henry frowned. "You know, Hester, I couldn't have done anything here without Carl. He's handled the Board and let me have the material and really made the work possible." That sounded as though he were agreeing that Carl was mediocre but had been a help to him who wasn't! He fingered the button on his shirt uncomfortably.

"Ah, Carl, take a bow!" Hester said, waving her hand to him as she led the way into the dining room.

"Carl, I am sorry I didn't take pains to show Cooper something about the work," Henry said, lingering a moment outside the dining room door. "I suppose it's just that all along I've wanted to be very sure I had something before I told anyone."

"Of course, Henry." Carl laid his hand on Henry's shoulder. "I understand perfectly, but you can see his side of it."

Henry felt better. Perhaps Carl was so used to his wife's jibes that they didn't draw blood every time, but if Liz ever said a thing like that to him . . . Her back was turned toward him, but her smooth head reassured him. Of course, he was a little different from Carl too. He went quickly around the table to seat Hester. Caesar thumped down on the floor behind her chair.

There were white calla lilies in the low pewter bowl in the center of the table and the damask cloth was bottle green. Hester had dyed the cloth herself. No detail was ever too much bother when she was planning a room or a dinner. Even the clear glass ash trays were a careful note.

"How beautiful, Hester!" Liz said, looking at the lilies. Then she found the gardenias at her place. "Oh, Hester, thank you."

"Well, after all, this is an occasion," Hester said. "We had to have flowers and wine to start you and Henry off on this trip properly."

Liz saw Henry's pleased smile. "I'll remember this if I see people suspicious of microcydin, Hester."

"They're bound to be that," Carl said. "There have been so many false hopes and disappointments in tuberculosis."

Mrs. Plew, who came in by the day, spoke to all of them as she changed the soup plates. Mrs. Plew's son was one of the patients in Henry's microcydin report.

Liz, eating the steak that Hester had ordered especially from town and not taken from the sanitarium larder as she did the meat for ordinary meals, tasted Hester's envy with it. Hester wished it were Carl who was going to present a paper.

Mrs. Plew poured wine into their glasses, beaming as she did it at this piece of fanciness.

"I wish you would take my fur cape, Liz. It's covered by insurance and it's just the right weight over your suit. Chicago can be so raw in early April."

"Really, I couldn't, Hester. Borrowing an evening dress is bad enough," Liz said.

"Don't be silly; that's one I haven't worn in ages. I remember a Medical Meeting we went to one spring in Boston. I took my new spring things, and I tell you, I nearly died of the cold. Remember, Carl? You bought me a fur neckpiece while we were there."

"Yes," Carl said slowly. "That was when I heard Minot present his work on liver."

"I swore then that I'd never go to another Medical Meeting; Carl could just go alone. Whew, it was stuffy! Most of the women kept themselves busy hunting down antiques or buying new outfits or having their hair and faces redone." Hester moved her hands contemptuously. "Do you have something to look for, Liz? It's absolutely the only way to go on a trip: have something to look for and something to bring back. I've picked up these little glass ash trays on different trips. They're really old cup plates, you know. One came from a shop in Connecticut and I found one in New Orleans." Liz looked curiously at the small pressed glass plate at her place.

"It has Henry Clay's head on it," she said.

"Yes. Isn't he a pretty boy?" Hester laughed. "The mold was made for his election campaign in 1844, evidently, and even though he lost the election, there must have been enough people fond of him to hang on to their plates. These are real flint glass, but it's imitated in an ordinary cheap glass. You can always tell the difference, though." Hester had an exact mind that went into such detail over things that Liz was always impressed.

"But, of course, you don't need things to look for to keep this trip from seeming pointless with Henry going to present something really important. Carl never did give a paper. Carl, we haven't drunk a toast to Henry!"

9

"That's right." Carl pushed back his chair slowly and stood up. Henry's eyes studied the stamens of the calla lilies in embarrassment. Hester's lips moved silently as though she would form Carl's words for him. Liz smiled at Carl. "To your success, Henry, and confusion to all disbelievers."

"Thank you, Carl." Henry was standing now. "To our very good friends to whom we owe so much. But I still feel, Carl, that perhaps I should wait till I can report more cases over a longer period, or explain why the stuff works only in twenty-five per cent," he said as he sat down.

"Why, Henry?" Carl Dalton brought his hand down on the table so heavily the china rattled.

"Good gracious, Carl!" Hester exclaimed, but she was pleased. It was Carl's mildness that she minded in him most of the time.

"It isn't any flash in the pan when you've watched them long enough to know those patients are cured. If you don't report it, someone else will come along someday and stumble on the mold. You don't claim that it cures every case, but, my God, Henry, to cure twenty-five per cent that we couldn't help before is a miracle."

"Yes, it is," Henry agreed solemnly. "I saw Mrs. Watson just this afternoon and she hasn't had any recurrence."

"That's wonderful, Henry!" Hester said.

Liz watched the slow color rise in Henry's face. That was the way he had looked the day the microcydin had stopped the growth of the tubercle bacilli in the test tube.

"Henry, I'll never forget the day you were sure about Lester Small," Carl said. Lester Small was the first human Henry had treated with microcydin since his outlook was already hopeless. "You came back into my office, and we just sat and looked at each other for a while. You were as white as those calla lilies. And then you said, 'I've got to tell Liz,' and you were out of the building like a shot out of hell, and I stood at the window and watched you run across the grounds." Carl took off his tortoise-rimmed glasses and wiped his eyes. "I wrote Hester that it was like being there when Pasteur saved the Meister child with the first inoculations against hydrophobia."

"What were you doing, Liz, when Henry came to tell you? Of course, I would be away when all the excitement happened," Hester said.

"I was washing clothes, and I never went back to take them out of the washer till that night," Liz said, remembering how Henry had looked standing on the basement stairs, telling her that Lester Small was getting well. She had gone to him with her hands still wet and they had clung together, and then they had gone upstairs to the kitchen and Henry had eaten the first real meal he had had in a week.

"Remember and tell them that when someone comes to write up the story of the man who found the cure for TB. It will be a lovely colorful bit," Hester said.

Henry shook his head. "Don't put it that way, Hester. It isn't *the* cure. Carl has some remarkable cures to his credit. It's just that microcydin has cured cases of miliary TB and tuberculosis meningitis that are a hundred per cent lost without it," Henry said.

Hester shrugged and smiled at him. "Don't let him be too modest at the meeting, Liz. My father might have had the credit for thinking of the tick as a carrier of spotted fever if he had spoken up. But, of course, his career was distinguished enough as it was."

"Yes, indeed," Henry murmured and held his lighter for the cigarette she was tapping on the back of her hand. As she inhaled, she seemed to draw a rarer atmosphere into her lungs than any they breathed.

"Hester, we better have our dessert right now if we're going to have any," Carl broke in, looking at his watch. "These people have about three quarters of an hour before their train leaves."

Hester drew on her cigarette with a deliberation that rebuked him before she jingled the little bell for Mrs. Plew.

The old uncomfortable feeling Liz often had in this house crept into her mind. Carl and Hester seemed to be always so opposed to each other. Her life and Henry's could never be like the Daltons'; she could never be bitter and waspish. Henry would never lose his fierce driving interest in his work. She had told herself all this a hundred times, but she shivered involuntarily.

"You know, I told Mrs. Plew to take the ice cream out of the dry ice as soon as we sat down to dinner, but it's still frozen so hard it chills you through, doesn't it?" Hester said, seeing Liz shiver. "Drink your coffee and it will warm you up." They had their coffee in the Sèvres china cups Hester had brought back from Paris the time she had stayed nearly a year.

Henry stood in the hall putting on his coat when Hester came up to him. Carl had gone in to answer the phone.

"Hester, this was so thoughtful of you and Carl," he began, but Hester stopped him with a twist of her lips and a scornful toss of her head.

"Henry, here's a note for you. Read it when you're alone," she said mysteriously, slipping it into his pocket. Then she was gone again to come back with Liz. Henry took it out of his pocket to read at once and then thought better of it.

"This was a lovely way to start Henry off, Hester," Liz said as they went out to the Daltons' car. Her new gloves were smooth over her hands and the gardenias on the collar of her coat were fragrant.

"Let's see, you'll be in Chicago Thursday, Friday, and Saturday, and you'll be home Sunday," Carl said. "We'll put off the pneumos until Monday."

Thursday, Friday, Saturday, and they would be on the train part of Thursday, Liz thought with disbelief. She was looking forward to the trip as though it were much longer. Carl made it seem as though it were nothing.

"We'll meet you and bring you home for a late dinner Sunday night," Hester said. "We'll be crazy to hear all about it."

"Oh, no, Hester, you don't have dinner at night Sunday, and Henry will be anxious to get over to the sanitarium. We'll just drop in and see you for a minute," Liz protested, not wanting to think yet about being back.

"You can go home right after dinner," Hester said firmly. "We want to see you before you lose your look of the city. Why, you'll be famous by that time, Henry!" Hester's voice was a little shrill. Liz leaned her face down to smell the gardenias.

"Well, if you had another steak like that one tonight, Hester, I might weaken," Henry said. He saw suddenly how much Hester wanted to have a part in launching the microcydin, and he couldn't be indifferent, even though he caught Liz's eye and knew she wanted to go straight home when they got back.

"Liz, don't get too tied up in the women's doings and have a wonderful time," Hester said to Liz as they walked toward the train.

"Don't wait for the train to leave. Thank you both for everything," Liz said, her foot on the step of the Pullman. She wanted to be gone now, she and Henry together.

POMEROY SENTINEL
Dr. and Mrs. Henry Baker will leave
tonight for a Medical Meeting in
Chicago where the Doctor will present a paper.

THE train moved slowly past the station platform and
the people gathered there, waving, smiling, holding up a
child to see the engine. The light caught the gilt in the
sign at the end of the station, giving it its last chance to
shine until tomorrow night. "POMEROY," the sign read.
"Pop. 7,150, N.Y."

Already people were starting to leave, dropping their
hands in their pockets, turning back to their own lives.
They had the disorderly look of an audience after a con-
cert: some struggling into their coats or already in the
aisles, anxious to be gone; only a few still in their places,
applauding.

Liz leaned close to the window to wave to the Daltons.
Someone had gone over to speak to Carl. Wherever he or
Henry went, there were always former patients from the
sanitarium, or families of patients. Hester stood quite
apart, her head wrapped in a scarlet scarf, her arms hug-
ging her white coat to her against the chilly spring night.
Her eyes watched the moving train and her face in the
station light was stark. Caesar stood beside her. His red
tongue, lolling from his mouth, matched Hester's scarf,
and his black and white spots, her black hair and white
coat. Liz rapped on the window, but Hester was looking

14

at the car ahead. Liz felt a moment of sympathy for her because she was not going.

The town drifted past the window, marked off by the gaudy neon signs over the drug store and the shabby Seneca Hotel and Burke's Insurance Co. Hester's loathing for this town colored each building more than any feeling of her own, but Liz had never thought of it as her town; it was only a temporary location until Henry's work on the mold was done.

When the tracks crossed the main street of the town, the little warning bell ding-donged steadily, as though ringing down a curtain, Liz thought with pleasure. And there at the crossing with his flag was Lester Small, the first patient to have the microcydin. She waved to him and he took off his hat.

"Look, Henry, there's Lester Small. That's a good omen."

"You bet it is!" Henry waved enthusiastically.

At the corner of Main Street was the sign "STATE SANITARIUM, 3 miles." And Liz remembered how they had driven into Pomeroy twelve years ago and she had said, "There's a sign. It's three miles up that road."

"Give me your hat, Liz, and I'll put it up here," Henry said. "What are you watching so hard? Anyone would think you hated to leave."

"I was trying to wave to Carl and Hester, but they didn't see me."

"Nice of them to go to so much bother, wasn't it? Carl got this drawing room for us and wouldn't let me do anything about it."

"Carl's a dear; he's almost as excited about this trip as we are. I want to take Hester something from Chicago, and I thought it would please her if I could find one of those little clear glass plates she collects. Of course, they may be rare and they may cost too much. She wouldn't want anything but an authentic one."

"Well, see what you can find. I'm going to take back some Scotch for Carl."

Liz leaned back against the seat and let the Daltons go out of her mind. "I almost don't believe we're off, Henry. I was thinking when I saw the sanitarium sign that we've been here twelve years."

" 'The groundwork of this study was begun twelve years ago . . .' " Henry declaimed in the slightly exaggerated voice of the public speaker.

"In spite of the great reluctance of the investigator's wife to forego the fleshpots of Babylon!" she took it up.

"But the work was carried on with her devoted and invaluable assistance!"

"Ah, we thank you," she said, clasping her hand to her heart and bowing. He laughed at the face she made, but he wanted to tell her how he felt about the way she had put in those years, but he couldn't find the words just then.

Liz went over to comb her hair in front of the door mirror, tipping her head to see the side. Then, as usual, she coiled her hair and pinned it into a knot without looking at herself.

"You should feel pretty good at this moment, Dr. Baker," she teased him. "I admit there have been times when I wondered if you would ever get to this moment."

"The most important quality in a wife is faith," he told her. He filled his pipe and lighted it, letting himself relax a little, cautiously; he had been so taut all week.

"I beg your pardon," she inquired. "Do I hear my faith questioned after fourteen years?"

He reached for her and swung her around to him, kissing her for all the things he couldn't say.

"This is just my idea of why people take these drawing

16

rooms," Liz said, raising her eyebrows at him and going back to the mirror to touch her lips with lipstick.

Henry watched her with pleasure. "You know, your hair is just the color of Atabrine; remember those lovely yellow capsules?"

Her mouth that was a little too wide in repose tightened. "I love medical allusions when you're describing a lady's hair."

He liked to see her gray eyes darken the way they did now. He and Liz had been working too hard to fool like this for a long time. But she looked thin.

"Liz, are you all right?" he asked with sudden concern.

"I'm fine," she said. Her eagerness to be off on this trip shone in her eyes and fanned color into her face.

"It must be that outfit, then. Is it new?" He eyed her over his pipe. "You don't look natural."

She smiled at his heavy attempt at interest. "It is the new thing, sir. 'Do not fear to defend new ideas . . .'"

He joined in with her, "'. . . even the most revolutionary. Your faith is what counts most.'" They were words of Pasteur's that he had quoted so many times Liz knew them too.

"But," he held up his pipe, "madam, may I remind you, 'You must have courage also to admit an error as soon as you have proved to yourself that your idea is wrong.'"

"Yes, but I haven't proved any such thing. I think this suit is an excellent idea."

"You're a sacrilegious wench, mixing Pasteur's words up with styles. Let's go into the club car while the porter makes up the berths. It's miles back," he added, leading the way.

Liz followed him as she had been doing ever since that summer she met him: back to the University town where he was an intern and they had lived on his small salary as

17

assistant in the bacteriology lab, and then to the sanitarium in Pomeroy so he could carry on his work. There was no leading him.

Henry opened the heavy door onto the platform between the cars, and they could feel the speed the train was making, rushing blindly through the dark. He reached back for her hand as she stepped across the passageway.

Something about the club car made you feel stagy, Liz thought. Even to yourself, you looked like a bright Pullman advertisement. Each person in the gaily decorated car assumed the attitude of the ad: the porter setting the two Scotch and sodas on the little table in front of the couple; the three men talking politics; the girl with the extra long legs in sheer black hose and the extra long dark red fingernails, tapping her ash into the ash stand; the man with the hand-painted tie and the three inches of too white ankle showing above his clocked rayon socks. Liz picked up *Life* from the empty seat and sat down. Henry sat beside her. The eyes of the young woman with the dark red nails flicked across at them, made note of what Liz wore, and moved away. The eyes of the man with the tie studied her ankles, moved briefly to her face and over to Henry's, then returned to the folder he was studying. We must look married, Liz thought.

When the porter brought their drinks, Liz raised hers ever so little, catching Henry's eye. "To the paper," she said soundlessly, and his eyes agreed, smiling. The paper he was going to give at the meeting in Chicago had become an entity, almost independent of them. For so long it had been a distant goal, then a beginning, but now that it was finished, it was a thing in itself, a thing to propitiate.

Henry leaned his head against her chair. "Don't let's stay long. Let's go on to bed. Somehow I'm tired."

"That's strange. You got to bed by four this morning."

"You were supposed to be asleep when I came to bed."

"I sleep like a cat!" she told him. "Let's go."

"It wasn't like this the time I went to the meeting to hear Perth," he said out of the darkness of his berth. "It was no fun at all with you home."

"I was home with Nancy," she said, remembering standing on the station platform watching the train go off and the bleakness that swept over her. She remembered driving back to their house on the sanitarium grounds and sitting with the baby until she fell asleep. There hadn't been enough money for two of them to go.

Then her thoughts went swiftly to Nancy—Nancy who was fourteen now and deaf, Nancy who had been healthy and well until the sudden severe attack of undulant fever. Liz lay still, swallowing against the feeling in her throat. She had used to cry by herself over Nancy, but Henry had come on her crying and said gravely, "We mustn't cry for ourselves, Liz, and it's so easy to do." She had flung back at him angrily, but he had denied to her for all time the relief of tears. Sometimes she fought Henry's strength.

But Nancy was alive. They still had her, and they might so easily have lost her. Henry had saved her with the same mold he had found for tuberculosis. "If we knew anything else to do, we wouldn't risk it, Liz, but we don't," Henry had said that night, and even now she remembered how gray his face was and how little beads of perspiration stood out on his forehead. And it had saved her, miraculously. They had been wild with relief and joy.

She had followed Henry into the little laboratory across from the kitchen. "I'll wash those jars and plates and slides forever and never mind again," she had promised extravagantly. "And cook eggs and peel potatoes for the agar till the cows come home. Oh, Henry, I'm so thankful for the molds."

And then when Nancy was getting well and they could breathe easily again, they noticed her asking things over. She turned her little radio up so the sound made the whole house vibrate, and she wasn't aware that it was loud.

"Many people are deaf and it doesn't spoil their lives, Liz. Nancy will learn to read lips and wear an instrument; it won't really handicap anybody like Nance," Henry had said.

No, of course it wouldn't, only she had been all right before the fever. Two years ago she could hear the wind in the pines around the sanitarium and now she couldn't, and there was that listening look in her eyes.

The silence grew and Liz knew that Henry was thinking of Nancy too. She could always tell.

"We ought to have a letter from Nancy in Chicago," Henry said.

"I know it's best for her to be at Greenholm, but I'm so glad she'll be home this summer," Liz said. "I want to get a new tennis racket for Nancy while I'm in Chicago." Her mind was very nimble.

"Get a really good one while you're at it," Henry said. He was quick at it too. If you thought of something you were going to do for her, the sense of pressure on your heart relaxed.

They didn't talk about Nancy's deafness very much and when they did, very matter-of-factly, vying with each other in the cool casualness of their tone of voice. They would be still like this, and after a while they would go on to something else. It was Henry who broke the silence.

"You know what I miss in these streamlined all-steel cars is the creaking of the wood. Remember how you'd lie in a sleeper at night, and when you went around a curve,

20

you'd hear the strain of the wood?" The light touch, oh, very casual.

"Mmm. You don't hear strain, you feel it. I feel safer in steel, thank you," she answered lightly enough, though the innocent word "hear" pressed on a nerve in each of them.

And then they were quiet again. Henry stretched his arms behind his head and pushed his feet against the end of the berth. Now he was glad that he hadn't waited another year to give his report. The patients the drug had cured were triumphant, positive cures. They would have died without it. And they had stayed cured. Lester Small had been working for two years. The drug prevented spreading. Those plates he had were good. And he had his control cases. He wished now that he had given it to the Abrahams boy; he might have lived. But if you were going to test a thing out, you had to stick to your rules.

It didn't work on them all. It hadn't touched the cases with cavitation. And in the mild cases rest did as much as the drug. But in some of the fresh spreads, or in the meningitis cases where every one of them was considered fatal, it had saved about a quarter of the patients.

If he could just have the proper facilities and three or four good men under him . . . and have enough money for Nance and Liz, of course . . . there was no telling where he could go with it. His hand tightened against the pillow.

"It's the greatest advance in the treatment of tuberculosis in the last three decades, Henry!" Carl had said.

But it wasn't all his. Perth deserved some credit. Henry was back again as a student assistant in the bacteriology lab seeing a stranger talking to Professor Dickinson. At noon old Dick had introduced him to Dr. Perth. "I have a luncheon engagement, Henry. I thought you might take

Dr. Perth over to the cafeteria. Dr. Perth is from the State Agriculture College." There was a patronizing tone in Dickinson's voice that told Henry he was giving Perth the brush-off. Perth had come down to talk to Dick about molds, and Dick was not impressed.

But he himself had been. Perth told him about an article in a British medical journal by a scientist who had isolated a mold that killed the bacteria taken from a boil. The man in England, Fleming, his name was, hadn't gone very far with it, and nothing had come of it. "But somebody's going to," Perth had said that day. Perth was growing molds of his own, but none of them tallied with Fleming's penicillium.

Dick had tried to scare them off. "There are hundreds of thousands of molds, and you might have to try every one of them before you found one that would work," he had scoffed. "And after you find one that prevents the growth of bacteria on culture plates, you've got to find one that animals can tolerate, and *then* you've got to be sure that you have one that kills bacteria in the human body without killing your patient!"

But maybe they *could* find that one. "I'd like to write that Englishman, Fleming," Perth had said over his third cup of coffee. "I can't get the possibilities out of my head." It was tough that Perth hadn't lived long enough to know that Fleming's penicillin mold had proved to be the lifesaving thing he had thought it might be, even though it had no effect on the tubercle bacillus.

When he thought back over all this, it seemed as though he had been fated to meet Perth and go up to Pomeroy and raise Perth's molds. He had grown discouraged plenty of times but never quite enough to give them up completely until Carl had his heart attack and was sick in bed for six months. Liz did her best but she couldn't swing the lab alone and he had had to let the molds go. That had been a bad time for him. The state declared him unavailable for the army because of Carl's illness, and he had felt restless and trapped. But even Carl's illness had had something to do with it. Because Carl had to spare himself all unnecessary exertion, he had gone with the contractor to inspect the cellar of the old part of the sanitarium.

"We'll have to get rid of the dirt here to get that mold smell out," the contractor had said, and Henry had noticed the rich growth of mold. After the contractor had gone, he went back and scraped off some of the mold and grew it on a culture medium, a little sheepishly. And that was it. He wished he could tell Perth about it, that it was really due to him after all.

Number 1241 he had called it at first, for the train he used to take back from seeing Liz when he was a student. Now he called it microcydin. He turned with the excitement of remembering the day when he went over his cultures and found no growth after four weeks. Even then he was afraid to believe it, but when weeks later there was still no growth, he was sure he had something. Some mysterious substance that the dirt mold produced had inhibited the growth of the bug. He remembered explaining it to Liz. You read of things like that happening to other people, Koch and Pasteur and Fleming and Fleury, and you imagined you knew what it would be like, but you didn't know until it happened with a mold you had grown and isolated yourself. He had put the plate under the low power of the microscope and looked again. And then he had called Liz to come and look. He broke out in a sweat now, just thinking about it.

Liz slid her hand up under the pillow and lay across the bed. She could tell that Henry wasn't sleeping above her. He was too excited. She was excited too. This was the pay-off. All the years together had worked up to this. Henry saying, "I can't get it out of my head, Liz. There must be a mold that will work with TB, and it might just be this." Henry coming back when they were all ready to go into practice and telling her a Dr. Dalton needed an assistant, in a little town in New York state. "The salary isn't much, Liz, but we get our living and he's interested in my ideas, willing to let me see what I can do if it doesn't interfere with my regular work. I can use the lab and he says our house . . . the assistant's house, that is . . . has an extra room I could use. He'll furnish any equipment. . . . Could you stand it, Liz?"

"How long would you stay there?" she had asked. "You mean for a year or two, Henry?"

"Maybe a little longer than that. It might take four or five years and then we might not have anything, I suppose. It might be just a wild dream. But, after all, Louis . . . you know, Liz, the one who wrote that book I have on tuberculosis. Back in 1860 he buried himself in a charity hospital in Paris for six years, working night and day, keeping records, doing autopsies. . . ."

"Did he have a wife?" she had asked, not the way Henry took it, just wondering, trying to see this Dr. Louis.

"I don't know, Liz. Oh, it's too much to ask, I know. The trouble with me is that I want everything: you and the chance to chase down the mold too."

"Of course it isn't," she had said quickly. "I want you to do what you want. I couldn't stand it if you weren't excited about your ideas. That's what I love about you." And it was, partly. She had never met intensity like Henry's before. Stubbornness, her mother had called it. "He seems such a stubborn young man, Elizabeth." "Yes," she had said happily, "he is a little," but she had been thinking of his arms around her and his lips and his clear brown eyes. She hadn't realized how stubbornly he could pursue an idea, how oblivious he could be of everything else when he was working. But she had learned.

It had meant that they could never get away for more than a day, that they were tied to the endless monotonous routine of raising the mysterious, ugly molds that might or might not turn out to kill disease-producing bacteria. She had learned how to transplant cultures because Henry couldn't always find time with the work at the sanitarium, how to make the everlasting medium, measuring it all more carefully than the ingredients of a cake. She had made a whole batch once, ten liters of it, only to have it spoiled at the last minute in the autoclave, and there were the dozens and dozens of horrid test tubes to clean before she could start in all over again.

One of the orderlies helped them and two of the nurses and the laboratory technician at the sanitarium, but the work went on so long and the nurses changed and new ones had to be interested in it so they wanted to do it; there was no money to pay them for the extra work. She thought of the daily washing of plates and jars and test tubes. She might be slapdash in her own kitchen but not there.

Lying in her berth yet moving through the dark, her mind ranged easily back and forth over the years. She hadn't known in the beginning that when a guinea pig died it had to be autopsied right away, or that they would have to get up at all hours of the night to inject the pigs, or that Henry would never come to bed without stopping to look at the cages of the guinea pigs.

"Daddy can't go, Nancy. I'll take you," she had said a hundred times. "Daddy can't come to dinner just now. You and Mother will eat together. . . . Maybe next summer Daddy will be through and we can go away on a vacation."

But any and all of it was better than the time when Carl was sick and Henry had the whole sanitarium on his hands. They had both worked every night in the lab until they were worn out. When she got sick with the flu, Henry couldn't do everything alone so he had had to give up Perth's molds.

"Oh, well, Liz, I was probably a fool to try to grow molds that may turn out to be nothing," he had said. "Why on earth I should think *I* could find something to cure tuberculosis when Koch couldn't! If I was going to do this, why didn't I stay on in bacteriology; why do I try to do clinical medicine too? Tell me that, Liz."

To have Henry doubt made the earth fall away under her feet. She answered quickly, because she knew Henry needed to hear just that, and sharply to cover over her own doubts: "Don't talk nonsense, Henry. You wouldn't have had the idea if you weren't meant to carry it out."

"If it weren't for you, Liz, I'd never have stuck at this," Henry had said many times. And she cherished the words even though she doubted that they were true. She was glad Henry couldn't see into her mind and didn't know the times she had wished that he wanted only a successful private practice in some city, with an office downtown where it would never bother her, and a nurse and a secretary and a house they had built. People would point it out and say, "That charming place belongs to Dr. Henry Baker." And they would have friends and time to do things with them. . . . She was thankful that Henry didn't know the childishness she was capable of.

But Henry had been right. "Lucky" he called it. "Come and look, Liz!" And she had gone and stared at the aqua-colored agar slants in the test tubes. But she hadn't looked so much at the test tube or the living guinea pig that should have died but didn't because of the microcydin, or even the living patients, as at Henry. "That's it, Liz. We've got it!" And now, day after tomorrow, he would report it. Other doctors would know what he had done.

"Liz?"

"Yes."

"You weren't asleep?"

"No."

"I'm coming down."

He sat on the edge of her berth and lighted a cigarette. His face looked worn in the sudden flare of the lighter. He had worked too hard, stayed up too many nights. After the meeting he must get rested. He handed her the cigarette and lit another for himself, and the two spots of light made a circle that drew them together.

"It's a funny thing, but all of a sudden I feel scared about the whole thing," he laughed.

"That's just stage fright. You won't be when you come to give it. It's all there, Henry, just as you've done it. There are people alive because of it." She sat up in bed. "I was just lying here thinking how it will be to have a famous husband."

"Goose!" He laughed, and she could feel the relief in his voice. "Don't let it worry you." He put out his cigarette. "You didn't really want to sleep alone, did you?"

"Oh, I can manage."

"All right!"

"No, Henry, don't go back up." She reached her hand out to him.

THEY had a table set up right after breakfast and Henry spread out his papers.

"Would it bore you too much to let me run through this, Liz, and time me?"

"Of course not." She glanced at her watch. She didn't always listen, for watching Henry's face. It was hard to understand how you could know every line and feature of a face and yet have to look again and again to correct your memory. Now it was difficult to remember how Henry's face had looked when they first came to the sanitarium. He had been a little thinner, not much; he was as he had been then, a long bony figure, but his hair had waved up from his forehead, and now the hair had grown back and a bare space over the temples showed his skull but at the same time seemed to give his face a stronger look. "Like Cicero," she had told him. He was frowning over his paper.

"Stop scowling," she murmured, and his forehead smoothed and his mouth and brown eyes managed to smile without interrupting his words. Then he was intent again.

When he was so absorbed was the time to look at any man's face, she thought irrelevantly. Joe, the garage mechanic, had had that intent look yesterday when he listened to the motor on the old car; any person did when he was drawn out of himself into his work. So many men must work at jobs that didn't ever take all of them. It showed in their faces after a while, in a slack bored look. Doctors, most of them, were lucky. Women were . . .

"Do you think that was clear, Liz?" Henry broke off to ask.

She nodded her head. "I'm timing you. Don't stop."

Henry continued, turning the typewritten page, knowing it so well his voice gave no pause. Liz took off three seconds for the interruption.

"Case of E.B.C. Male, forty-one. On admission this patient was comatose, fever 104.6; typical signs of left hemiplegia . . ." Henry disposed of the bare statement of facts without any change of voice. But, listening to him, her whole mind cried out in anguish against such cruelty of life that smote a man down as suddenly as the gods used to do in Virgil. How could Henry deal with such tragedy day after day and not feel the uselessness of life? Sometimes the sanitarium cast a shadow all day on the eastern side of their cottage and she felt that shadow on her own spirit. From her porch she could see a corner of the porch of the Women's Building with the beds ranged across the back, and she could feel the weariness of lying in bed in her own body.

Maybe it was because of Nancy's illness that she had grown afraid of the very look of case records when she saw them piled on Henry's desk. Last week she had picked up some records that had fallen on the floor, and putting the sheets in the manila folder, she had read, "Patient expired 12/24/36." Just before Christmas! How had the family endured Christmas? Perhaps the patient was old, tired of life. But hunting through the record she had come on the words, "aged nineteen." She had walked away from the pile of records and Henry's desk down the path from the house until she was out of sight of the sanitarium and could run across the field behind.

"This case illustrates," Henry's voice went on. He was

using this case as a tool to prove something. The patient was cured of his tuberculosis, but he was slowed up. "Some damage to the brain . . ." He would go on living but in a lesser way. Perhaps he would rather not live than have to live more dully than before. How horrible to be less than you had been.

"Case of G.B.A. Female, thirty-five. This patient did not respond in spite of . . ." Liz watched the country running past the window and tried not to feel too deeply about this woman she had never seen, whose name she did not even know, but who was like herself, wanting so many things, loving someone, perhaps hoping she was pregnant or fearing she was, looking into the mirror and trying her hair in a different way, looking at herself with strangeness.

"Autopsy revealed an erosion of an artery in . . ." Liz saw the bare land beyond the train window covered with netted veins and arteries, the cunning and beautiful complexity of organs that were no longer needed and the blood staining deep into the ground. The heart . . . Why did they use the heart as a symbol of love? A stylized, pretty red heart bearing no resemblance to the mass of dark red muscle with tubes running to and from it. "The collapsed lung . . ." And she saw it hanging like some shriveled sack on a tree they passed, or tunneled through and riddled with erosion like the dirt bank rising up from the tracks. ". . . and confirmed the diagnosis." Henry's voice dropped. The words seemed to make a click as though a key turned in a lock. But what small comfort to confirm a hopeless condition. How cold, even if it did help some other case.

Henry's voice continued. "In these hundred cases the treatment . . ." Her mind wandered thinking of all that the word "treatment" took in that Henry never stopped to think of: the phone call from the hospital in the night. It didn't disturb his sleep. Nights were the times when Henry worked on his obsession. She thought of his voice over the phone, anxious, concerned, but calm, painstakingly asking the horribly physical questions: "Was she nauseated? Has she urinated? Any headache?" She could almost ask the questions herself. Henry would stop only to wash his hands or change his shirt and get a cigarette before he was hurrying over to the sanitarium, leaving the slide under the microscope, the light streaming in the laboratory because he would come back to it in a few minutes or a few hours or the next day. But it wasn't easy, and it ceased to be dramatic or noble or anything but exasperating drudgery.

Henry was at the summary now. "This antibiotic produced by an earth mold has proved successful in the treatment of tuberculous conditions of certain types. These few cases seem to indicate . . ." There was a triumphant note under Henry's quiet tone. He laid down the last sheet, trying to hide the question in his eyes, his eagerness.

"Half a minute to spare!" she told him. "It was splendid."

Henry was relaxing ever so little. He leaned his head back against the seat as though the tightness of his neck muscles eased.

"And you think it was all clear?"

Shamelessly, she answered without hesitation. "Yes, I did, Henry." But it was no falsehood, knowing Henry. Henry was clear about what he thought, like mid-afternoon light through a northern window.

"Well, I guess that's all I can do about it." Henry slapped the pages against the table, letting himself feel a little good, a little confident. He laid his box of slides that he would show with the paper on the pile of sheets.

"Aren't you a little pleased, yourself, Henry?" she asked, smiling at him.

"Well . . . the paper could be better; some of it's crudely put together," he said slowly. "But what it says is true and, damn it, Liz, when you think of the people microcydin has cured, it makes you feel sure this is only the start. It's a 'true scent.' "

"It's a lot more than a scent."

"Yes, I guess we've come farther than that. It was the true scent when I scraped off the mold." And both of them were silent, remembering different things.

"I'm glad we're getting away for a little," Liz said. "Medical Meetings are to doctors and their wives what picnics are to children, don't you think, Henry?" They were too serious. She wanted to be gay on this trip. They had waited so long for it.

"In a way, I suppose." It was hard for Henry to drop the paper so quickly. "They're more important than I used to think. You don't read the stuff that's reported on at the meetings until months later in the journals. Remember that time when I heard about Lindsey's work and came home and used it on the Reid boy?"

Liz preferred to keep the light tone and not to think of the Reid boy who died anyway a few months later.

"There's something quaint about all the doctors and their wives setting off on their spring pilgrimage."

"How does it go?" Henry tried now to match her mood with a burlesque of Chaucer. " 'Whan that Aprille with his shoures' sooty . . .' Something about rooty-tooty . . . 'So pricketh them nature in their corages—Than longen folk to go on pilgrimages . . .' "

They both laughed. "You misquote more tag ends of

32

things, Henry. It gives you a very false air of erudition."

"Alwus belittlin'," he complained.

"Now I'll sit in the lobby and watch the doctors and their wives and think 'pricketh them in their corages'!" Liz said.

"I'll be glad to see the old crowd again. We're lucky that so many of them are coming," Henry said. "I can't wait to see Paul Foster as the full-fledged psychiatrist!" He grinned. "Paul ought to be good; he used to analyze himself and Kay, and I guess he tried to analyze me too."

"I suppose Kay is as stunning as ever," Liz said. "Remember, Henry, how impressive she used to be? She always seemed older and more intelligent than the rest of us, and wore better tailored suits and cashmere sweaters and bought new books instead of renting them. And then, of course, she had no children and could take courses at the University. I can see Kay and Paul living in New York."

"And Johnny Holmes is head of surgery at Woodstock now," Henry said, going on with his own thoughts. "I can remember the time in the operating room when Johnny knocked over the rinse basin and drenched the chief! I must remind him of that."

"Henry, do you realize that we haven't seen any of them, at least I haven't, since we left Woodstock? That's twelve years. They'll be middle-aged, almost."

"Well, so are we, 'almost,' I suppose, to idle observers." He laughed at her.

Liz glanced at Henry. He looked a good deal older, but it was becoming to him; he looked more certain. She leaned over so she could see herself in the mirror, but she couldn't remember how she had used to look. She wore her hair differently then. . . .

"I've dreamed of going back to one of these meetings

some day, Liz, with this thing in my pocket, so to speak, but I didn't know whether I ever would. When you think of the thousands of poor devils who've done just as much work without ever quite hitting on it, like Perth, it . . ."

"You live right," Liz said flippantly, but Henry was serious.

"I've been so busy living and breathing and thinking microcydin, I hadn't stopped to think about being the one to discover it until last night." Henry sounded embarrassed.

"Well, wasn't it a nice thought?"

"Liz, why should I be the lucky one?"

"Think how you've worked, Henry, for only barely enough to live on all these years!"

"That was nothing to me, Liz. I didn't want to do anything else, really. Think of you putting up with it. If all those years had gone for nothing, I would have hated it most for you."

"But they didn't. Thank Heaven! Look, we're almost in," Liz said, as the roof of the station darkened their bedroom.

Part Two

"Everybody was there . . . famous researchers, oc-cupants of celebrated chairs, heads of great clinics and great hospitals, Distinguished Foreign Guests. . . . There was every variety of physician and surgeon . . . but mostly physicians come from everywhere for the purpose of learning something . . . and for the fur-ther purpose of having a good time.

"For this was a convention, the autochthonous folk festival of the Americans that is part professional forum and exchange, part vacation, and part debauch."

BERNARD DEVOTO

CONVOCATION

I T WAS so good, Liz thought, to swing up the avenue of a city in the spring dusk. After a Main Street you knew as well as your own face, it freshened your spirits to walk past towering buildings whose names and occupants you didn't know. She had not spent a cent nor spoken to a human being, but she felt as though she had just come alive.

As she turned in at the hotel, the uniformed attendant whistled and a taxi shrieked to a standstill in front of the awning. People, strange people, well-dressed and breathing health and prosperity, went up the stairs with her and separated in the lobby. She took a childish delight in asking for her key and the mail at the desk. But there was no letter from Nancy.

"Liz, Liz Baker!" Someone called her by name. The slender, gray-haired woman coming toward her, in the gray suit that matched her hair and the gray-green hat and gloves, the very color of the molds when the sun struck them, couldn't be someone she knew; but the woman was smiling and holding out her hands in a way that was familiar.

"Charlotte Holmes!" Liz cried out, and a young man in the lobby, seeing them meet, wondered at women's enthusiasm for each other.

"I thought that was you, Liz, when you went over to the desk, but I waited until you turned around. You look just the same, and I don't suppose you have a single gray hair."

But Charlotte wasn't the same, Liz was thinking as they talked. The change was more than the extreme slimness of her figure or the scallop of gray hair under the wisp of a veil, it was the little air of planned elegance that she had never had in the old days.

"It's simply wonderful to see you, Liz!" Charlotte squeezed her arm. "We came out on the train with the Bottsfords, remember? No, I guess they came after your time. Do you realize that John and I are the only ones of our crowd that stayed on at Woodstock? There's John now."

"Henry says he's head of surgery, Charlotte! How splendid!"

"I am proud of him," Charlotte admitted, arranging her fur on her shoulders. A satisfied little smile shortened her mouth into a firmer line that was not so youthful.

"Well, Liz, I'm glad you got here. Where's Henry?" John asked, kissing her. He had been good-looking in the old days but too thin and gangling, and his hands always stuck too far out of the sleeves of his intern's coat. Now there was no angularity and his sleeves were long enough. His face was a trifle heavier but had the same warm smile.

"I was pleased to see that Henry's on the program, Liz. That's a good thing for him."

"Yes," Liz said, but she minded John's fatherly tone.

"The Hamiltons are here, and Kay and Paul Foster," Charlotte said. "We're all going to get together in Alice and Bill Hamilton's room before dinner." Charlotte leaned a little toward Liz and lowered her voice. "I told John we shouldn't go there because Bill always drinks too much at these meetings, and nobody can do much about it if he's the host."

"I'll tell you, Liz, Bill's a great boy," John said. "I don't suppose you'll find a bigger-hearted fellow anywhere, and I hear he's doing very well in Pittsburgh, but he's hitting the bottle a little too hard."

Charlotte looked at her watch. "I think we better go up, John." And Liz remembered how, when they were at someone's house of an evening, Charlotte used to look at her watch and say, "John, we've got to go; remember you have to be in the operating room, scrubbed up by seven tomorrow morning!" Charlotte had always wanted John to get ahead. There was the time when she didn't buy anything for herself all winter because she was saving for a trip home and then bought John a microscope with her money instead. And they had to crowd the dishes so it could go in the china cupboard.

Charlotte and John stepped into the elevator without thinking about it, but it gave Liz a sense of pleasure: the fragrance of the women's perfumes and the scent of the clean starched linen of the men mingled in the crowded cage. The woman in front of her wore fresh violets.

"We'll see you in a few minutes in the Hamiltons' room," John said as they stepped off at their floor, and Charlotte smiled and nodded. It was all very gay. Liz wondered if the other people in the elevator heard and envied her. But, of course, they had their own plans for the evening. People met old friends and went to cocktail parties and out for dinner all the time. They didn't live the way she and Henry had lived. At home at this hour she would be getting dinner ready or working in the lab till Henry came, and then she would do the dishes and go in to help him some more. But now she was free from all that.

Her feet made only the sound of a cat's paws on the thickly carpeted corridor. She turned the big key in the lock of their room and felt her own identity as she never

39

could in their house at the sanitarium. She moved around the room humming, throwing her gloves and hat on the dresser, slipping out of her high-heeled shoes. It was easy here to remember that once, years ago, she had wanted to be a dancer. Henry never could take her love of dancing seriously and, little by little, she had ceased to believe in it herself except as a childish fancy.

The phone rang, but the sound was different from the insistent querulous ring at the sanitarium, and she answered it eagerly.

"Is this Mrs. Henry Baker?"

"Alice Hamilton!"

"Oh, Liz, I've been trying to get you for the last hour. Come on up here; we're in 1620. Bill has seen Henry; that's how I knew you were here. He says he looks wonderful. Paul and Kay Foster are here and John and Charlotte Holmes. Isn't it marvelous that we all came! Hurry now."

"We'll come the minute Henry gets back," Liz promised.

She and Alice Hamilton had lived in the same apartment house when Henry and Bill were interns, and had their babies that first spring. Alice went back to nursing and often parked her baby at their apartment, and she took care of him with Nancy. But since then they had known only what could be scrawled on a Christmas card or conveyed by snapshots of growing children. Bill and Alice had four. The last snapshot showed them all in front of a long rambling stone house they had built in Pittsburgh just before the war.

When Henry didn't come in a half an hour, Alice called again, so Liz left a note for him and went up. She could hear voices and laughter as she walked along the corridor, and when she knocked on the door, it was thrown open instantly.

"Here she is now!" John Holmes announced as he drew

her inside. "Charlotte has been telling the girls that you look exactly the same," he explained to Liz. "And Kay and Alice couldn't wait to see you."

"Don't you believe him, Liz. You're more beautiful," Bill Hamilton called out from the end of the room where he was mixing drinks. "I'm fixing one for you." It was so natural to have Bill acting as host and paying compliments just as he used to do that Liz laughed. And he still wore resplendent ties. . . .

"Liz, darling, I'm so glad to see you!" Alice said. As she kissed her, Liz was aware that Alice's trim little figure had grown plump. Her dark eyes were the same, but the skin was wrinkled ever so slightly at the corners and she used more make-up. Instead of the braid she used to wear, her dark hair was curled and piled high on her head, too elaborately to go with a nurse's uniform, but she was the same bubbling little person.

Kay Foster sat smiling, waiting for Alice to be through. "Hello, Liz," she said quietly, shaking hands with her. "I'm glad you haven't changed; I was afraid you might have."

"You haven't either, Kay, except that you've cut your hair and look younger." It was Kay that she was most glad to see, she thought. She was glad to see them all. It was as easy to pick up where they had left off as though they had never moved away from Woodstock.

"Where's Paul, Kay?" Liz asked.

"Lobbying, I presume. He always has a few axes to grind at a Medical Meeting," Kay said. "He'll probably run into Henry."

Bill handed Liz a drink, and she sat on the edge of the bed beside Kay.

"We never drank anything but beer in Woodstock, did we?" Kay asked.

"You mean we couldn't afford anything else," Bill said. "Here, John, let me fix yours."

John held out his glass. "That's not bad stuff. A Grateful Patient give you that, Bill?"

Bill laughed. "No, but I did have some of the smoothest brandy you ever had on your tongue from a G.P., one of my old ladies. It was her dead husband's stock and pre the first war!"

"Well, now I begin to see why you went into geriatrics, Bill," John said.

"Isn't it dreadful that in all these years we've never been to the same Medical Meeting before?" Charlotte said, turning her back on the men. "It isn't my fault. I always tag along. I love them."

"I do too," Alice said. "And it gives Bill a chance to get away and relax, but he took the oral part of his Boards today so this is the first time he could really let down. Now I hope he'll get rid of that little cough he has."

"Liz, you heard that Sam and Rachel Reiner are divorced, didn't you?" Charlotte asked. "I just thought I'd tell you before you see Sam. He'll be here."

"No, I didn't. I'm sorry. I always remember the fun we used to have at their apartment. Remember?" Liz said.

"Do I? I remember all those records they had," Alice added. "Remember how he used to play the violin and Rachel sang?"

Charlotte said, "It's a pity they've broken up. Why, all my ideas about Jews are colored by knowing Rachel and Sam. In fact, I don't remember that we thought about their being Jewish then. John says he thinks all the good these books on the 'Jewish problem' do is to make everyone self-conscious."

"There's Henry and that sounds like Paul with him."

John went out in the corridor to welcome them and Bill followed. Liz could hear the gladness in Henry's voice.

"Who says women squeal and act girlish when they meet? Listen to the uproar they make!" Alice said. "Isn't this wonderful; I tell you, I feel as though I were back in my twenties."

"Let's go to the Pump Room for dinner on account of we never had enough money when we were in our twenties," Charlotte said. "Except Kay, and she suffered with us."

Kay shook her head, smiling. She still had that aloof air, Liz thought, and the exaggerated look of figures in *Vogue*. Her straight dark hair fitted her head like a cap and gave piquancy to her high cheekbones. Kay was never like anyone else.

"What makes you sure you want children?" Kay had asked suddenly that winter before Nancy was born. "I don't think I'm the maternal sort."

She had known the answers in those days. "You'd hate it if you couldn't have any," she had told Kay.

"That's certainly a negative way of reasoning," Kay had said. Funny to remember exact words they had spoken so long ago.

"Of course, you want a child, Kay; you don't want to miss out on something that's a part of a woman's life. I'm going to have four," she had said glibly, she who had only been able to have Nancy. But after all these years she could still remember the swift sweep of color in Kay's face. Kay had waited much longer than the others before having a child.

As though she felt Liz's thoughts, Kay met her eyes with an amused little smile that covered itself abruptly with a look of disinterest as she looked away. Liz followed her glance and saw Paul coming toward them. He was as

43

light as Kay was dark, and taller—the tallest man in the room.

"Elizabeth," he said, taking both her hands. "You look wonderful! Kay and I have been waiting a long time for this." Paul had a way of putting more meaning into a name or a gesture than anyone else. Liz remembered the boys teasing Paul about his charm.

"Thank you, Paul. You're looking very fit yourself," Liz answered, but warmed by that same charm.

"Hello, Mrs. Foster." Paul touched Kay's head, and Liz saw her jerk back and then lean over to the table for a cigarette.

"Light?" Paul asked, but Kay had her own lighter.

"We've been having a grand time catching up on things," Liz murmured to fill the awkward moment. She was glad to see Henry and Bill.

"Brought him back to you, Liz," Bill said thickly.

"I'm glad you came on up without waiting for me. I felt guilty when I saw the time," Henry said.

"I knew you had met someone and forgotten all about the time."

"I ran into old Dr. Williams, the pathologist from Presbyterian, and I wanted to talk to him about some of this stuff. . . ."

"Nope, no, you don't! No shop talk," Bill objected. "Come on back, fella. You're way behind the rest of us and you gotta catch up." Bill picked up one of the girls' hats and put it on his head as he and Henry went over to the dresser where Paul and John had taken refuge.

Henry was enjoying all this, Liz could see. It was a relief to him too to get away from the sanitarium and the everlasting lab work.

"Bill's just like a little kid when he gets off like this at a Medical Meeting," Alice exclaimed. "I don't see anything wrong with it either, because at home he's under such a strain all the time."

Charlotte turned to Kay. "John and I were talking about what fun it would be if you all did get here, and I said to John, 'What on earth do you suppose we'll talk about without that old topic of where we'll settle and whether to go into private practice or stick to teaching?' I can remember when no one knew where he was going."

"Paul and Kay had a wild idea of going to North Dakota once, I remember," Alice said.

"I wish we had gone. I would have liked it, I think," Kay said.

"And you and Henry were going to Henry's home town in New York state, I thought, Liz. We were thunderstruck when we heard you'd taken that sanitarium job," Charlotte said.

"What changed your minds, Liz?" Kay asked.

As though it were only last week, Liz remembered. "We were all set and even had an apartment leased in Buffalo. Henry went on a month before we were to move to see about a connection with the health office while we were getting started, and when he came back he said, 'You know, that isn't really what I want to do at all.' So!"

"Heavens, and you threw up all your plans just like that?" Charlotte asked.

"Just like that," Liz said, smiling. She felt good about it now.

But Kay pursued the subject. "Did Henry just decide he wanted to go into sanitarium work?"

"It wasn't so much the sanitarium work as it was that he would have a chance to try to find a mold that would cure TB. And there we've been ever since," she finished, waiting for them to ask if he had found the mold. But they didn't.

"He does private practice, too, doesn't he?" Alice asked.

"You can't do that in a state job," Liz answered briefly.

"Still, I suppose your expenses are so much lower than if you were out on your own and had an office and a house. Really, when I think what Bill makes, more than we ever dreamed of, and how little we have to show for it when we've paid our income tax and our bills and all, I just don't know whether it's worth his working so hard," Alice said. "Besides, I hardly see him he's so busy."

"I know what you mean," Kay said. "Paul leaves the house at eight in the morning and I don't see him until around seven-thirty in the evening, and we're out for dinner three or four nights a week, at least. Oh, it's a charming arrangement. But I manage," she added.

"That's the way it is with John too," Charlotte said. "Isn't it queer that the last time we were together we were so busy taking care of babies or trying to get a sitter and learning how to run a house and make ends meet that we females didn't have an extra bit of time, and now, twelve or fifteen years later, we have time to burn?"

"And the men are busier. John's just run ragged. You know he does private practice besides being head of surgery, and it's just too much!"

Kay's voice cut in sarcastically. "The dilemma of the middle-aged woman of the middle classes. It's always found at the decadent end of an age, I believe. You should hear Paul on the subject."

"Well, I don't know about that, but I liked it better when we were young," Alice said.

"How original of you. Most people do," Kay told her.

"Will you look at Bill! He's just having the time of his life." The tone of Alice's voice was a little anxious. Bill had put on Charlotte's fur neckpiece. The hat and veil had slid over to the back of his head, and he was standing beside Paul with an owlish expression on his face.

A knock broke in on their talk.

"That's Samuel or I'll miss my guess," John said.

Sam Reiner stood in the doorway. "Hello, John, I found Bill's note and came right up. Hello, everybody! Liz, it's good to see you. Kay, was it fifteen years ago that you beat me at tennis? Hen, you old son of a gun, you came out of hiding at last. I see you're on the program. Good for you! How's the psychosomatic, Paul?"

When he had been the rounds and had his drink in his hand, he said suddenly, "Say, do you know who's here? I just met him in the lobby and I could hardly believe it. As a matter of fact, I didn't know him until he spoke to me first."

"Who, Sam?"

"Peder Hansen!"

"That transfer doctor from Norway," Charlotte cried out.

"The Nazis didn't get him, then!" John said.

"No, but he spent some time in a concentration camp. He's going to study over here for a while and try to get his health back. He sure needs to. Remember how healthy he used to look?"

"He always looked as though he went skiing every day," Kay said.

"Remember how polite Peder was? I loved the way he'd bow from the waist," Charlotte demonstrated.

"He's nothing but skin and bones now and he walks with a cane. But his face lit up when he saw me."

"Let's have him paged! Here, I'll do it." Paul took the phone.

"You know, we're never going to get anything to eat if we wait for Peder," Charlotte said. "I think we ought to

47

telephone and at least make reservations. It's a quarter of nine, now."

"That's what I love about going to a Medical Meeting. It doesn't matter when you eat," Alice put in. "Bill, send for some more ice, and you'll have to get the glass in the bathroom for Peder. Oh, I'll have to take over. Bill is fine up to a point, then he lets everyone shift for himself." Alice's face was flushed. Her voice had a shrill note.

"Relax, Alice. I'll take over," Sam said. "Lady bartenders aren't allowed in this hotel."

"Why don't we eat right down here in the hotel? It's raining and we'll have to wait to get a taxi," John suggested.

"Sure, swell! Call up and tell them to phone us when they have a table. How many are there? Nine . . . ten with Peder. Tell 'em twelve; we may pick up someone else on the way," Sam said.

"No, don't pick up anyone else. We want to think we're all in Woodstock again," Alice objected. "Open the door, somebody. The smoke in here is so thick my eyes sting."

"I don't say that, Paul. What I claim is . . ." Liz heard Henry's voice and saw him sitting on the arm of the chair, talking shop.

"Liz, Henry told me about Nancy's deafness," Sam said, standing beside her. "He says you're wonderful about it."

"Oh, no, I'm *not,* Sam. I can't see why it had to happen to her." In spite of herself, Liz's eyes filled with tears. The frantic surge of anger against fate that she knew so well rose in her, making her hand tremble as she opened her bag for a handkerchief. She never knew when it would assail her like this. "One of my hot flashes," she always said apologetically to Henry.

"I know," Sam said gently. "It's a damned crime." They seemed alone, cut off from the gabble in the rest of the

48

room. Liz stared at the flower arrangement in the print over the bed until the moisture dried from her eyes. Sam jingled a key in his pocket. "I suppose you heard about Rachel and me?"

"Yes, Sam, and I'm so sorry."

"I am too," he said ruefully. "I miss the kids like everything. I miss Rachel too, for that matter."

"Are the children with Rachel all the time?"

"No. Rachel's singing for radio, you know. She's good too. The children are with her mother. I can't take care of them where I am. You know I've left the Foundation?"

"No, we didn't. Are you out in practice, Sam?" In the old days at Woodstock they had said "out in practice," and it had seemed dangerous and exciting and a challenge after the confines of the University. She had been anxious for it and, still, she and Henry had not gone out in practice. Her mind came guiltily back to what Sam was saying.

"I'm head of the Research Department for the Lieter and Wainwright Pharmaceutical House." Sam shrugged. "It has its points."

"Maybe you and Rachel will be together again."

"I'd like to think so. We weren't having any kind of a life in New York on what I made at the Foundation and, naturally, Rachel took up her singing again. I don't blame her. She has too much talent to waste, but we didn't see much of each other. Rachel had her own friends. But I'm doing better financially now!" He smiled at her boyishly.

"And have everything to work with," Liz added, thinking of the Mason jars that had once held fruit and the old tin sink that she and Henry managed with in their homemade laboratory.

John turned around from the phone. "They'll call us.

Probably be a half an hour. That'll give everyone time for one more drink."

"Not me. I'm in a lovely glow now!" Alice said. "John, please don't give Bill any more. He's had enough," she murmured in a low voice.

"Say, I ran into Durkin from Columbia downstairs and he told me a story . . ." John began. "It's pretty good. Ladies can listen too."

In the shout of laughter that followed the story no one noticed the slightly stooped figure that paused in the open doorway. When Liz glanced up, she touched Sam's arm.

"Peder! Here's Peder, everyone!" Sam went over to the door. For a sudden, startled instant no one spoke. Then they all talked at once, in embarrassment.

Peder looked like an old man, and they all knew that he was younger than any of them in the room. There was something odd about his jaw. When he smiled, you didn't notice it so much. His skin was an unhealthy color and his collar looked much too big for his neck.

"This is wonderful to see my old friends from Woodstock!" He spoke with the slight formality and the same marked accent that had seemed so interesting twelve years ago. His blue eyes smiled, but the white teeth were no longer flashing. There was a gap between the first two in the lower jaw. "Alice and Kay and Liz . . ." He remembered them each by name. "This is truly wonderful!" he said again. "I was in the city, so when I saw there is to be a Medical Meeting, naturally, I come. I had no idea, no hope I find most of my American friends together."

"Well, you found some all right, Peder, and you're in time to go to dinner with them," John said. "Sit down and have a drink."

The conversation went on again. "I'd never have recognized him. I don't see how Sam did," Kay murmured.

"He looks so old," Charlotte said. "He looks sick."

The phone rang. "They'll have a table in just a few minutes," John announced. "We'll have to go right away."

Everyone moved at once, as though it were a relief to be doing something to take their minds off what time and the war had done to Peder.

Alice said, "Of course, Bill is really tickled pink that we didn't go to the Pump Room. He hates all that stuff, and yet, he'll pay just as much and more to sit in a smoky place like this and eat a lobster."

"Alice, please! Speak reverently of lobster," Paul protested. He was sitting at one end of the table with Liz and Alice on either side, putting in a polite comment at the right time, but he was trying to hear what Henry was saying halfway down the table.

"Isn't this just a man's dream of paradise?" Charlotte said, waving her hand at the room. "Fish nets and old bottles and lanterns and big-bottomed wooden chairs."

Paul lost the drift under the girls' chatter, but he was watching Henry. Hen looked older and showed strain like the rest of them, but he looked alive. The old feeling about Henry stirred in him, a feeling he had thought was laid for good and all. He and Henry had roomed together in the fraternity house and later in the interns' quarters. He had used to envy Henry; Hen had always known what he did know and what he wanted to know. They had both been bright enough, but Henry was more sure. He himself had sometimes worried that he seemed brighter to professors than he was. He still had that feeling with patients now and then.

It was like Henry to go off up to a little sanitarium in the woods and stick there because he had something he wanted to work out. Hen had done what they had all toyed with in their minds, the old Arrowsmith idea. He wondered how it had worked out for Liz and Hen.

"What's it like living in a sanitarium, Liz?" he asked.

"Not too exciting, Paul, but after listening to Charlotte and Alice, I guess it's simpler than private practice. And Kay says you're so busy she doesn't see much of you. Of course, I see Henry at a distance all day, and he has his laboratory in a room in our cottage."

Kay's saying that gave him a twinge. It was as much her fault as his that they didn't see more of each other. "Is Hen going on up there, Liz, or is he thinking of moving now? I haven't had a chance to talk to him yet."

"We haven't talked very much about it either, Paul. Henry's been so absorbed in this work he's been doing that he couldn't plan ahead, but we don't plan to stay there indefinitely, of course." She felt her voice trailing off into vagueness and she longed so for definiteness. "This work of his has got to the place now where I imagine it will take him away," she said and let a little importance color her tone.

"Henry has his Boards, of course, hasn't he? You almost have to have them in this day and age if you're going to specialize," Paul said.

"No, he hasn't." All the importance oozed out of her voice and mind. "You can't imagine how busy he's been. And, of course, aside from the sanitarium work, there is a big educational and preventive program." There! Henry would never tell him. "You have no idea . . ."

"What Henry ought to do, and it would be fun for you too, is to go back to Woodstock for a year and brush up before he takes his Boards."

That was like Paul. He always had a plan, Liz remembered.

"But I rather imagine Henry's passed them by now, and you just weren't aware of it," Paul said.

What was there about Henry that she wasn't aware of? Paul didn't know how closely they lived together. And how did Paul think they would finance a year back at Woodstock? She had no income of her own as Kay did. She looked down the table and saw Henry talking to John and Peder. Paul's eyes followed hers.

"Same old Henry!" he said. "Always burned up about something."

"Always the same thing," she corrected. "Ever since he knew his mother died of tuberculosis when he was little, he's meant to find something to cure TB, I think."

"And now he really thinks he has it?"

Liz bristled at something in Paul's tone: the hint of skepticism. She hesitated, thinking of the hours they had spent discussing the title of Henry's paper. "Microcydin, a Cure for Tuberculosis." "We can't say that, Liz. It doesn't cure the pulmonary cases. Maybe it will if we give it over a longer period . . ." "A New Hope for Tuberculosis," then, she had suggested. "Too euphoric for a medical title," Henry had objected. So they had called the paper "Microcydin in the Treatment of Tuberculosis." But thinking of Lester Small and Mrs. Graves and the French Canadian boy, thinking of Nancy too, she said to Paul, "Yes, he does,"

Paul was used to drawing inferences from intonations and silences. Liz's hesitation was not lost on him now. Perhaps she was fed up with Henry's obsession; the two of them must have had a rather thin time of it up there both socially and financially.

"Henry's had some wonderful results," Liz went on.

Paul wondered if Kay ever spoke of him with such pride.

"I'm anxious to hear his paper. Can't the four of us run away one of these evenings for dinner so we can really talk?"

"We'd love to, Paul. After Henry's paper is over. He can't really relax till then," she said, smiling for Henry's foolishness at having any qualms at all.

"Paul, do you think there's any harm in taking seconal once or twice a week? Charlotte thinks it's dangerous. But it's better than lying in bed and not sleeping, isn't it?" Alice asked in that tone women always use when asking advice from a doctor who is also their personal friend, a tone that dares him to disagree.

"Well, it isn't the seconal in itself so much as it is the habit," he began, but Charlotte interrupted.

"John and I read every night before we go to sleep. It seems to work just as well."

"It would depend on what you're reading, I should think," Kay said, feeling under no obligation to be particularly pleasant to Charlotte.

Alice looked uneasily at Bill. He sat by John down at the other end of the table and there was no way that she could say anything to him. She had known he would get drunk. He always did at Medical Meetings. And, after all, by noon tomorrow he would be as alert as any of them, listening to the papers and taking notes and meeting people.

But tonight he would be difficult. She would have to put him to bed. She wouldn't go to sleep herself until she heard his heavy breathing. Then she would take a magazine into the bathroom and read a while with the door closed until she felt like sleeping. Sometimes drinking so much made him amorous and he would call her "honey" and beg for "just a little loving, honey," with his voice slurring the words so they made her shiver. He was hurt if she put him off, and if she let him come to her, lying stiffly with her face turned away from his breath, he fell asleep almost as soon as he had loved her. Then she could slip away.

Sometimes she sat at the open window, letting the cold air blow in on her, until the memory of Bill in the early days of their marriage came back and crowded out this present time: Bill on call at the University Hospital when she was night supervisor; never sparing himself when he had a really sick patient; giving another transfusion when there didn't seem to be any use; the time he had worked all night and when the patient looked better about four in the morning, walking down the corridor with her saying, "We did it, honey; darned if we didn't. Give us a kiss on it!" She would have died for young Dr. Bill Hamilton then. She would still. When she got to that point, she had forgiven him. She heard him cough and frowned a little.

"How'd you like being the big boss, John?" Bill asked so loudly that the people at the next table turned to look at them. "Yes, sir, pretty lucky for you that McCall had his coronary!"

Alice could hear Henry trying to get Bill on another subject.

"Well, it's quite a job, I can tell you," John said, taking no offense.

Kay, sitting between Peder and Sam on the other side of the table, was silent. She felt so removed from the rest. The next time John and Charlotte and Liz and Henry, all of them, were together at a Medical Meeting she wouldn't be here. She would never go to another. There was no point in going on with Paul. She didn't mean enough to him. Their life together had no real vitality. Sometimes she had difficulty feeling any vitality in anything she did. Paul brushed it aside when she tried to tell him how she felt. "We've got to the age where the edge dulls a little,

Kay, that's all. Facing it is a part of maturity. Some people would rather hide that from themselves and never grow up—plenty of people. I had a man in the office today . . ."

But it didn't dull for everyone. It hadn't for Liz and Henry. When Paul had said Henry was coming to this meeting, she had decided to come, just to see Liz and Henry after all these years. There was something about Henry . . . about the feeling between him and Liz that she had envied back in Woodstock. She had to see if it had lasted. Her glance flicked a little rudely over Charlotte and John and Alice and Bill to Henry.

"Remember that case on 2 West that last year, Henry?" John said. "We argued about whether he could stand operation or whether we ought to let him go. God, I remember we got worked up over that bird. There was practically a civil war in the record room. And then Heath operated him and he died on the table."

"I have thought of that case many times in the war," Peder said. "It is amazing what operations men can come through."

"I guess you know better than any of the rest of us what the human body can stand, Peder, after what you've been through yourself," Sam said. Sam was always the one to say the thing the others only thought to themselves.

"I do know this," Peder said, and his precise tone caught the attention of them all. "The human body can only stand what the human spirit will stand."

"Tha's it," Bill said emphatically, nodding at Peder and drawing his face into a sagacious expression. "We're too damn busy with bodies . . . curse of doctors, forget all about the spirit. Paul's got the inside track going into psych . . ." He had two tries at it before he got the word out . . . "psychiatry."

They laughed then and the serious moment passed.

Alice busied herself with her lipstick, and Kay looked at her with distaste. Liz warmed toward Bill for the first time that evening. Oh, that *was* it; she felt sometimes that Henry was so everlastingly absorbed in sick bodies and the microbes that infect them.

"You don't forget the spirit and the morale when you're dealing with tuberculous patients either," Henry said quietly.

"All kinds of patients," Paul put in, but to Kay his tone had too professional a note.

"No dessert, just another cup of coffee," Charlotte told the waiter, sitting up a little straighter and passing her hand down over her stomach to remind herself that it must be kept flat.

"How about a liqueur for everyone?" Paul conferred authoritatively with the waiter.

"What's this 'Charlotte de pomme monseigneur'?" John asked, reading from the menu.

The waiter sketched the form of the dessert in the air with his pencil and explained in broken English that it consisted of a fruit mold with a sauce.

"Bring that to the gentleman over there," John directed, pointing to Henry. "He deals in molds."

The confused waiter nodded vigorously and wrote it down amid the laughter.

"I've had enough molds. I'll have a chocolate sundae," Liz ordered.

"Someone gave me the address of an antique shop," Charlotte told the girls. "It's supposed to have a rather good collection of old glass. I thought I'd run over there tomorrow morning. Any of you interested?"

"I am," Liz said. "I want to try to find one of those little antique glass cup plates for a gift. Unless they're too terribly expensive."

"Well, last year at the meeting in New Orleans I picked up some authentic cranberry glass for the window on my stairway. It's really stunning and I saved easily a hundred dollars. John's suspicious of all antiques and even he thought so. Maudie Becker . . . her husband is in GU surgery . . . had been looking for some, and she was just wild when she heard what I paid for mine!"

Liz thought of Hester saying tartly, "Whew, it was stuffy! Most of the women kept themselves busy hunting down antiques or buying new outfits or having their hair and faces redone." Hester was right in a way. She had been so glad to see all of them, but now, after only a few hours, she felt too separate from them. The eager rush of enthusiasm they had all felt was dying out like Fourth of July sparklers. Why did they keep protesting that they hadn't changed? Of course they were changed. Alice was so bothered about Bill's drinking and Charlotte couldn't talk without quoting John. And Kay was so quiet, almost as though she weren't well. She was lighting a cigarette, and the flame made her fingers look translucent and deepened the eye shadow under her eyes.

Liz glanced down the table at Bill and looked away quickly. He was like a funny paper picture of himself with that cigar. Peder's face was a relief from Bill's, but it was so old . . . no, not old, worn. At least Peder could talk about the spirit. The rest of them . . . it wasn't just that they had grown older, but they had grown so secure and prosperous and well fed. In the old days they had been so insecure, so far from prosperity, so unsure about the future.

"Where's Heine Bates now?" Sam was asking.

When they used to get together at the Homestead that served waffles and sausages for seventy-five cents, they used to argue about medical things. Now they were talking about personalities, and positions and possessions, she thought illogically, amusing herself with the alliteration. Liz took a spoonful of the ice cream in the silver sherbet in front of her. It had a sweet, flat taste and it was lukewarm, like the talk at this dinner. She laid her spoon down.

"Kay, are you thirty-six or thirty-eight?" Charlotte asked abruptly. "I remember you're either a year older or a year younger than I am."

Kay was slow in raising her eyelids. "You really have a remarkable memory, Charlotte. I'm thirty-eight."

"I was thinking you were younger. I'm thirty-seven," Charlotte said with a pleasant sense of superiority.

The waiter poured the liqueur into the tiny glasses in front of each one. It had a blunt edge against the glass.

"Remember the time the old codger that had the prostatectomy gave you the bottle of Johnny Walker, John?" Sam asked.

"And we saved it to drink whenever anybody made up his mind about what he was going to do next," John said.

"We drank to you on the Buffalo deal, Henry, but we never did drink to the sanitarium job," Sam remembered. "We finished it on Paul and New York."

"Well, better late than never!" John said, lifting his glass.

Liz took a sip, letting the fiery liqueur lie on her tongue. She was glad they had gone off up to the sanitarium. Henry hadn't grown complacent like John; he never would be, nor satisfied with mediocrity as Carl Dalton was. She and Henry were as close together as they had been in the beginning; even closer. Maybe it was working so hard that had kept them safe, and making only enough money to scrape by and not having time to plan for the future. Why had she ever minded? They were lucky, she and Henry.

She must tell Henry so to make up for the times she had been silent and moody and felt bitter inside. She had kept it to herself, but Henry had always known.

"I know it's no fun, Liz, but we've got something. We can't blot out now," he had said sometimes and gone back into the lab with his shoulders a little slumped. And after a while, after Nancy was in bed and the ironing she had left till night was finished, she had made some coffee and sandwiches and taken them into the lab on a tray, and without saying anything Henry had known she was with him again.

Henry set down his glass. He was thinking how close he had come to going to Buffalo to practice. And if he had, he would never have come back like this with a contribution of his own. . . .

"How does it feel, Henry, to have an almost grown daughter?" Charlotte interrupted his thoughts. "Are you putty in her hands the way John is?"

"Well, I . . . it's a nice feeling, Charlotte," he said slowly. He supposed the girls were talking about their children. That would bother Liz. He glanced down the table at her. Liz met his eye, smiling. She looked so young and pretty tonight. It was good for her to get away; she had looked tired on the train.

"Georgie, he's the little fellow . . ." Charlotte rattled in his ear. "When he hears John's car in the driveway, he's down the stairs like a flash. . . ." Henry smiled appreciatively. He was as bad as Liz about wincing every time the word hear was mentioned. At least Liz wasn't nagged by the persistent thought that if he had given Nancy the microcydin in smaller doses or stopped it sooner, her deafness might have been only temporary. But how could he have known that? Perhaps he should have put it into his report in more detail. "Further observations have inclined us to the opinion . . ." His mind shaped the sentence.

"John, are they doing as many phrenicectomies now on the TB service?" Henry asked, glad to get away from his own thoughts to the talk of medicine. That was what he had missed so.

But John wasn't interested. "I don't really know, Hen. I don't get up there any more. The surgery interns rotate, of course. Hobson is the head of chest surgery now; he's a fine operator. By the way, Paul, do you know Kerns in New York? I think he's the most likely man for the chair of surgery at Chicago."

"Did you see that Nickols went to California?" Sam asked. "Albrecht will take his place, don't you think, John?"

Henry sat back, listening. These were names he didn't know. He had been off up in Pomeroy with no knowledge of academic appointments or interest in them.

"Albrecht hasn't his Boards," John said. "That held him back in the army too."

Henry lit a cigarette. He didn't have his Boards either. "How were the Boards today?" he called down the table to Bill who was quietly nursing his glass.

"Shimple," Bill said, closing his eyes and lifting his head as he said it. "Shimple, Hen. Don't you worry."

"Thanks, Bill," Henry said. Then he noticed that Peder was taking no part in the conversation either. He sat smoking, listening to the talk around him. He must feel shut out of all this talk of appointments too.

They drifted through the lobby toward the bank of elevators.

"Don't you wonder if every man you see is a doctor?" Charlotte asked. "Tomorrow they'll have their badges on and then you can tell. I think it's fascinating, but, of course, I think you can really tell when a man's a doctor; there's just something about him!" she finished vaguely.

Alice tucked her arm through Bill's. "Let's go on up, Bill."

"S'too early yet, Allie. Dutch Willis is here; I promised I'd look him up at the bar. You 'member Dutch, Hen?" He disengaged Alice's arm gently. "Le's all go an' have a drink 'fore we go up."

"Thanks, I've got to see Dr. Borden before the committee meeting tomorrow," John said. "But I'll look in there with you. Borden usually makes the bar along about this time. See you tomorrow, Liz, Alice. Henry, I'll be on hand to hear your paper. It's three-thirty, isn't it?"

"Yes. I'm going around to get a program right now," Henry said. "See you."

"I wish they wouldn't," Alice said to Charlotte. "Bill's so tired he needs to go to bed." She wondered at Charlotte's unconcern. But John would never drink too much, she thought resentfully. "I think I'll stop and get a magazine before I go up."

"Here, I have a program, Henry," Paul said. "There's some good stuff there. You're coming up to the room with us, aren't you?"

"I think we better not tonight, Paul. I've got a couple of things I want to look over. But it's good to see you two. We'll get together tomorrow night," Henry said.

"Call me, Liz," Kay said. "But not before ten!"

The elevator was crowded and they didn't speak. Then they were walking down the corridor to their room.

"Did you mind coming back up so early?" Henry asked.

"It isn't really early. No, I wanted to. It was good to see them but . . . they've changed, Henry, haven't they?"

"Oh, I don't know," Henry said, but she could tell that he was thinking about the program.

Already the room seemed uniquely theirs. Henry pushed the button by the door and, just as though they were at home in the cottage, Liz hurriedly turned on the light by the armchair and the desk light and snapped off the overhead lights.

Henry threw himself across the bed with the program.

"How does it feel to see your name on the program?" Liz asked. She slipped out of her suit skirt and hung it up in the closet. "Does it give you a scary feeling?" she teased. Henry hadn't heard; he didn't answer anyway. She stood in the doorway of the closet. Charlotte's suit must have cost over a hundred dollars. . . .

"I'll be damned," Henry said. "There's a paper here on 'A New Mold with Antibiotic Properties, A Preliminary Report' by Stockton, Grayson, and Fenton." There was something odd about Henry's voice. Liz went over to the bed.

"Henry, what does that mean? You don't think he could have found our microcydin, do you?"

"He could have," Henry said slowly. "Everyone's stirred up about antibiotics now. The dirt in his cellar could have it too."

"But we must have found it a long time before he did," she said.

"I hope so, but we worked several years on the wrong scent, you know."

Oh, yes, she knew. How well she knew. All those cultures she had transplanted, all those Mason jars lined up in the room they could have had for a guest room or a sewing room or a study. All the test tubes and data. And all the Perth molds thrown out in the end. And then the whole performance over again when Henry started to try

63

his own mold. Henry had been as excited as he ever was about Perth's molds. She had been excited too when the microcydin had kept the bugs from growing in the test tube. Assurance came back to her.

"But, Henry, it can't hurt your report!"

"I don't know. Whatever Stockton's reporting must be related to microcydin." He read the title aloud again, and Liz seized eagerly on the words: "A Preliminary Report."

"Well, yours is more than that. You have cases that have stayed cured for two years, Henry!" Liz was talking to Henry as she would to Nancy: "You have all those lovely woods to play in; you don't need a back yard like the girls in town have."

But Henry was like Nancy and refused to be consoled. "Of course, I can only claim twenty-five cases out of a hundred cured, Liz!" He wanted to be contradicted.

"Think of the twenty-five though, Henry! Think of Lester Small and that woman from Auburn with the four children, who could go back to her children well!" And she was warmed herself, thinking about her. Henry had the X-rays of her lungs made into slides to show with his paper.

"But it isn't the twenty-five, really. It's the other seventy-five. Why didn't it have any effect on them? You see, Liz, I can't answer that. That's what I told Carl."

"And you say that in the paper, Henry."

"Yes." He turned a sheet, hunting. " 'Although eighteen of these cases seemed comparable on all points to the cases of Group A, with no worse involvement of the lungs, they did not react favorably.' Maybe I should have waited until I could prove why it didn't work for those before I reported." He turned toward Liz and his face was worried.

"Don't be silly, Henry," she said sharply. "If you had waited, someone else would have reported it. Even if this man on the program did isolate our microcydin, he won't be ahead of you with it." She was like a mother fiercely championing her boy against another.

"If they really did isolate microcydin . . ." Henry said slowly. "Oh, hell, we don't even know that he's tried it on tuberculosis." He turned a page and was lost in his paper.

Liz undressed quietly. She tied her dressing gown around her and remembered how many times she had worn it at night, washing test tubes. She leaned her head against her shoulder and fancied that some faint smell of the mold clung to the material. The mucous membrane of her nose prickled and she sniffed as she was always doing in the lab. Psychic again, she told herself, but her eyelids felt suddenly dry and red.

Like the ladies in the ads on the soap boxes, she thought as she picked up the stockings she had worn and went briskly into the bathroom and drew water in the basin. When they were washed, she hung them on the towel rod, not caring whether they dripped on the hotel bathroom floor. You had so much time to do all the stupid little chores when you were worried or unhappy; it was when you were busy living that you didn't have time for them. She heard Henry stacking the pages of his paper together on the desk and went back into the room.

"Some of my results amaze me every time I go over them, Liz." His voice sounded confident again. "I'd be a fool if I didn't report them. If this Stockton had found a mold that would do as much, he'd probably be reporting 'A Cure for Tuberculosis.'"

She felt herself snatched back from an abyss onto safe ground, but she had no quick words. She lay on the bed, watching him.

"The next few years I'm going to put in finding out why microcydin doesn't work on those other cases." He was putting his papers back into the brief case that looked too new. Then he stopped and hunted out one particular sheet. As he read, he shook his head over it as though he were worried.

"Christ cured only a few out of the millions of people that were sick, but everyone was convinced." She didn't look at him as she said it.

Then Henry laughed. "Oh, Liz, as a scientist's wife you are wonderful! If pushed too far, you go back to faith healing!" He laughed so long she sat up and looked at him severely. Anyway, he felt better.

"Liz, did I ever tell you that I'm thankful for you?"

"No," she said promptly. "You seldom even act it."

"Well, I am," he said.

But when Henry had turned out the light and gone to bed, the room seemed filled with an uneasy dark. The lights from the street came in under the blind. They were used to the silent darkness that wrapped the sanitarium grounds at night. Liz knew that Henry was wide awake, going back and forth over his paper. What if someone else really had found Henry's mold? If all those years had gone for nothing? She turned restlessly away from the light and fell asleep.

Henry's thoughts broke away from his paper at last, and he remembered Hester's note that she had given him so mysteriously. He had forgotten it until he put his hand in his pocket at Bill's, and there was no chance to read it then. He went over to the closet, finding his coat easily in the light from the street, and took the note into the bathroom to read so he wouldn't wake Liz.

Dear Henry,
    I can't let you go off on so important a trip without writing more than I could say tonight. You are not apt to come back to this little place for long. Many things will be open to you after such a brilliant piece of work. I want to see

you go on to bigger things. But I want you to know too how much you have meant to me.

I was suffocated with dear, good, easygoing Carl. Sometimes, I felt as though I couldn't breathe and then I would have to go away for a bit. Living is meant to be more strenuous than that. And then you came and let in a breath of air. You lived vigorously and the life around you quickened. It affected even Carl. Did you notice that I spent more time again at the sanitarium? Nights when Carl was in town playing poker with his cronies and I couldn't sleep, I have walked past the light in your laboratory window and known you were working, doing something that would amount to something. In your work I lost my stultifying sense of futility in the life here.

You will put all this aside as the wanderings of an older woman, Henry, and I am much older, old enough to be your mother, but in some matters age does not count. Our minds understand one another. We are both ambitious, motivated by the same urge that Carl could never understand.

"Fame is the spur that the clear spirit doth raise
(That last infirmity of noble mind)
To scorn delights and live laborious days."

To want to make your mark in the world is something that Carl doesn't see, but I want you to know that I am with you in spirit in this important moment of your life.

Hester.

He sat on the edge of the tub with the letter in his hand. He couldn't see Hester writing a letter like that; it didn't seem like her. But he had known she was interested in the work from little things she had said, and the other night when he left he could see how much she wanted to have a part in it. It touched him to think she should get such a lift out of the lighted windows of the lab. He looked back at the note to see how she had put it:

"In your work I lost my stultifying sense of futility in the life here." You couldn't really blame her for feeling that way; the institutional life was dull and Carl was pretty easygoing and uninspired for an ambitious taut-drawn person like Hester.

He had said something of the sort about Hester to Liz once, and Liz had said, "Hester didn't have to marry Carl, and when she gets fed up, she dashes off wherever she wants to." Liz had no sympathy for her, but he could see how Hester felt.

Those lines of poetry she had quoted were a little beside the point, but he turned the page and read them again:

> "Fame is the spur that the clear spirit doth raise
> (That last infirmity of noble mind)
> To scorn delights and live laborious days."

The last was true enough. He and Liz had lived laborious days, but Fame hadn't been the spur. He remembered that day he had come back to school after his mother's death, when he was eight. He had felt uncomfortably set apart from the others, and the teacher had made it worse by putting her arm on his shoulders when he stood beside her with his excuse note. The whole class seemed to look at him from a respectful distance; only Tony and Walt came up to him in the cloakroom and asked him about it. He could remember now the smell of the damp jackets and rubbers and the look of the shiny pine wainscoting. "Did you see her die?" Walt had asked, and he had had to say no, that she died at a sanitarium. "Did she die of tuber-culosis?" Walt had wanted to know, stumbling over the word so that Tony snickered. Then Walt had asked, "Don't the doctors know how to cure it? They oughta."

When he had told Paul once, long ago, that his interest

in tuberculosis had dated from that day, it had sounded a little sentimental. But Liz had understood why he had to try to find something to cure tuberculosis. That was spur enough.

To Hester a man should want to make his mark in the world. She cared so much for success, and to her, lack of success meant mediocrity. Well, he wanted to make his mark too.

He got up stiffly and turned off the light. Then he replaced the letter in the pocket of his coat and went back to bed, somehow cheered by Hester's words.

ENTERTAINMENT
FOR VISITING WOMEN

WHEN Liz woke, Henry was already out of bed. She could hear the shower running in the bathroom. She lay still, watching the cord of the window shade move in the spring air. Sunshine broke into separate colors on the edge of the heavy glass ash tray and spilled a little warmth on the impersonal taupe carpet of the hotel room. There was a spot of ink on the rug, round like a half dollar. But it wasn't on her rug and she need do nothing about it. And then her mind moved in from the outer to the inner sense of the day.

This was the day Henry gave his paper. That was why they were here. "Twelve years ago . . ." the paper began. Then she remembered, someone else was giving a paper on antibiotics. She wondered if it came before or after Henry's and stepped out of bed to the desk to get the program. She moved over into the sun, where the carpet was warm under her bare feet, to look through it.

The other paper came before Henry's. The three men's names attached to it looked like a brigade leagued against the single name, Henry R. Baker, M.D., under his title. She tucked the program back into the blotter and went over to the window and leaned on the sill like a woman in a tenement. She couldn't look out onto a city street every day.

Beyond the sharp corner of the many-windowed wall across from her she could see a patch of Lake Michigan. Twelve stories below, traffic moved and squealed and came to a sudden stop at the insistence of a distant, piercing-sweet whistle, then moved again. A woman crossed the street with a child hanging to her hand. The lights changed before they got all the way across and they were marooned on the island in the middle of the street. The cars rushing past them on either side made them look helpless. Liz heard Henry open the bathroom door.

"Hello, my lovely wanton, I hoped you were still asleep," Henry said and came over to her. He put his arm around her and his hand came gently under her breast. "Want a shaving kiss," he asked, kissing her.

"Henry, they'll see us across the courtyard."

"Let them. We're only a man and a woman in a hotel room to them. They don't know that we've found a mold to cure tuberculosis!"

She knew by his fooling that he felt good and excited and eager to give his paper, that he had stopped worrying over the other one. Everything was all right, and she felt suddenly good and gay herself.

"I must get dressed," she said.

"I'll have breakfast sent up to you so you can be luxurious." He didn't say to make up for all the drudgery at the sanitarium.

"No, I want to go downstairs with you. Wait for me." She didn't say because I want to be with you as long as I can today; we're together in this.

He said, "You'll have to hurry then."

"I'll only be a minute." As she left the window, she saw that the lights had changed on the street below and the woman and child were walking across a path of safety laid across the sea of traffic, like the dry land across the Red Sea.

71

Before she turned on the shower, she heard Henry whistling in the bedroom.

In the lobby there were many men wearing badges with their names on that showed they were doctors attending the meeting. There were more older ones, she thought.

"I don't think it's a healthy profession, Henry," she said. "Look at that doctor!"

Henry grinned. "He looks a little haggard, all right."

There were wives with badges too.

They went downstairs to the coffee shop and ate by themselves. "I think that's Harley Apgar over there, Liz. He's head of tuberculosis research at Johns Hopkins."

Liz considered him as she drank her orange juice. "He looks bright," she concluded. "Are you going to talk to him about your work?"

"Well, I'd like to. I'll wait till after I give my paper; he might be interested then," Henry said.

He could ask Henry to come to Baltimore to work on tuberculosis research, Liz thought to herself. Nancy could go to that school for the deaf there and be near them, then. Dr. Apgar, whom she had never seen five minutes before, became suddenly a benevolent and powerful saint. Especial grace rested on his pin-striped gray suit, and the heavy pink plastic rims of his glasses were halos.

"That's Halstead, Liz; see over there, paying his check? He did the work on the estrogens. A beautiful job. He's going to talk this morning."

"Oh," Liz said, looking appreciatively at the unprepossessing little man with the box of slides under his arm. "Do you know him?"

"No. I heard him at that other meeting I went to. I haven't been around enough to know many men except those from Woodstock," he said.

"It's high time you did."

"You can't do that kind of a job and get around too. But from now on I hope to get to these meetings so I can talk to some of these men who are working in the same field."

Liz finished her coffee happily. "From now on." It would be very pleasant.

Someone called to a man just coming in the coffee shop. The group at a table in the corner shook hands with him and made a place for him. They were all talking at once. That was what Henry had missed, Liz thought.

"I'll come back to the room at noon, Liz, and get your blessing," Henry said as they stood in the lobby. "That Stockton paper comes at 11:30. I'll come up after that. Mine is in the afternoon session."

"Don't have me on your mind, Henry. I'll probably be with the girls and you'll want to have lunch with someone. I'll see you around five, in the room. And if you can't get there, just leave a note at the desk."

"Well, maybe that's the best idea. I'll be just in time to hear Halstead's paper if I go in now," Henry said. She could see that he was beginning to be tense again.

She nodded. "I'll go up and write Nancy. Good luck!" she couldn't help saying though she didn't need to. Henry knew she wished him that. They tried not to say obvious things, but she lingered a moment after he left her, watching him cross the crowded lobby. Tomorrow, people would say, "That's Baker, did the work on that mold that cures tuberculosis." Standing there by the magazine stand, she thought she had never loved Henry so much. There was nothing little about him or dishonest or self-seeking. And she was awed again by the miracle that he could have worked out this thing by himself.

"*Sun* or *Tribune*, lady?" the man at the newsstand said

sharply. "Oh, the *New York Times*," she said on an impulse of superiority.

"Yestidday's. We ain't got today's yet."

"The *Tribune*, then, I guess," she said and paid for the paper she really didn't want and folded it under her arm as she went over to the desk to ask for mail. There was a letter from Nancy. The round handwriting looked so good to her and on the other side, around the flap, the straggling initials Nance always put on her envelopes, S.W.A.K. Liz carried it upstairs to her room to read. She wished it had come before breakfast so Henry could have read it.

The beds weren't made and the room had a disheveled air. It seemed less their own than it had last night. The sun had moved away from the window sill and the courtyard was cold in the shadow. She ignored the unmade beds and sat down to read Nancy's letter.

Dearest Mother and Dad:

I'm so glad you are *both* away on a vacation *at last!* Think of the poor molds all alone! And the guinea pigs! [Nance loved the exclamation point.] It was my turn today to sit behind the glass door and have the rest of the class read my lips. We can say anything we want so I said: "My father has found a mold that can kill TB bugs." One or two could read my lips right away, but most of them thought they were wrong when they read the word mold. It was nice for a change to be on the knowing side instead of the reading. Afterwards, Miss Allen asked me if it was really true. I said yes it was, and that you had gone to a meeting to tell other doctors about it this week. I felt very proud.

Can I come home the middle of May if I get a good grade in lip reading? I get tired of being with mostly deaf girls. I guess I forget I'm deaf too. I want so to be with you at the sanitarium for spring.

Thank you for the new sweater, Mom. It's a beauty.

Worlds of love to you both,

Nancy

P.S. Be sure to go to a night club! You might collect a souvenir for me, or an autograph of the orchestra leader if he's one of the famous ones.

Liz sat entirely still for several moments, then she gave a little moan and shook her head slowly back and forth. Her throat ached. She folded the letter and put it inside her bag. It wouldn't help Henry to read it before he gave his paper. She was glad now that it hadn't come before. He could read it tonight. "See, Henry," she would say, "she'll never think of herself as deaf." She had told him that before. And he had said, "We want to be careful about that though, Liz. Some people who are deaf, older people particularly, make it harder for themselves because they don't admit it. They're too proud to wear an instrument and they're a nuisance to people." Henry said to patients: "You have active tuberculosis. Let's face it and plan to beat it." Henry was very gentle with Nancy but very firm. Just the same, Nancy was used to hearing, and she went on hearing with her mind. That was important.

They would talk about Nancy's coming home in May instead of June. Perhaps they would call her up tonight. Nancy could hear quite well on the telephone. It would be so good to hear her voice. A wave of longing washed up in her mind. But maybe Henry would feel that Nancy ought to finish the term. The first two weeks she had been so unhappy and wanted to come home, and Henry had written her two or three times a week, but he had kept saying, "We mustn't let her run home to us."

"Don't forget how tired we get of the molds, Nancy, and yet we have to stick with them," Henry had written her.

75

And, of course, he had been right. Nancy had come to like the school.

Thinking of Henry, looking at Nancy's deafness through Henry's mind, made her feel better. By the time Charlotte called about going to the antique shop, Liz's voice was gay. "I'll meet you downstairs in the lobby in five minutes." And she felt gay as she and Kay and Charlotte stepped into the taxi.

"Alice said she was going to stay in bed and sleep some more," Charlotte said. "John said Bill was really plastered last night. He went around shaking hands with perfect strangers at the bar and I don't imagine he quieted down very early. Alice probably had her hands full."

"That's hard on Allie," Liz said.

"Well, I just wouldn't stand for it," Charlotte said.

"And that would settle it, of course!" Kay mocked.

But Charlotte was unaware of any sarcasm. "Kay, I wonder if Paul couldn't do something to help Bill," Charlotte asked suddenly. "Doesn't Paul think drinking like that is due to some maladjustment? I mean, that's what you get in books."

"I wouldn't know," Kay answered. "Paul isn't apt to offer his advice unless it's asked for, you know, especially to old friends."

The taxi stopped in front of a three-story red house with a black slate mansard roof, black window frames, and a massive black front door. The fancy black ironwork around the roof and down the front stone steps gave the house the faintly raffish air of a respectable matron decked out in sheer black lingerie. Each of the long plate glass windows that looked on the street was filled with antique glass: amethyst, amber, milk, and cranberry.

"Look at that glass!" Charlotte exclaimed. "No, I'll pay for the taxi. This is definitely my trip!"

Liz knew when a doorman opened the door that everything at Arundel's would be expensive.

"It's fun to see it, anyway," she told Kay.

"Personally, I loathe old glass," Kay said. "I don't think it can be compared with some of the new Steuben or Orrefors. And I don't think it fits into a modern background. This, for instance. Did you ever see anything sillier?"

But Kay might have been a Victorian lady herself as she stood by the long window, a snood covering her short hair, old gold bangles over her gloved wrists, holding a glass dog in her hands.

Charlotte had met someone she knew in the hall. "I might have known you'd be here bright and early! I remember the old silver you went off with at that Medical Meeting in New Orleans." Charlotte's voice came through the room.

"Well, I . . . I'm rather interested in glass cup plates," Liz told the man who came up to her.

"We have quite a nice collection. Will you just follow me upstairs," the slender, colorless man in the studiously casual clothes told her.

Kay and Charlotte seemed occupied so Liz followed up the spiral staircase, letting her hand touch the polished mahogany rail, half pretending for an instant that this was her home and that the large old rooms opening off the upstairs hall belonged to her.

"In here," the man said, stepping aside to let her cross the threshold of a gloomy west bedroom. A canopied bed faced the white marble fireplace. Two mahogany bureaus flanked the windows. A black haircloth sofa stood before the fireplace and two stoop-shouldered rockers confronted each other vacantly across a marble-topped table. An Aubusson carpet stretched its faded pattern from baseboard to baseboard. Liz stood a minute looking around the room, and her guide waited for her admiration to force itself into speech. When she said nothing, he gave a little dry cough.

"These are all museum pieces, of course," he observed, laying his ringed hand on the marble top of the dresser.

No trace of living lingered. The occupant of this room must surely have been carried off for burial long ago and the bedspread smoothed up over bare mattress and bolster. Liz walked away from her thought to the bow window at the north end of the room. The light was heavy but it filtered into the room through a hundred pieces of clear glass: glass compotes, cake plates, figurines, glass hats and slippers. The clear glass could draw no sun from the gray-white light, but it gave a spurious sense of warmth.

"How much are the little cup plates?" Liz asked.

The man's mouth twitched, as though it had been waiting eagerly to answer. "Twenty dollars the pair. We don't sell them singly. Of course, no one has any use really for a single one."

"I am matching some that a friend has. I only need one," Liz said.

"What pattern is your friend collecting?" His tone, or was it a slight emphasis, distrusted the friend.

"The Henry Clay pattern; it was cast for his campaign for president in 1844," she said stoutly, pleased that she could be so definite.

The man's eyebrows raised. He took one of the little plates that leaned against the window and held it up to the light so Liz could see the head of Henry Clay. "Quite perfect," he murmured.

78

"I suppose it is the real flint glass?" Liz asked, trying to sound knowing.

For answer he snapped the edge of the tiny plate with his thumb and finger and a perfect pendant of clear sound hung suspended for an instant in the room. He reached for the companion plate.

"Your friend," he said with that same faint derisive emphasis, "will be delighted with these."

Liz hesitated as though considering. She could hear voices downstairs and the sound of the front door opening and closing. Hester would be delighted with these two plates, but she couldn't afford them. She was aware of the man straightening a plate on the window shelf, shifting his feet, discreetly but with impatience.

"They are perfect, but I couldn't consider buying a pair." She handed the little plate back to him.

He was slow in taking it. "I doubt if you will be able to find another pair to match your friend's. Unless, of course, you would be satisfied with imitations." His tone of voice assumed that she would be.

She turned away from him and walked toward the door, toward the voices of people who could afford to pay twenty dollars for a pair of cup plates. He replaced the second plate on the window shelf and the thin sound of glass against glass reproached her. She was conscious of every sound in the dead air of the deserted bedroom. He cleared his throat; now he was coming down the stairs behind her, scornful of her, sneering a little perhaps. She felt that she was fleeing in front of him and deliberately stood still with her hand on the railing. Then she saw Kay in the hall below.

"Kay!" she called out.

Kay turned. "Oh, there you are. Come and look at this silver teapot."

Relief flooded through her. Liz turned to the man behind her. "Thank you," she said and smiled at him.

"Don't let me break this, for Heaven's sake!" Charlotte said, getting into the taxi with a cranberry glass decanter. "I do think it's a beauty. And you know everyone doesn't know about Arundel's. The dean's wife told me about it."

"I'm pleased with this silver teapot too. I suppose it was some of that silver they shipped over from England during the war," Kay said.

Liz felt empty-handed. She wished she had found something to buy. She remembered what Hester had said and repeated it as her own, "I think the only way to go on one of these trips is to have something to look for and something to bring back."

"I know it. That's true. I always bring something special back from places," Charlotte said. "I told Alice to meet us at Fields' at one. We'll just about make it."

They had to wait a few minutes for a table, the room was so crowded. But Liz liked the waiting. The orchestra drowned out the clatter of dishes and silver and the sound of voices, mostly women's. The covered dishes carried past on trays sharpened her appetite. She thought of the noons at the sanitarium when she heated canned soup and made a sandwich for lunch. Henry came when he could, and they ate at the kitchen table. He read through a case record as he ate or an article in a journal, and she read too, one of Hester's magazines. If she had spent all morning in the lab, she came with a wad of Kleenex in her pocket for the exasperating running of her nose. When it was bad, Henry noticed it and was conscience-struck. "Sunday, Liz, I'm going to tend to that serum for you. It's stupid to let it go and have you sniffing all the time." But he forgot. Somehow, they never did it.

"Four," the lunchroom hostess said and led them

through the maze of diners to a table by the window. Alice found them there before they had finished ordering.

"I'm a little late because I walked all the way down here. You know at home I get out in the garden every day in the spring, and I just felt boxed up in that hotel," Alice said. She looked very smart and younger than her age and gave no sign of the two sleeping capsules she had taken at four in the morning.

"Did you see anything of our husbands?" Charlotte asked.

"Bill was going to hunt them up for lunch. I saw Paul and Henry in the lobby and told them Bill was looking for them."

Then Henry wasn't nervous, Liz thought. The other paper wasn't worrying him. She felt enormously free and relaxed. "I think I'll have the fresh mushroom soup and crab salad and coffee," she said. What fun to be sitting here having luncheon with Alice and Charlotte and Kay. She had been too busy helping Henry all these years to do things with the women in Pomeroy. She had little idea of who they were or what they did. Henry's work had held them so tightly together that they hadn't needed other people. But it was hard now to think of anything to say. She sat back and listened.

"I'm doing over one of the girls' rooms," Charlotte said. "And I want to leave the walls turquoise and change the rest of it. The walls are the shade of this sample." She laid a small swatch of wool on the tablecloth, tilting her head to look at it. "This is from an old evening cape that I had the painter match."

"Are you going to have it modern or Early American?" Alice asked with immediate interest.

"Be modern about it; you can do a much smarter room," Kay said.

Charlotte took a sample of red wool from her purse and laid it next to the snip of turquoise. "This on the armchair and then eyelet embroidery curtains," she said dreamily.

Liz's glance wandered out across the tearoom. She felt cut off from these women whom she had known so well as girls, and yet a sense of familiarity with some other experience teased at her mind, another time when she had sat like this, her fingers crooked around a teacup, talking woman talk . . . but she couldn't remember.

Alice and Charlotte and Kay had come along for the trip, she thought. Nothing was expected of them except to look attractive and keep themselves amused with shopping or a play or buying antiques and be charming over cocktails with Dr. and Mrs. So-and-so. That was their only connection with their husbands' work. That made them ideal as doctors' wives in practice. She would have to learn to be more like them.

The conversation had veered to Russia. "Our Medical Auxiliary had a review of that book on Russia. . . . I can't just think what it was," Alice was saying. "Oh, you know, that diary by the man who wrote the book about the Wayward Bus."

"Steinbeck," Kay prompted.

"Yes, that's it. Well, honestly, when we got through, I guess we all felt that if they just had some doctors and their wives go over there. . . . I said to Bill, why couldn't there be an international Medical Meeting in Moscow?"

"I imagine Stalin would go for that idea," Kay said.

"If they had it in Russia, only the men would go anyway," Charlotte said.

"I think the men enjoy Medical Meetings more if they take their wives, though, and it's good for you both to get off together where the office can't reach you. Like this meeting, I think it's lots of fun, don't you?" Alice asked.

This meeting wasn't the climax of days and months and years of work for them, Liz thought. Everything didn't depend on it. She glanced at her watch. Henry might be up in the room going over his paper. He would have heard the other paper by now. She wished she knew how it would affect Henry's. It was one-thirty. If she went right away, she could see Henry before he left for the afternoon meeting. What was she doing here when Henry might need her? She laid her fork on the plate and took a final sip of coffee.

"I'm sorry, I forgot that I said I'd be at the room at one-thirty. I'll have to run and I'll see you all this evening."

"Why, you can't make it, Liz. It's one-thirty now! You're late anyway," Charlotte began.

Liz was already hurrying across the dining room, counting her money for the bill. She was impatient at the wait for the elevator, but once down on the main floor she streaked through the crowd and out to the street. She looked so frantic the policeman on the corner whistled for a taxi for her. What had she been thinking of? Henry hadn't said he wanted her there, but he might.

As she went down the silent corridor to their room, she told herself that she was being foolish. Henry would have gone to lunch with Paul and the others. He wouldn't be back; she might as well have stayed and finished her lunch. But she had to be there anyway. She got the door unlocked quickly and swung it back so hard it slammed against the closet door.

"Henry!"

SCIENTIFIC SESSION

AFTER the first paper that morning, Henry and Paul went out in the lobby.

"Seems like old times, Hen; like coming out of old Speedy Bullitt's class."

"Sure does. That was darned good, but it made me realize how rusty I am on everything but the contents of the thoracic cavity. On anything else I feel like Rip van Winkle."

"Well, why not? That's your specialty. What's your next move, Henry?"

Henry dropped his cigarette in the jug by the elevator before he answered. "I don't know. I suppose I'm hoping this work I've done will open up something. If I had enough money to swing it, which I haven't," he said with the humorous grin Paul remembered, "I'd like to get a teaching job on the TB service at Woodstock or any other decent teaching institution. I've learned a lot of things they didn't tell us when I was there. And, of course, I'd like to go on with this work on the mold."

"Well, if it makes a big enough splash, maybe you can," Paul said. "Tell me about it, Hen."

He was back, miraculously, in their room at the fraternity house, Hen turning around from his desk and straddling his chair backwards to say, "Look, Paul, why can't you give a patient with . . . ?" Henry's mind was always playing around with an idea, questioning and reasoning. Hen's marks hadn't equaled his own, really, and sometimes a professor had been annoyed with his questions, but Henry never cared much about marks.

Paul listened now in amazement. "You mean you took those molds of that guy at the State Aggie and kept 'em going for eight years?"

"I kept trying to find others. We had to do it in such a small way, you see. I gave up on Perth's molds about the time penicillin came out. But when penicillin didn't work on TB, we went to work again with a mold of our own. I felt sure there was some mold that would kill the tubercle bacillus. I know Liz thought I was nuts, but she helped me all the time."

"Just you and Liz did all that lab work?"

"We had a little volunteer help from a nurse and an orderly now and then, but otherwise we did it alone."

"You must have thought you were the Curies," Paul muttered.

"Well," Henry smiled. "Thinking of the Curies helped some when we got discouraged."

Paul smiled too. "We call that identification with the myth in my lingo, Hen. There's a lot of that. I suppose that's one of the biggest reasons a lot of boys decide to be doctors." But Henry wasn't put off.

"Maybe you're right. I used to think if Louis could bury himself in that charity hospital in Paris for six years collecting his statistics, I could hold tight a little longer."

"You've stayed twelve years by my calendar."

"Yes, but the Pomeroy TB Sanitarium is paradise compared with the charnel house Louis worked in. Besides, I had Liz."

"That's right," Paul said.

"And about then, like all those stories, this mold from the dirt started to do things."

85

As he talked, Paul grew excited himself. "You mean, Hen, this stuff, what do you call it?"

"Microcydin."

"This microcydin has cleared the lungs absolutely in twenty-five cases?"

"Yes. It saved Nancy's life too. She had a severe case of brucellosis."

Men milling around in the corridor disappeared into the ballroom where the papers were being given, but Paul and Henry still stood by the radiator along the wall. The second paper was over and crowds surged back into the hall.

"Who've you told about this, Hen?" Paul asked.

"Nobody, really, but the head of the sanitarium. Perth's dead, you know. I really wanted to carry it a longer time to make sure of the cures. You see, I can only go back a little over two years. I hesitated about making a report so soon, but I wrote to Dr. Hancher at Hopkins. He urged me to report the work and gave me a place on the program."

"Why didn't you report Nancy's cure right away? Anything that will cure severe brucellosis is terrific. I have a patient now whose child died of it. I'm treating her for her guilt complex because she let the child have the raw milk."

"Oh, it was only one case and not scientifically controlled. You see, I had Nancy on sulfa and then I gave microcydin too. But it cured her. And, Paul, Nancy lost her hearing."

"God!" Paul said softly. He saw the changed expression on Henry's face. He looked suddenly fifteen years older. "Why do you think it was the microcydin stuff that made her deaf?"

"Because I've seen some temporary auditory disturbance in a couple of TB patients I gave it to in smaller amounts."

"Does Liz know?" Paul asked and the next minute could have bitten off his tongue.

"No. I hope Liz doesn't have to know for years," Henry said. "I'm only mentioning Nancy's case in my paper as an example of further possibilities to be explored."

"God, Henry," Paul said again. "You've paid enough for it."

"Yes," Henry said. "So has Liz."

"Hi, Paul! Henry Baker, as I live!" Someone they had known at Woodstock came up to them. And they went in together for the next paper.

Paul wasn't interested. He sat in the darkened room and thought about Henry. Suppose Henry had found a cure for tuberculosis. No suppose about it; he had found it. He had twenty-five cures. Why, his name would be one of the "greats" in medicine: Henry Baker who had used to room with him, who sold textbooks and worked as assistant in bacty to make enough money to stay in school; Henry Baker who was so absent-minded they used to rib him at the house and tell him he'd never remember to propose to a girl. And then he came back one week end married to Liz. Liz and Hen had moved into that two-room apartment in the old Cheney Apartments. It was Henry's getting married that had decided him to get married. He and Kay and Liz and Henry had been pretty close those two years.

Paul remembered a remark of Kay's one time after she had been in one of her moods. "Kay, what in Heaven's name do you want out of marriage that you don't have?" he had asked her in bewilderment. And she had whispered with her face on his shoulder so he could hardly hear her, "Paul, I want you to love me the way Henry loves Liz."

He had been a little hurt and dumfounded. "Kay, I

love you more than Henry could possibly love Liz," he had protested. "He gets so wrapped up in the patients on TB that he forgets everything else. Sometimes he doesn't go home for thirty-six hours."

He remembered how she had lifted her head and looked at him the way she still did when she felt he didn't understand her. "That doesn't have anything to do with it. Every man has to have his work or his art, or should have. But there just isn't anybody else in the world for Henry but Liz. Not even himself."

Paul shifted in the uncomfortable seat. On the screen the smears of blood cells followed each other, but he didn't see them. He was thinking so hard about Kay. Then he went back to Henry.

Pretty nice at forty to come out with a piece of work like that! By tonight everybody would know about Henry Baker. Old Hancher must have been excited when Henry wrote him. Henry deserved success after all those years and knowing he had caused his child's deafness. It wouldn't be easy to carry that thought around with you. He remembered now that Liz hadn't gone on about Nancy very much, the way women did.

As the lights went on for the conclusion of the paper, Paul leaned over to Henry. "Do you want to stay for the next one?"

"You bet I do," Henry said with a grin. "That's right in my back yard."

Paul took out his program and read the title: "A New Mold with Antibiotic Properties, a Preliminary Report."

"I'll meet you afterwards, then. I want to catch Ransom," Paul said and went on out.

Once the paper was started, Henry was unaware of anyone around him. Four words floated across the heads of the men in front of him and sounded through his mind so loudly they deafened him for a minute to anything the speaker was saying: *"A microorganism isolated from the soil."* A dirt mold like his. *"We have called this bacteromycin."* Unconsciously his hand went to his collar, pulling it away a little from his neck, and his fingers against his own skin were cold. For a moment he couldn't see the man on the platform standing above the reading desk. The man's voice blurred and became inaudible to Henry as though the loudspeaker had failed. Then the words were clear again, terribly clear, pounding in on his brain: *"Strikingly similar in its properties to penicillin except that it is far more active against gram-negative and acid-fast bacilli."* That was true of microcydin! A sickening certainty grew in his mind. The bacteromycin was different from his microcydin though it was of the same family of molds. He leaned forward, his lips parted a little. His heart beat so loud it was hard to hear the speaker. *"At the present time, all the therapeutic possibilities of bacteromycin have not been determined but it has been successfully used in some of the lower animals."*

Without knowing it, he had been holding his breath. Now it came from his lungs as though he had been running. The man next to him glanced at him and moved a little to the other side of his seat. But he, Henry Baker, had used microcydin on humans, one hundred cases, even on his own daughter.

". . . and in various diseases of man, to show that it is a compound of proved value."

The speaker was discussing the method of production. For a few seconds Henry forgot everything in his concentration. Their work had been done under the best circumstances with trained bacteriologists, but they had the same difficulties he and Liz had had.

"Bacteromycin is produced more effectively in agitated

submerged than in stationary or surface cultures. . . ."
They had found that out. He thought of Liz shaking the
big jars until she was exhausted.

He nodded his head following the description of the
complicated process of production. Once, not knowing that
he did it, he spoke aloud, "Yes." A refinement on his own
technique delighted him. He could do that. Perhaps he
could obtain a purer form that way. Of course! He hadn't
thought of that. His mind followed, almost ecstatically
freed from all personal coloring. A dozen questions he
would like to ask crowded to his mind. After the lecture
he would go up and ask the speaker. When a slide was
thrown on the screen, he was breathing so hard the man
next to him looked at him in annoyance.

*"In this brief preliminary report we cannot go into de-
tail. The results of studies now under way will be presented in communications in the near future but it was
thought wise to present in a general way certain remarkable results obtained with bacteromycin. Since 1942 . . ."*

He had started early in '41. The excitement that had
held his mind suspended and impersonal faded; now his
personal feelings rushed in, clouding all clear thought.

*"Since bacteromycin was found to be active against
mycobacterium tuberculosis it was then tried on inoculated guinea pigs. . . ."*

Henry sat farther back in his seat. He thought of the
guinea pigs in the basement of the cottage. And suddenly,
irrationally, he thought of Liz saying, "I hope I never
hear the squeak of a guinea pig again as long as I live."
Sweat poured out on his face and on the backs of his hands.

*"Very cautiously, it was tried on patients in terminal
states."*

"Don't call them terminal, Henry," Liz had cried out

one day. "You can't be so sure that they are." Henry shook his head as though to escape from the thought of Liz.

"*. . . We have had very hopeful results and although we cannot say positively, we are inclined to believe that this may be our best ally against tuberculosis. This slide will show the results of two control groups in two types of tuberculosis.*"

As the speaker finished, the usual applause began. Some were already hurrying out. The dignitaries at the back of the platform stood clapping. The president of the society came over and shook the speaker's hand. And then, slowly, like a kind of ground swell, applause grew all over the room. Men were talking aloud and clapping at the same time. An interest approaching excitement, rare in such meetings, was apparent. Someone was clapping the speaker on the back. "A cure for tuberculosis," someone said.

Paul had come in well before the end of the paper, when the speaker was explaining the technical details of the production of bacteromycin. It sounded like Henry's stuff, called by a different name. Paul raised in his seat, trying to see Henry. This was a pretty definitive piece of work unless Henry had priority. For an instant he felt a kind of relief; Henry hadn't quite made it after all. A red flush of shame spread under Paul's skin. He thought quickly of what this would mean to Henry. It was enough to make a man crack, like Morton and Wells who spent the rest of their miserable lives fighting for priority in the discovery of ether. But Henry would never fight for any priority. . . .

"Do you suppose they've got it this time?" a young man next to Paul asked him at the end of the paper.

"What?" Paul asked, deep in his own thoughts.

"A cure for TB. You must have been asleep. It's hot enough in here to put anyone to sleep."

"I don't know," Paul answered a little stupidly. Then he saw Henry still sitting in his seat.

A sense of numbness kept Henry from feeling or thinking. He chewed the inside of his cheek so hard the flesh bled, and the salty blood moistened his mouth that was too dry for saliva. The occupants of the seats beyond his crowded past, and when one man trod on his feet, he stood up. His stunned brain told him he should applaud and, belatedly, as the clapping was dying down, he clapped with hands that felt brittle. He stopped in confusion, realizing that he was the only man in the room still clapping.

He hesitated a moment in the aisle; he should go up and congratulate the speaker, tell him of his own work, but as he hesitated, the speaker, surrounded by a group of men, left the platform. Two men with buttons in their lapels saying PRESS came past Henry.

"Get some sort of a statement from him!" one of them said.

"This is the big news of the meeting. Tell Sam to give it the play."

"What's the guy's name?"

"Stockton. Here it is on the program," Henry said, holding out his program to the news reporters.

"Thanks." The reporters went out to the telephone.

It was too late to see Stockton now. He would look him up this afternoon after he gave his paper. Was there any point in giving his own paper?

On his way out he felt a hand on his arm and turned quickly. It was Paul. "Henry, I heard the last part of that damned paper. Let's go get a drink."

"Oh, thanks, Paul, I . . . not just now."

"Hello, Henry and Paul. Bill's looking for you." Alice appeared suddenly beside them in the lobby.

"Hi, Alice," Henry said. He left her to Paul and walked rapidly through the crowds to the elevators. He had to get away from everybody, upstairs, alone where he could think, where no one could see him. He hoped Liz wasn't in the room.

LIZ closed the door quietly behind her. Henry had moved the writing desk over near the window. His papers lay all over it. His slides were spread out on the white spread of one of the beds. Henry was in his shirtsleeves and his collar was open at the neck. He looked abstracted and as though he hadn't slept for days—the way he looked when Nancy was sick, or the day he gave the first of the microcydin to Lester Small.

"Henry," she said, "what happened?" And then she knew. Her legs were suddenly weak. Her lunch rose sourly in her throat. "Stockton's paper, Henry?"

"Yes," Henry said. His voice was quiet. "It's a beautiful piece of work, Liz. They did everything we did so much better. They found their mold without so many false starts; it isn't microcydin at all; they call it bacteromycin, and it's more effective."

"Than microcydin, Henry?" she asked in a small voice.

"Sounds like it. It's the darnedest thing you ever heard of, Liz. It's really funny in a way!" His voice broke. The sound made her shiver. "Theirs cures some cases of tuberculosis too."

She sat down on the other bed and saw that the pillow was dented in and the spread mussed. Henry had thrown himself down on the bed when he first came in.

"What are you doing now?" she asked in a dry voice.

"I've been going over this paper of mine to see how it reads in the light of the other one. We've got more cases over a longer period, but our percentage of good results is not as great as theirs even with our larger doses. Really, the only point in giving the paper at all is to add to the general knowledge of molds," Henry said.

"You mean, our microcydin won't ever be used to cure people?" Her voice seemed to come from across the room, as though someone else asked the question.

He shook his head. "Why should it be? They report better results with smaller dosage with their bacteromycin, Liz." His voice was impatient as though he were explaining something to a slow pupil. He had no right to give it to her so brutally, but she might as well know now. The bitterness he felt got into his words and burned Liz as he spoke. "I can imagine what Hester will say!"

"Good glory, why Hester?" she said sharply.

"Because she hates failure so."

"I don't like it either. What are you changing?"

"Oh, I'm changing the tone a little. I sound as though I were Balboa and the first white man to see the Pacific."

"Leave it that way. You were. When did they find their mold?"

"Late in '42. We were a few months ahead of them in that, but it doesn't make any difference; they found a *different* mold, Liz, don't you understand? A dirt mold but with different cultural characteristics."

Liz was silent, trying to take it in. Finally she said, "Have you had any lunch?"

"I don't want anything. I couldn't choke it down if I tried."

She went over to the phone and ordered some lunch. She wondered how much it would cost to order lunch à la carte and sent up as well, but she didn't ask. Henry sat staring out the window. She went over to the desk and picked up the first page of the paper.

"Henry, you've written all over here so you'll never be able to read it!"

"I had to change some of it. I sound too sure of myself, as though nobody else knew anything about it."

"Why shouldn't you sound sure?" She wished he wouldn't just sit there. She remembered the morning and Henry saying, "We're only a man and a woman in a hotel room." That was what hurt. They had felt themselves more, a very special man and woman who had done something special.

"Damn me, anyway, Liz, why would I go off up to Pomeroy and try to do something in a half-cocked way without any real facilities? You should see the set-up and equipment Stockton and his men had for raising the molds and taking off the bacteromycin."

"There was nothing half-cocked about our way. We grew enough to get microcydin to use, didn't we? If we'd found the most effective mold, it would have seemed remarkable and fine. Well, it still is!" This was the way to talk to Henry now. When he left to give his paper and she was alone, she could really look at this thing and see it for what it was. It helped her too to sound firm.

She took out the old portable typewriter that had been Henry's in college and, putting in a fresh sheet in the typewriter, began to copy the first page. Henry had written an explanatory paragraph.

Until this morning, when it was my privilege to hear Dr. Stockton's presentation, I believed my dirt mold to be unique, but Stockton, Fenton, and Grayson reported a mold that appears to be more effective. The great similarity in cultural characteristics and in the clinical effect leaves no doubt as to the close relationship of the two. Their results would eliminate any reason for reporting this mold which I have called microcydin except that it will throw a little more light on the importance of this group of molds in the future therapy of tuberculosis. . . .

Liz's face was set grimly as she copied the words. Her fingers struck the keys angrily. Why did he have to say it out so plainly?

Henry's lunch came and he went on reading over the pages of his paper. The room was oppressively still except for the angry clackity-clack of the old typewriter. She stopped.

"Go on, Henry, and eat. You look ghastly now. Henry! Henry, please."

He sat down and ate the poached egg and a slice of toast. He drank the coffee black and pushed the table out of his way. Liz felt him standing looking out the window. She finished typing over the altered pages and stacked the sheets.

"You'll have to change your shirt and it's a quarter after two."

Obediently he took off his shirt as though he were glad to have something to do. He tied his tie badly and had to retie it. Then he put on his coat. Mechanically he arranged the slides in the slide box.

"I guess I'll go," he said.

"I'm going to hear you."

"No, Liz!" he said sharply. "Please don't. I don't want you there."

"All right. I'll go down to the mezzanine with you anyway."

They were silent in the elevator. On the mezzanine doctors with badges passed them or stood in groups talking. The doors at the end of the balcony opened and closed, and with each opening came the sound of the speaker's voice.

"Well, I'll go on in so I'll be there," Henry said.

"Maybe you better." She caught his hand an instant quickly. His was cold and it frightened her.

"I'll be upstairs when you get through, Henry."

He nodded. She waited, hoping he would turn around, but he went on in.

She didn't go back upstairs. Instead she sat in one of the chairs along the corridor and tried to look as though she were not at all interested in the room with the closed doors. She wished she had put her hat on or brought her gloves. She didn't really believe Henry's paper would just be passed over. The work behind it must show, the fact that he had done it on his own. No one could overlook those cases that were cured. The other paper couldn't have everything Henry's had. She felt suspended in hope, waiting.

The closed doors at the other end began to impress themselves on her: their heaviness, the bottom panel bracked and scarred as though a whole family of children had kicked it, the grooved paneling, the heavy silver knobs, one on each door. They looked fateful and yet promising, like the double doors of the living room at home on Christmas Eve. They looked final, like the doors closed on the room where her grandfather had died.

Someone opened the doors with a clatter, setting the stoppers on them. Men began pouring out, each one with his name badge that he would take home to his children when the meetings were over. The children would finger it a minute for its satin ribbon and the gold printing, maybe even pin it to a sweater or playsuit, and then discard it, and it would be picked up and tucked in a drawer. It wasn't easy to throw away anything so official looking, and years later, when they moved or cleaned house, it would pop up again.

Some of the men came out for a smoke and stood discussing the last paper. She wished she would see someone she knew, Paul or Sam. No, not Paul, but Peder.

"Going in for this one, Joe?" one man asked another.

He shook his head. "I've had enough for today. They've been corking, haven't they?"

One man hurried by with a brief case in his hand. He looked at his watch as he passed, for all the world like the Rabbit in *Alice in Wonderland*. A sick-looking young man went by, reading his program as he went. She imagined that he had had TB and been cured. Of course, he would be going in to hear Henry's paper.

Then the roar of talk in the big room quieted. The same man came out and released the door stoppers.

She got up hurriedly and slipped inside the doors just as they closed, quite like Alice following the Rabbit. She sat down quickly on a seat against the back wall, hoping that people would take her for a woman physician, that she looked that intelligent.

The men on the platform at the far end of the long room appeared small and insignificant. It was hard to make out which was Henry. Back of them hung a large white screen. It made a pitiless background that dwarfed the men in their gray and black suits.

A little figure in gray was talking, explaining some change in the next day's meetings, and Liz wondered if the delay made Henry nervous. The next day sounded as far off as life after death. Her eyes came back to the screen. The blank expanse yawning there could stand for all that was still unknown in medicine. Each man threw little marks on it, strange graphs and figures like Henry's, but none of them were permanent. They died out and gave place to others.

The man was announcing Henry: "Dr. Henry Baker,

State Sanitarium, Pomeroy, New York." She wished she could see Henry's face more clearly. The light was poor. He placed his paper under the reading light and his hands were more illuminated than his face. His voice, giving the formal greeting, didn't sound like Henry's. The loud-speaker gave it a rasp; was it nervousness or despair or bitterness that it amplified? She clasped her hands over her bag as though it were something to hang on to.

"I don't want to stay for this; it's more of that anti-biotic stuff we heard this morning," a man in front of her whispered noisily to his companion, and they both went out.

"Until this morning, when it was my privilege to hear Dr. Stockton . . ." Henry's voice changed and became more natural ". . . leaves no doubt as to the close relationship of the two molds."

He was cutting the brief history. He had skipped the part about "twelve years ago." She wished he hadn't. It may have been personal, but they should know how he, how they both had worked. Why didn't he say, "My wife and I, day in and day out, for twelve years"? He made it sound cut and dried. "I first became interested in the possibilities of molds through Dr. Perth of the State Agri-cultural College. Dr. Perth was apparently the first man in America to be aware of Fleming's little-appreciated report." Henry felt so badly that Perth had died before he found his mold; he felt he owed him so much. ". . . When none of the extracts from Perth's strains or from penicil-lium proved effective in treating tuberculosis, we began to work with a dirt mold.

". . . In a cruder way than Stockton and his co-workers with inexperienced operators . . ." But devoted operators, Henry. Even Jake, the orderly, was devoted, and Miss Symes and your wife, Liz. . . .

". . . By 1941 it was possible to test the extract on the mycobacterium of tuberculosis. The results were so spectacular and the amounts needed so small that we gave the extract from the dirt mold the name of microcydin. The balance of 1941 was devoted to testing the extract on inoculated guinea pigs. (Slide, please.) This slide shows . . ."

Liz was glad of the dark that fell on the room, for the statistics on the sheet. They didn't show up very well from the last row, but they were something on the yawning white screen. Henry's voice was better now, warmer, more sure.

The big doors opened and closed with a squeak as a latecomer slipped in. The squeak was like the squeal of the guinea pigs in the basement. Oh, you got used to it. Henry wasn't even aware of their squeaks. Nancy used to stop and listen when she was a tiny tot and say, "Bunnies, Mummie!" Henry told her they were guinea pigs, but she went on calling them bunnies. And now she wouldn't be able to hear the squeak. Liz wondered if Nancy used to take in more things through her ears than most children, or was it just that now that she was deaf they remembered her hearing so well? The squeaking guinea pigs had helped to save her life.

". . . This slide . . ." Up in the corner were the initials L.S. for Lester Small. The curt columns of dosage, temperatures, and pulse, and all the rest of it, couldn't begin to tell the story. And this was Henry's best case. She wished that he could throw a picture of Lester Small standing at the crossing with his stop sign and tipping his hat and smiling as they rode off in the train. Henry had finished with the case.

"The success of this case encouraged us to select a group of cases . . ." There was no applause. She had dreamed

101

that they might rise in an awed body when Henry told them about Lester Small, that he had been about to die and was well now.

". . . The following slide shows our results in one hundred cases. Of these, twenty-five were cured or greatly improved. There remain the seventy-five upon whom the mycrocydin seems to have had little or no effect." Must he say it so bluntly? He looked at the unsuccessful cases as squarely as he looked at Nancy's deafness. She didn't. She pretended.

The lights were on. Henry seemed strangely alone and defenseless standing there on the stage. She felt her love for him rising in her, reaching across the room to protect and sustain him. It didn't matter about the other paper. She knew what he had done, alone by his own efforts. How could she ever have minded any of the drudgery or the low salary or the sanitarium? She wanted to tell him that the years weren't wasted, they had been so close together.

Henry lifted his head and faced the sea of faces. He seemed to be looking across them to her. It was hard to sit there and not go to him.

"We encountered more untoward effects than Dr. Stockton reports from bacteromycin. This may be because we have used the microcydin on more cases or because bacteromycin is less toxic. In certain instances, vertigo, rash, kidney disturbances caused us to reduce the dosage below an effective level and in two cases to discontinue the therapy altogether. Auditory disturbances were encountered in six cases. In this connection, as a matter of record, in one desperate case of brucellosis with a failing heart in a thirteen-year-old child . . ."

Liz caught her breath. She held her bag against her mouth. Brucellosis was the other, technical, name for Nancy's disease.

". . . where sulfonamides had proved unable to cope with the disease and microcydin was given, the patient recovered but permanent deafness resulted. . . ."

Nancy! Henry was talking about Nancy in that calm, toneless way. Nancy's deafness was due to their microcydin. He had known that all along and not told her. Her own ears pounded. She closed her eyes against the tears that burned under the eyelids.

On the stage Henry paused as though he too found it difficult to go on. But the pause was lost on Liz. When he continued, his voice was quiet. ". . . This report may serve to confirm the importance of earth molds in the therapy of tuberculosis." His voice was low, too low to be heard clearly at the back of the room. He hesitated as though he had something more to say, but the light, signaling the limit of time, flashed. He nodded, and it seemed to Paul, listening in the fifth row, that he bowed to the inevitable, and, picking up his papers, walked off the platform.

A tiny scattering of perfunctory applause rattled over the audience. The chairman of the program shook hands with him.

"Poor delivery!" a man near Liz said. "Still in an experimental stage. I'll let them work with it a while before I try it on any of my patients."

"Since penicillin, they're going mad over molds. They aren't the answer to everything by a long shot," an old doctor grumbled.

"What was his name?" one man asked another, turning his program.

"Don't know. Never heard of him. Barker, something like that."

✦

Liz slipped out in the crowd. Henry would go right upstairs as he had this morning. She didn't want to see him. He would be sunk, but she couldn't help him. She never wanted to hear of microcydin again. If Henry had never touched it, Nancy wouldn't have been deaf. But she might not be alive, either, another part of her mind insisted. How could you tell? Maybe she had passed the worst of it; maybe she was getting better without the microcydin. Henry didn't know.

She walked out of the hotel without her hat and turned unseeingly up the avenue. The smell of the molds was in her nostrils so strongly that she sneezed and fumbled in her bag for her handkerchief. Her head or her eyes ached. She wished she were . . . not back home; home meant the sanitarium and the lab and the molds. It meant Hester sneering at mediocrity. There was no place to go. She walked faster, not looking in the shop windows or at the people she passed, only wanting to get away. She could turn down to the lake and sit on the sand. She could cry there and nobody would know her, but she had lived too long with Henry to cry. "We mustn't cry for ourselves, Liz, and it's easy to do."

The heels of the pumps she had bought for this trip pounded against the pavement. Her lips that had lost any trace of lipstick were caught between her teeth and her eyes stared coldly at the people coming toward her up the street.

HENRY stepped down off the platform and went to the projector table to get his slides. The next speaker, who was handing his slides to the operator, nodded and said, "That was an interesting piece of work you did."

"Thank you," Henry said. As he picked up his slides, he dropped one. The thin glass fell with a slapping sound against the floor, cracking into pieces that were held together only by the strong passe partout tape that bound the slide.

"Oh, that's too bad," the other man exclaimed.

"It doesn't matter; I'm through with them," Henry said as he picked it up.

The chairman called the next speaker to the platform. Henry shoved the sheets of his paper into his pocket, then seeing that he would have to go past the platform to get out, he sat down quickly in a seat at the end of the first row. It would seem rude to go out now.

The speaker had begun, but Henry heard no single word. He wiped his face with his hand and found it wet. He could smell his own perspiration soaking into his suit and noted with surprise that his feet and hands were clammy. He wondered impersonally how the paper had gone, if Dr. Stockton had heard it. He could still feel his heart pounding and he wished he had hurried out for a drink. His mouth was dry and he felt parched. There was a pitcher of water on the table on the platform, but he had not even seen it when he was standing there.

He wondered what Paul had thought of the paper. He wished now that he hadn't told him so much about the work. It would be published in the journal, eventually. At least there would be a record of all he had tried to do, filed away in the archives, along with the record of the efforts of the generations of doctors, each with his little grain of fact to add to the great impersonal total, only a rare person here or there finding something new or important enough to mark an advance. He had thought he might be one of them. But not he, Henry Baker. Stockton, Grayson, and Fenton had found something better.

"How did it go?" Liz would ask. "Tell me what people said." He hoped fiercely that someone would say something to him about it so he could tell Liz. "An interesting piece of work," the man speaking now had said. Liz would make a face at that. Or she wouldn't ask. She would be solicitous and do things for his comfort, like this noon, but waiting to hear all the same.

Thank God he had told Liz about the Stockton paper, but he had still hoped somehow then. Liz had hoped too. He had still had his paper to give. Now it was over. He doubted if it had caused the slightest flurry of interest. It seemed preposterously childish now that he should have thought that the two of them could have discovered something as effective as penicillin, that they could name it, as you name a child, and give it to the world.

If his paper had come first? No. People might have been as excited about microcydin at first as they were about bacteromycin, but the other paper would have wiped out its importance anyway.

He pushed his hands into his pockets and stretched his legs out in front of him. Yet where had he been wrong in doing as he had done? His mind went back to his first interest in molds when Perth came down to talk to Dick. But he shouldn't have kept at it so long. He had had no right to put in twelve years working on something that someone else would have found sometime, anyway, and with less effort. He had had no right to drag Liz along with him. It was thinking of Liz that made it so hard. Quickly his mind moved to the Daltons so he wouldn't have to think about Liz.

He thought of Carl, Wednesday night, proposing a toast, and Hester smiling, her sharp, bright eyes meeting his, holding his; her saying, "The first time there's been anyone here who wasn't satisfied with complete mediocrity." He had never warmed to Hester, and yet she had managed to connect him with that exciting medical world she had known in her father's house. Now he had let her her down. He minded this disappointment for Hester too. Hester would resent it because it would seem to tie her more closely to failure and unsuccess. He shifted uncomfortably and pulled in his feet.

The lights came on and the paper was over. He hadn't heard a word of it. The Scientific Session was ended for the day. He was glad to be interrupted in his thoughts. He glanced at the men around him, but he didn't know any of them. A white-haired man whose badge said Louisville, Ky., nodded to him and said, "Extraordinary things, these molds! Interesting paper."

"Thank you," Henry replied, grateful for his speaking to him. He followed the crowd out into the corridor. He lingered a little near the entrance, hoping that Dr. Stockton might be looking for him. He would like to look over Stockton's data a little more carefully, but more than that, he would like to talk to him about molds.

"I wish to congratulate you on your paper." A dark foreign-looking man stepped up and shook Henry by the hand. He spoke with a pronounced accent. "You haf been more deeply interest to find a cure for tuberculosis than

Dr. Stockton. He was interest in what bacteromycin could do in any direction. You haf had one end in view."

"Yes, I have had," Henry said, touched by the man's earnestness. He tried to read his badge and made out only Switzerland before the man had given his hand an emphatic pump and gone off.

"Henry, we've been waiting for you!" Bill and Sam came up to him. "Paul's looking for you too," Sam said.

"Swell, Hen. It was swell," Bill said. Henry remembered that Bill hadn't heard the paper this morning.

"Gosh, Henry, I want to hear more about it. I supposed you were just running a sanitarium. I had no idea you were doing research too." Sam had his arm around Henry's shoulders. "It stands on its own, a piece of work like that." Sam knew how he felt. He was trying to say, "Never mind about the other paper."

"Thanks, Sam," Henry said. "Sam, you don't know Dr. Stockton, do you? I'd like to meet him."

"No, but I'll hunt him up. That shouldn't be hard. I'll circulate around a little and see." He leaned closer. "Why don't you let the son of a gun look you up?"

They went on, and Henry stood aimlessly in the crowd, looking as though he were waiting for someone. He saw Paul coming across from the elevators.

"Henry, you need a drink! You've been through enough for one day." He put his arm through Henry's.

"That was a real piece of work!" Paul said as they waited for their drinks at a table in the crowded bar. Why did they say "piece of work"? Both Sam and Paul. But that was all it was: a piece of truth. "I can't begin to tell you how impressed I was with it!" Paul felt self-conscious as he said it, and yet he meant it. The drive, the stubborn persistence that had kept Henry at it all these years, the courage was what it came down to—to try it in the first place was heroic—but when he tried to get it across to Henry he felt foolish. There was something about Henry's stillness that stopped him. Henry had ordered his drink as though it didn't make any difference to him, almost as though he were doing it in his sleep.

"The thing that I can't get over, Hen . . . ," he began with a fresh cigarette.

"The thing you can't get over, Paul, is that I was fool enough to let myself in for such a blow, that I went off up to Pomeroy and tackled a problem like that by myself. Liz and I: she did half the drudgery. You're not impressed by what we found, by microcydin. It's worthless because another man has found something better. Let's forget it!" He took a gulp of his drink, and it had no more taste to him nor effect than so much tap water.

"I don't blame you a bit. Stockton's report was enough to blow the ground out from under you. And it was tough having that powerhouse of big names from a university back of it," Paul said. Henry's bursting out like that was better than having him just sit there. "Just the same, Hen, I'm perfectly sure your work won't be entirely brushed aside."

"Why are you? There's nothing to keep it alive. You'll never hear of microcydin again, brother. Just bactero-mycin." It annoyed Henry that he remembered the name bacteromycin so easily. "You heard the applause, the real excitement this morning. When I finished this afternoon, there was just lukewarm interest."

Paul turned his empty glass slowly in his hand. "The same," he said to the waiter. Henry took out a fresh ciga-rette, and Paul leaned across the table to light it for him. Seeing Henry's face lighted for an instant was like the sudden strange second when your eyes caught the eyes of a driver of a passing car. You seemed to see deeply, intimately, and then you were past. He had always thought of Henry as a selfless individual, spurred on to research to find a cure for TB, his mother dying with it and all that. But he wasn't entirely selfless. He had his ambitions too. The sense of inferiority Henry had always given him ebbed a little; he felt closer to Hen than he had in all the years they had lived together in Woodstock. Henry was indulging in his share of self-pity right now, or he didn't know the signs.

"It's incredible that there could be two molds so much alike," Paul began. "There's John. Come on over here, John," he broke off with relief.

"Henry, that was nice work!" John turned to the man with him. "Dr. Helmer, I want you to meet Dr. Foster and Dr. Baker. Dr. Foster left the cloister and is in private practice in psychiatry in New York. And Dr. Baker gave the paper this afternoon on the new antibiotic."

"Oh, yes," Dr. Helmer said politely. "I didn't hear it. That's a little outside my field of interest, you know."

"Dr. Helmer is in Washington," John explained to Paul and Henry. "With the Crippled Children's Division."

While they were ordering their drinks, John saw someone else he knew. "Excuse me just a minute; there's Welborn. I've been wanting to see him. I'll ask him to join us."

"It's amazing the way psychiatry is growing in importance," Dr. Helmer said to Paul. "A sad commentary on modern life, isn't it, really?"

"Don't put it that way, Dr. Helmer. We psychiatrists feel that these same problems and difficulties have always been present, and the wise physician has done what he could to meet them, but . . ."

"Dr. Welborn has an engagement. I was glad to get a word with him, though. He's chairman of the Board of Regents of the College this year," John said.

"That's your drink there, John," Paul said.

"Oh, thanks. I was about ready for this one. Well, Henry, I bet there's a weight off your mind!"

"Yes. I'll listen to your paper tomorrow with a free mind." Henry pushed back his chair. "I have to go and find Liz. Glad to have met you, Dr. Helmer. See you, John. Thanks, Paul." Henry went swiftly between the crowded tables out of the dimly lighted room into the lobby. He couldn't stand any more of that. He stopped at the desk to ask for mail. He wished there had been a letter from Nancy. That would help Liz. But there wasn't any letter.

It was five-thirty and Liz would be upstairs waiting for him, wondering why he didn't come. But he was in no hurry to see her. She would know it hadn't gone well from his slowness in coming up. He stopped at the counter and bought cigarettes and spent nearly half an hour at the transportation desk, arranging for their return Pullman space. Then he stepped into the elevator.

A man wearing a badge got out on the twelfth floor with him. He glanced at Henry and then turned in the opposite direction. Had he heard his paper? If so, he hadn't been impressed. Perhaps he hadn't been there.

Henry went down the corridor to their room. At least he could tell Liz what Paul had said, and the doctor from Switzerland. But Liz would know how it really was. He wished to God they hadn't done everything together. If you were going to work at a thing like that, you ought to have sense enough to do it alone.

IT WAS close to five when her blind walking took Liz past the house with the sign ANTIQUES hanging over the steps. She went by at first and then came back to peer through the dirty window glass at the clutter of objects crowded on two horsehair-covered chairs and a marble-topped table. Sad brown portieres looped back at either side of the window, and on the right-hand curtain a fly-specked sign proclaimed in crooked letters "Rare Bargains." She might just look at the glass, Liz thought. She still had to take Hester something.

She wouldn't tell Hester that the report had gone badly. She would say three other men had discovered a mold that Henry thought was better but that he had made a real contribution. That was what you always said, a contribution to science. Henry's experience was greater than that of the other men. . . . Why shouldn't it be? He had learned by treating Nancy! She stood still at the top of the stone steps and held on to the railing until the paroxysm of her mind eased. Had Henry told Carl and Hester about Nancy? Perhaps he had said, "I'm not telling Liz, naturally."

A chipped enamel plate held by one screw to the central panel of the door bore the words WALK IN. This place was as different from Arundel's where Charlotte had taken them as the way she had felt yesterday was different from the way she felt today. She opened the door boldly and walked in, attended by the jingling of a bell far off in the back of the house.

The front parlor and back parlor had been turned into

one long tunnel of a room that was jammed with old things. There was no attempt to group like objects or separate the merely shabby or secondhand from the few genuine antiques. Prices were marked in pencil on stickers. A sign on the wall below a cracked oil painting sounded the first cheerful note: "Look around: you will find something you want."

A man opened the door at the rear. He looked shabby and disheveled, secondhand rather than genuinely old. His glasses were patched with black adhesive tape. His coat was a different color from his vest or trousers.

"How d'you do," he said around a dead cigar.

"How do you do. I was looking for some old glass."

"That's right. You look. There's some over there on that sewing machine and that table. We've got a bunch of it. Look at this!" He indicated two sections of a bookcase propped on a radiator and filled with glass pieces, everything from a pitcher with Niagara Falls in gold lettering to an old brown gin bottle. The proprietor raised the glass front of one of the sections and stood waiting without haste or interest.

Liz minded the silence in the room. "What I was really looking for was a Henry Clay cup plate."

"Let's see, somewheres here I've got a little glass saucer." He removed his cigar and laid it on the edge of the sewing machine while he pulled out a drawer of an old secretary. "Little stuff in here." He and Liz looked together, moving the glass tiebacks and the odd stoppers and sandwich celery dish a little.

"It's all white and red in here," he said, as though only now arriving at the decision. "Sure you don't want some pretty red glass? That's what most ladies come looking for."

"No," Liz said, turning away. "I want clear." She felt

suddenly that she had always wanted something different from what other people wanted—life with Henry, even when it meant making so little money and working all the time. How had she been so sure? "Why don't you let Henry get started first?" her father had asked, and she had said, "Because I couldn't stand to wait all that time. I want to help him." She stood in the dusty, cluttered room and looked with a little pity at that person she had been.

"Red glass is awful pretty in a window," the proprietor commented from the rear of the room.

"Yes, I know it is. I like it too, but . . ." There were other ways of living your life besides slaving over an obsession. If she had waited a little . . .

"But you're fixed on one thing! Well, it pays to know what you want."

Not if you were going to question yourself twelve years later.

The proprietor had reclaimed his moist cigar. "I know I had one little glass saucer here cause I used it for an ash tray. I maybe carried it back to the office."

Liz followed between the furniture to what had once been a butler's pantry. A rolltop desk fitted under old dish cupboards and was covered with a litter of papers. He lifted the blotter.

"There!" He held up a small clear glass plate and, turning away from her, blew the ashes and cigarette stubs off on the floor. "There you are. I knew I had one. It's got that President's head you wanted, too." He held it close to his eyes. "No, he didn't get to be President, that's right. He just missed out."

Liz took the little plate. She and Henry had just missed out too. They had found a mold but not quite the right one.

"How much is this?" she asked cautiously.

The proprietor's mouth sucked in around his cigar. "How does a buck strike you?" He looked around, hunting for something else to use as an ash tray.

"Do you have another like it?" Liz asked. "People usually sell them in pairs."

"Nope. That's all. You're lucky I had that. Had it ever since I started the store."

Now that she had it she could be critical, slow to take it. "Is it real flint glass?" she asked.

"Lady, you can search me. It's glass an' it'll break if you drop it, that's all I know."

Liz took a dollar from her purse, but she hesitated, fingering the cup plate. She was in no hurry to go. When she went out the door, she would have to go back to the hotel, she would have to see Henry.

The man was puzzled. "You want I should wrap it or can you put it in your purse?"

"Oh, I'll take it as it is. Thank you." She made her way back through the furniture to the front door. On the street she looked at the cup plate more closely. There was a little crack that she hadn't noticed before. She held the glass as the man at Arundel's had done and snapped the edge with her gloved finger. It gave a small flat clink, and she slipped it carelessly in her purse. She was sorry that she had bought it; it was imitation, and Hester would see that at once and smile that special contemptuous little smile she had for things or people that were ordinary or mediocre or not quite a success. Let her. It fitted this trip. Maybe it fitted them, her mind insisted. She turned back to Michigan Avenue.

Henry would be waiting for her in the room, wondering what had kept her all this time. She thought of him sitting at the desk, looking the way he had this noon, and quickened her walk, hardly waiting for the light to change before she crossed the street, pulled to him as she had been all these years. Then, deliberately, she walked more slowly.

Liz unlocked the bedroom door without tapping or calling. Henry wasn't back yet. She needn't have worried about him. Then she saw the roses in a vase on the dresser. Beside the vase was an envelope addressed to Mrs. Henry Baker, Room 1216.

From Henry. He had known how she would feel. "In spite of the way it worked out, I thank you. I love you," Henry was saying. She took the card out of the envelope, and scribbled in the meaningless handwriting of florists was the name "Hester."

She tore it across and dropped it in the wastebasket. Then she saw the pinch bottle of Scotch on the desk. There was a card with it that read, "With pride and congratulations, Hester."

Liz slipped the card back in its envelope. She put the vase of roses beside the bottle on the desk. Then she opened the window so the fresh night air could drive out the heavy fragrance of the flowers. She had a gaunt, sickish feeling. Slow tears came to her eyes and she let them come. Pity for herself contracted her throat.

She was tired of thinking of things Henry's way. His nobility had always made her ashamed of her own selfishness. But was it nobility? Hadn't he really wanted to be the one to find a cure for tuberculosis as much as he had wanted to cure it? He didn't mind the endless drudgery because it was what he wanted to do more than anything. He said so himself. He was as obsessed as any man hunting gold. It hadn't really mattered to him that it had meant making only enough to live on, that it had tied his wife down. In all these twelve years this was the first trip they had taken together. Once he had found the microcydin, he hadn't cared about anything else.

With sudden resentment she remembered that he had never tended to a vaccine for her allergy. "I'll run some tests, Sunday, Liz. We can make you a vaccine that will settle that." But he had never got to it. If she had had something that he could have treated with microcydin, that would have been different!

She remembered the night Nancy was so very much worse. Henry came out to the kitchen while she was getting some supper that they wouldn't be able to eat anyway. Henry's face. His saying, "I got the call through to Dr. Soames in New York. He doesn't advise moving Nancy, even by plane. From what I could tell him, he thought the outlook was about hopeless. He said they didn't have anything else to suggest for fulminating brucellosis beyond what we've done."

She remembered how she had been spooning water on the eggs she was poaching to make the yolks coat over. "Did you ask him about trying our microcydin?"

"No, Liz, he doesn't know anything about microcydin. It will have to be my own responsibility. If we knew anything else to do, we wouldn't risk it, but we don't. I don't like to take care of my own child, either, but Carl gave up two days ago, and there just isn't anybody here who can do anything for her."

They had sat at the table almost in silence. She had known Henry was making up his mind the way he always did—by himself. She remembered how she had asked as he got up from the table, "It couldn't make her worse, could it?"

"I don't think so, Liz," Henry had said. "And it probably won't help either."

They had been up all night. She had fallen asleep in her chair. Henry had waked her and brought her a cup of coffee when it was daylight. "Nance is better, Liz," he had whispered as though he were afraid to say it aloud. "I'm going to give her another dose at ten o'clock." He had given it the next day and the next. They had been thankful they had enough on hand.

He had given too much, and it had made her deaf. And given Henry another case to put in his paper.

The phone rang and she answered coldly, thinking it was Henry.

"Liz?"

"Oh, Kay."

"You didn't sound like yourself. You haven't forgotten you're coming down to our room before the banquet?"

"No, but Henry isn't back yet. He may be too late."

"Well, if you're ready, why don't you come on down?"

"I'm not dressed yet," she temporized.

"Come as soon as you can. Paul says Henry's paper was splendid. He was terribly impressed."

"Good," Liz said. She could imagine Paul telling her to say that.

"Have you seen Henry since the meeting, Paul wanted to know," Kay asked.

"No. I just got in." Paul was wondering how Henry had taken his disappointment. He was pitying them.

Liz took out the black evening dress she had borrowed from Hester. "Because, after all, it's foolish for you to buy one, Liz; you never go any place where you need one." It was a good thing that Henry hadn't grown any heavier so he could wear the dinner jacket he had had in Woodstock. The feeling of it in her hands bothered her. You couldn't live with a man so many years and touch his clothes unfeelingly; she laid it quickly on the bed. The coat to the suit Henry had worn on the train to save his new one had slipped off the hanger. As she picked it up, she saw the blank envelope sticking out of the inside pocket. She took it out and unfolded it.

Dear Henry,
    I can't let you go off on so important a trip without writing more than I could say tonight . . .

She turned the sheet over and saw the signature. It wasn't meant for her to read. Hester must have given it to Henry that night before they left. She turned to the beginning and read it through very slowly, then she put it back in Henry's pocket.

Why hadn't he said something about it? It was like a silly crush note a girl wrote to someone. But Henry must have taken it seriously enough so that he didn't want to talk about it. Perhaps he thought she wouldn't understand it any better than Carl. He had never seemed to like Hester, but maybe he did after all. He had thought of her this morning after the paper. He had said, "I can imagine what Hester will say." Perhaps she really did mean something to Henry.

Liz walked away from the closet and Henry's coat with the letter in its pocket, to look out the window at the wall across from them. This was like an installment in some soap-box opera that other women turned off their vacuum cleaners to listen to and waited till the next morning at eleven o'clock to hear what the woman in the serial was going to do. As cheap as that. What had made her so sure that she and Henry were so close, that she knew him so well?

She heard Henry's footsteps coming down the corridor, then their signal, three taps on the door.

"Liz?" Henry called softly.

Liz snatched up her bathrobe and fled hurriedly into

the bathroom. She turned on the water full force into the tub and pretended not to know that Henry was back.

"Liz!" Henry tried the knob of the bathroom door. It was locked. She wasn't anxious to see him.

"Hello," she called back, forcing her voice to sound natural. "I'm in the tub. I'll be right out."

She finished her bath slowly and unlocked the door.

"Kay called, Henry. She wants us for cocktails before the banquet. She said Paul was greatly impressed with your paper."

"He told me so," Henry said. "He tried to make me feel good." Henry was sitting in the chair by the window. Any other time she would have gone over to him. Instead she stood by the dresser and brushed her hair, letting it make a veil over her face through which she could watch Henry's reflection in the mirror.

"How did your paper go, Henry?"

"It was just another report of some work on a mold close enough to bacteromycin to be its brother, but a weaker brother, you understand." Henry's voice was dull. She waited, coiling her hair into a knot at the nape of her neck, watching the mirror. Henry would notice her silence and say something about it, and then she would tell him that she had heard the paper. But he seemed absorbed in his own recital.

"It's reception was nothing like Stockton's this morning. If my paper had come out this morning, it might have stirred up some excitement, but it was clear to anyone who heard both reports that microcydin isn't as effective." He lit a cigarette. She should say something. Henry was waiting, looking out the window. "They have a better mold; I'm not trying to deny it." He turned around from the window.

"Liz, can you stand it? After the way we worked, the

way you worked all these years. After my paper, I sat there and thought about that."

His voice bothered her, but she only said, "There isn't anything else to do, is there?" She slipped Hester's evening dress over her head and leaned closer to the mirror to fasten her earrings. Henry was staring out the window again.

She said, "You saw the flowers and the Scotch?"

"Yes, I saw them. Would you mind dumping the flowers in the wastebasket, and I'll take the Scotch to Paul's and get it drunk up."

After what seemed a long time, Liz said, "Henry, if you're going to Paul's before the banquet, you better get dressed." Why was she making it harder for Henry? "Would you rather not go?" she asked more gently.

"I can't sit here all night and lick my wounds. Besides, you've waited a long time to have some fun."

"Don't worry about me," she said. If he heard her, he made no answer. He went into the bathroom and turned on the shower. But he didn't step in right away. He was glad to be by himself. He had dreaded coming back to Liz, dreaded her disappointment. Why hadn't she said more about the paper? She was trying to make it easier for him by her brusqueness, trying to act as though it didn't matter. A sudden cold anger not for his own but for Liz's disappointment seized his mind. He opened the bathroom door.

"Why don't you go on down? Tell 'em I'll be there. Tell 'em I was held up talking to some men who were thrilled with my work. Tell John, particularly, that the room was so full you tripped over them." He closed the door, and there was no sound but the spray of the shower. She had never seen Henry like this. His voice had never had that tone.

The shower stopped. She heard the shriek of the rings on the shower rod. "What about some clean clothes?" Henry called. He hadn't expected her to go ahead. "Don't tell me I should shave again. I've got to look like the absent-minded researcher," he said, studying his face in the mirror.

"You look all right," she said.

He dressed in silence, and she fussed around the room, picking up the suit he had worn, tidying the bathroom, holding her long skirt above the damp tiles. Sooner or later she must tell him she knew about Nancy. It would have been easier when he first came in. Now it lay between them, separating them.

"Well, we might as well go," Henry said.

She picked up her bag and gloves, and together they went down the corridor that she was beginning to dread.

"I don't know why we do this when neither of us feels like it," Liz said.

"What would we do instead?" Henry asked.

COCKTAIL HOUR

PAUL leaned against the dresser where he had been pouring drinks. He held his glass in one hand. They were all there except Liz and Henry. John had brought up a doctor and his wife from Boston and three of his young men from the University. Sam had a woman doctor with him. There was no real talk, just bits tinkling dully, like the ice cubes knocking against the thick hotel glasses.

"Sam, you heard Hen's paper?" Paul asked, a little louder than he needed.

"You bet," Sam said, frowning a little. "That was a great piece of work, I'll tell you!"

"And work that I'm afraid isn't going to go for anything, considering Stockton's," Paul added. "It sounds as though Stockton has a mold that is a good deal more effective than Hen's."

"Oh, yes, Stockton's work is really a significant contribution," the woman doctor who had come with Sam said a little importantly. "We had heard about it at Hopkins, but we hadn't seen the actual protocols, of course. Tremendous potentialities!" She was rather uncommonly good looking as well as bright, which circumstance added weight to her remarks.

"Yes, but I was thinking about the human angle," Paul persisted, bringing them back to Henry. "You know, this is a tragedy for him. It means that his work, all the sacrifices he and Liz have made over these last twelve years, is obliterated. If you could have seen his face this morning! Frankly, it worries me to think what this is going to do to him," Paul said, stirred by his own words, not letting himself wonder whether Henry would like to be talked about and explained.

Everyone in the room was stirred by Paul's speech except Kay and Peder. Kay sat over on the bed, watching Paul. She knew he was enjoying it in a way. He was sincere enough in his sympathy, but he had always envied Henry. Peder frowned in his effort to understand.

Bill swore softly as he poured himself another drink, a little stiffer than Paul poured them.

"What's it about, Charlotte?" Alice asked in an undertone. "Oh, that's terrible," she said when Charlotte had told her. "Liz looked just the same at first, but, you know, at lunch today in the bright light I noticed how much older she looked, and really too thin, don't you think?"

"I don't imagine they've had much fun off in that place either," Charlotte said. "It must be pretty deadly and an awful place to bring up a child; no advantages, I mean."

"Why deadly?" Kay asked. "I envy them. Their lives have had some meaning. They've done the thing that we all talked of doing when the boys were interns but didn't do when it came right down to it."

"I can see you and Paul up in a place like that!" Charlotte laughed.

But Kay wasn't amused. "Well, that's what I mean; you can't see us."

Peder put out his cigarette. "Why do you emphasize the human angle? There is no place for the human angle in medical research. It cannot enter in. Henry knows that. What he wants is to cure most numbers."

Kay studied him, thinking what a relief he was. He made Paul seem sickly sentimental and patronizing to

Henry and Liz. That was it; to feel sorry for Henry made Paul feel better himself. He had been jealous of Henry.

"Peder, Henry isn't thinking about the human angle; that's Paul's own dramatic little idea," Kay said in a clear voice.

Paul never let Kay see that she had irritated him; he didn't now. He said in a calm voice, "You can't discard the human angle, Peder; maybe in Europe, but not here, thank God! The individual is still important here."

"It does bring Henry to the end of a blind alley," John said. "You see," John explained to his guests, "Dr. Baker has been working as assistant at a little state sanitarium all these years just to have the opportunity to carry on his work with a mold he believed could cure tuberculosis. He won't want to go on there, I don't suppose, and yet he'll really have to until some better sanitarium job opens up for him."

"Does he have his Boards?" Alice asked. She felt so good now that Bill had taken the last of his. He felt sure he had passed them all right. Dr. Osgood had practically told him so. Bill was so easygoing and so busy, of course, that he had kept putting them off, but she had kept right after him.

"No, he hasn't," Paul said. "He only had the extra time in bacteriology and his internship before he went to this sanitarium. But he's a good man. He'll do well anywhere and make a living. But he's just an example, I suppose, of a lot of men. . . ." Paul's voice took in everyone. He was sitting on the edge of the dresser now, squinting a little through his cigarette smoke. "What I'm wondering about is what happens to a man and woman who put all their eggs in one basket, so to speak—risk everything on one idea. The only ones we hear about are the Curies and the Dicks, the people who win in such a gamble. What about the others who lose, who don't get anywhere? What does it do to them?"

"The men who run for President and don't get it, you mean," Charlotte put in.

It was a good question for argument at a cocktail party; it could outlast the last drink, but Kay cut Paul short.

"You know, my dear psychiatrist, they'll be here any minute, and there'll be that horrid hush in the air if we've been talking about them."

Paul caught the displeasure in her tone. Kay couldn't stand to have anything said about Henry.

"The reason I was saying all this," Paul continued, "is that I'm afraid he's feeling pretty badly let down, and I thought it might help if we showed a little interest in his work. You know, draw him out a little, ask him questions about it. . . . It really is an absorbing story from the human side."

The talk tinkled again among them. Paul was filling Peder's glass.

"I'll have another, Paul," Kay said, chiefly because Paul thought she drank too much as it was. He took her glass and their eyes met. "Give poor Henry a hand for effort anyway," she murmured, mocking him, and saw him flush.

There was a knock at the door and, in spite of their intentions, there was an instant's guilty hush.

It was all so like the night before, Liz thought. If you went to cocktail parties two or three times a week, you would lose all track of time. It was feeding the guinea pigs night and morning and transplanting the cultures and getting three meals a day that kept your day in order.

"Liz, may I present . . ." Paul introduced the doctor and his wife from Boston and the woman doctor and the three younger men. It was a game. The last one introduced had to say something besides "how d'you do." Or you said something to him. The short young man whose name she hadn't heard clearly knew the game. He spoke first.

"I was greatly interested in your husband's paper this afternoon," he said politely. "I have an appointment in July at the Rossman Tuberculosis Sanitarium in New Jersey. Dr. Foster tells me you and your husband live at a sanitarium."

"Yes," Liz said, smiling. "It's not too bad, really. Are you married?"

The young man smiled. "Well, I hope to be. There's a separate cottage for the assistant on the grounds."

"Ah, yes," Liz said. "Partly furnished; heat, light, and water free."

"That's right. It sounds wonderful to us when it's so hard to find a place to live."

"Oh, it has its points," Liz agreed. "But you mustn't stay too long."

The young man looked at her quizzically. "Dr. Foster tells me you helped your husband in the work. He was telling us a little about it before you came."

She could see how it had been. Paul must have guessed how Henry felt about the other paper. He had dramatized their work so everyone would be interested. How like Paul, only . . . Two or three of the men were standing around Henry asking him questions. She moved so she could see Henry's face. Did it make him feel better?

"What part of the work did you do? Before you were married were you interested in research?" That was one trouble about a cocktail party—the man beside you stayed by you like grim death.

She didn't help him and he found it a little difficult.

"No, I majored in Romance languages and was interested in dancing. But you don't have to have much preparation to learn how to wash jars and feed guinea pigs. I became very clever at it."

The young man laughed. He had started out to be polite, but he was enjoying her now. Liz knew that he would write his girl about her. He would say, "They seem to have had a lot of fun, and the doctor has managed to do a fine piece of research. . . ." When you were at that stage, it was so good to look at an older doctor and his wife who seemed interesting and successful and still in love. It made you feel sure of your own future. It was good that you couldn't tell what their years had really been like. She didn't want to talk to this young man any more.

"Why don't you go over and talk to my husband about it? He would be so pleased that you were interested," she said.

"Oh, I can't bust in on him now. He's busy talking to Dr. Gardiner from Boston."

"Go ahead," she said and turned away. She felt suddenly so much older than this boy and able to dismiss him if she would.

"Liz, aren't you proud of your husband! Dr. Walters couldn't get to the meeting, but I've been telling her all about Henry's work," Sam said, coming over to her with his companion.

"Most extraordinary," Dr. Walters said. She had personality and a good deal of it permeated her voice. But there was something about her that made Liz think of Hester. The brown orchid on the impeccably tailored collar of her white evening gown allowed no truck with mediocrity either.

"Dr. Walters knows Dr. Stockton who gave a paper on antibiotics today," Sam said. He paused a second as though suddenly uneasy at mentioning it.

"Oh, I know him very well!" Dr. Walters filled the pause. Liz found herself wondering what Dr. Walters' first name would be; nothing like Mary or Liz or Peg.

"Dr. Walters is going to see that Henry and Dr. Stockton get together. So few people know anything about molds, they ought to enjoy talking to each other."

"How nice, Sam. Henry would love that," Liz assured him. "Did you tell him?"

"I will. Come on, Eunice, we'll go and talk to him right now." Eunice was her name. That fitted her better than a more commonplace one.

"Your idea seems to have been good," John said to Paul. They glanced over at Henry, sitting on the arm of the chair, talking to the doctor from Boston and the younger men and Sam and his friend.

"Better for him to talk about it," Paul said, adding ice to John's glass. "When he came out of that meeting, he looked as though he'd been hit between the eyes."

"I wish he had given his paper this morning," John said.

"It would have caused more of a stir for the moment anyway and got his name known a little," Paul said.

"It's amazing the way so often separate investigators, working quite separately and independently, hit on the same thing," Dr. Walters said in her clearly modulated voice. "There's something almost cosmic and preordained about it. You feel as though 'the time were ripe.' "

"Well, my work wasn't quite as spontaneous as all that," Henry said with a slow smile, but he didn't go on.

"It's fascinating, sir," one of the young doctors said. "It should make chest surgery much safer, I should think." He didn't say whose mold would, Henry noticed.

"It will," Henry agreed with enthusiasm.

✦

Liz sat down beside Kay.

"Henry's the lion of the party," Kay said.

"He was feeling pretty flat after his paper. What did Paul say about it, Kay, really?"

"Paul said it was the most damnable thing he ever heard of. He said he didn't see how Henry could sit there and listen to that other paper. When it was over, Paul looked around and saw Henry standing there clapping."

Liz could see Henry too. He wasn't small. He wouldn't minimize another man's work, but it would hurt him all the same. As Hester had written, he had wanted to make his mark!

"It's you I've been thinking about, Liz. You've given up so much so that Henry could do this work."

"Oh, you don't think about it when you're doing it. Just now and then, when you get fed up."

"You probably know it, but I wanted to tell you, Liz. You've been awfully fortunate just the same. You've been so together. Paul and I have grown farther and farther apart. I have no touch with Paul's work; of course, I couldn't have, but we just don't seem to have any desperate need of each other." Kay shrugged her shoulders ever so slightly and looked so poised, almost amused, that it was hard to believe she had used a word like "desperate."

"Oh, Kay, you can't say that. Paul couldn't do the work he does with badly adjusted, unhappy people if he didn't have you at home."

Kay's lips discounted such an idea. "Thanks, Liz. I don't know why we talk about me anyway. I was just having my little moment. There are plenty of married people who don't matter vitally to each other—you know, bone of my bone, flesh of my flesh, that kind of love."

Liz felt embarrassed. Kay leaned toward her and her face lost its poised amusement. The lines in her forehead deepened. Her face was thin and harried. The darkness under her eyes was not eye shadow after all, but the sign of unhealthiness of body or soul.

"I . . . we've been so busy, Kay, we've hardly had time to think about our love," she said.

"Of course you haven't, because it was there. It was there in Woodstock. I used to feel it." Kay sat back and picked up her glass.

"That woman doctor Sam is with is good looking, isn't she?" Liz said in the pause, to cover the moment of seeing too deeply into Kay's mind.

But Kay paid no attention. "When I die, Paul will feel badly, but my death won't take half of him; that's what I mean. That's the way it would be with you and Henry. Do you understand, Liz?"

"But if anything happened to you both, you'd find you were closer together than you think," Liz fumbled. "Nancy was terribly sick with undulant fever, Kay. When she got better, she was deaf. I . . . couldn't have stood it without Henry." But as she said the words, the meaning went out of them; she remembered that Henry had caused that deafness with microcydin. And he had tried to keep her from knowing it. She hardly noticed Kay's little murmur of sympathy. Kay touched Liz's hand, but Liz did not feel her touch. She looked over at Henry. The men were standing, ready to go.

"According to Stockton's paper the stuff is much less dangerous than penicillin," the man from Boston was saying.

"But you reported some injury to hearing, didn't you, Henry?" Sam asked.

"Yes," Liz said clearly from the other end of the room. "He gave it to our child, Nancy, and it made her permanently deaf."

She hadn't known she was going to say it. She hardly knew what she was saying until the last word. Then she looked at Henry. His was the only clear face in the room. He was staring back at her. She lifted her head and met his eyes.

There was movement in the room. Everyone was talking; fragments of sentences came to her: "Banquet at eight . . . quarter after now." "Thank you, Paul." "So nice of you to have us, Kay." "Nice to meet you, Mrs. Baker."

Sam came over to her and squeezed her hand. She was glad when he went on; she felt stupidly like crying. Why had she said that? In front of everyone. She had hurt Henry.

"Why don't you and Henry come out and have dinner with Paul and me, Liz? We aren't much interested in going to the banquet, are you? They're all alike anyway," Kay said. "I'll talk to Henry." Liz felt rather than saw Henry and Paul coming toward her across the room that had been so crowded a minute ago. Paul's arm was around her, but she stood stiffly.

"Henry, I was just asking Liz if you and she wouldn't rather go some place to eat with us instead of to the banquet?" Kay said.

"Why . . ." Henry started to answer.

Liz didn't want to be with Paul and Kay. She spoke quickly. "We don't get to banquets very often in Pomeroy. I wouldn't miss it." She used someone else's voice. "I have to go up to the room first. We'll see you." She didn't look at Henry. "Thanks, Kay and Paul. It was fun."

"We'll go on down, then," Kay said, a little hesitantly. "We'll meet you there."

ANNUAL BANQUET

Now they were walking down the corridor to the elevator. Henry was silent. "I didn't want to go to the banquet or out to dinner with Kay and Paul," Liz said. "I wanted to be by ourselves." Before Henry could answer, the elevator door opened in front of them, like some decision.

"Down car," the attendant said, white gloved hands waiting on the lever. Liz stepped inside the crowded elevator and Henry followed. She wished it didn't have to land at the lobby floor, but when it did, she stepped out and waited for Henry.

"Let's go outside," she said, not looking at him.

"All right," Henry said. "You're sure you don't want to go to the banquet?"

"I couldn't."

"Cab?" the doorman asked. Liz shook her head, and they turned toward the avenue. She had to hold Hester's black net skirt in one hand so it wouldn't drag on the pavement. She should have brought a wrap, but if they went back up to the room, they would stay there, and she wanted to get away from the hotel. It was a warm April evening, warmer than it would be at the sanitarium.

"Do you mind missing the banquet?" she asked, looking straight ahead.

"No," Henry said. "Liz, I didn't want you to know about Nancy because it was easier to feel it was her disease that caused the deafness. That was hard enough to take." Henry's voice was tight and slow as though he was thinking each word. He went right to the point.

In a store window a manikin on an exercise machine bicycled up and down, up and down, getting nowhere.

"Yes, it was easier," Liz said. "Because you can't be sure that Nancy wouldn't have got well anyway." She heard herself and was shocked at her own cruelty, but she seemed to have nothing to do with what she said. She . . . wanted to hurt Henry.

"I'm certain that she wouldn't have survived without microcydin," Henry said. "And I was afraid to give less than I did. Liz, you can only do what you think best at the time, and then you can't look back."

How could he always be so certain about what was right, she thought. They walked to the corner before he spoke again. Then he said, "How did you know?"

"I went to the meeting and heard your paper."

"My God!" After a moment he said, "I had to put it in the report for the protection of others."

When she said nothing, he added, "All case records are made up of human lives, Liz. All statistics and all knowledge—you know that."

She didn't answer. He sounded too impersonal. He had an answer for everything, one that satisfied him. He was like a stiff figure in a play, who came out and said his piece, somebody not quite real. Henry had changed in these years. His work had changed him. She had been too close to see the change until now.

"Liz," Henry touched her arm. "I'm sorry you had to hear it that way. I know how you feel."

But he was comforted by the feeling that he was doing the right thing anyway. And part of his mind was putting it down in his report, using it as material. His work had come to mean more to him than anything else.

"When you read the paper to me on the train, you left out that part about Nancy," she said in a low accusing voice, feeling that she was being childish but feeling she had a right to be.

"Yes, I did. But what good would it have done to tell you, Liz?" His tone was gentle and reasonable. She hated the reasonableness. "Sometimes, Liz, that summer when we realized Nancy was deaf, I felt as though the stuff were a kind of Frankenstein's monster, but I had to put that out of my mind to go on with the work."

"I'll never be able to forget what it did to Nancy," she said. "And now it isn't even going to do you any good. The other mold is better." The words were said. But why not say them? They were true. Let them face it.

Henry dropped his hands in the pockets of his dinner jacket. He turned his face away from her and looked across the street. He didn't blame her for being bitter, but Liz wasn't a child; she would have to face the fact that Nancy was deaf . . . she never really had . . . deaf because of the microcydin. "And now it isn't even going to do you any good," she had said. The words had a small, shrewish, taunting sound. He hadn't wanted any good for himself, God knew, . . . or had he, really? "To want to make your mark in the world . . . ," Hester had written. Well, was there anything wrong in that?

They had to wait for the traffic light to change, and he realized guiltily that they had walked the entire block in silence.

"Liz, there's a cafeteria over there. Let's get some coffee."

She had to lift her skirt a little higher crossing the street, and Henry took her arm.

People looked at them in the cafeteria, but not too curiously.

"You sit down and I'll get the coffee," Henry said.

There were plenty of tables, but all of the white-topped tables were so naked under the fluorescent lights. Those by the wall were as exposed as any, so she sat down at the nearest one and leaned on her elbows. Henry stood out in the short line. His evening clothes were a soft black against the harder grays and browns and khakis of other men in the line. His face was grave, shut in. She looked away because his face hurt her. When she glanced back at him, he was coming toward her, carrying two coffee cups, slopping them a little on the tray. He set them down on the table.

"Sure you don't want something more?"

She shook her head. The coffee was hot and tasted good and she said so.

"I'm going to get a doughnut to go with it. Have one?" Henry asked.

"Yes . . . , thank you." Her tone was colorless.

When he came back, she said, "There was a letter from Nancy today." She took it from her evening bag and gave it to him, but she knew it would hurt him.

"Let's go back to the hotel and call her up," he said, folding the sheet and slipping it into the envelope.

"It's too late there. It would be after ten their time."

"We'll call her tomorrow evening then."

Liz finished her coffee, remembering the last time Nance came home. She saw her as she stepped off the train: Nancy's hair had seemed darker than she remembered and she was wearing it longer; her quick, bright smile lighted her face when she saw them. She seemed more theirs in that first moment than any other time. They had walked together over to the car, asking her about the

136

trip and school, talking too fast without remembering to turn their faces toward her. Nancy didn't answer right away, and they had realized that she hadn't heard them. They had known again what they had forgotten in the pleasure of seeing her, that she was deaf. Liz set her cup down on the saucer and her eyes came back to Henry.

"Are you ever going to tell Nancy what caused her deafness?"

"Yes, someday, Liz." Henry's tone was patient. "Liz, let me carry the load on that score. Don't you too." He crumpled his napkin and laid it on the table. She pushed back her chair and started to stand up. The heavy legs of the chair caught the hem of her black net dress, and as she stood up, there was the penetrating sound of tearing lace. She sat down quickly with a little cry.

"What happened, Liz?"

"I tore Hester's dress," she said, gathering the torn skirt together. Henry paid the check and they went back out on the avenue, turning in the direction of the hotel. She was cold and shivered a little.

"Here, put my coat around you," Henry said, taking it off.

"No, I'm fine. You can't walk up Michigan Avenue in your shirtsleeves."

"I don't know why I can't." He laid it around her shoulders and it felt warm.

"Thank you," she said, and they walked the block in silence. Henry looked straight ahead down the street. She gazed abstractedly at a window of women's shoes, the fine kinds: high, thin heels; slender, cut-out straps of leather; the little plaque beside each pair bearing rounded, arty-looking figures, $29.50, $30—prices no wife of a doctor with an obsession on molds would hope to pay. She had never cared before, but tonight she didn't brush the idea aside as unimportant. The beautifully turned suède shoes, no sling-strap, open-toed affairs but elegantly covering toe and heel, were more than shoes; they were the grapes hung above Tantalus that bobbed too high every time the hand reached for them.

The last time she was home her mother had said, "I do think you should spend a little more on yourself, Elizabeth. You buy too cheap things." She hadn't minded in the beginning when they were all starting out, but twelve years of it was a long time. And it had been for no good at all.

"I couldn't have stood it, Liz, if we hadn't got anywhere," Henry had said on the train. Well, they hadn't. And there was nothing to do about it. Why didn't Henry say something? What was he thinking? Of course, he was sunk about the other man's work. He had counted on success. He had said, "If I thought someone else could do it better, and would do it, I'd give them my findings." But he hadn't meant it. He had wanted to be the one.

She had wanted some fame out of this too. She had wanted to write her mother and father and say, "Now you can see what Henry was doing all those years. He wasn't mediocre. . . ." (No, don't use that word. That was a horrible word that Hester had used. Well, then, that Henry had done a distinguished piece of work.) "I knew what I was doing when I married Henry." Then she was as bad as Henry. They weren't selfless like the Curies. They both had been thinking of more than just the patients the mold could help.

It was a long time since that night that Henry had come back from his trip to Buffalo and told her what he wanted to do. "It boils down to this, Liz. Do we want to think of how we can get a good practice and make a good living or do we want to see what these molds might do for thousands and thousands of tuberculous patients, even if we don't make more than enough to live on?

"We don't either of us care too much about . . . houses and cars and . . . oh, vested interests, do we?" he had asked with a fine sweep of the hand.

And she had said, "No. Oh, Henry, you know we don't." She had made a face at the stuffiness of such things. They had gone out to the kitchen and had a late supper and uttered high-sounding phrases, "It's only if you lose your life in some real work that you find it," and they hadn't sounded exaggerated or funny because it was so late and they believed them. She had felt so lucky to be married to Henry who had such nobility of purpose. She had thought he was like the men who were his ideals: Louis and Laennec, and far less naïve than Arrowsmith.

But was he, really? He could make mistakes and be self-seeking and thoughtless. She glanced at Henry beside her, looking at him coldly as though he were a stranger. He looked middle-aged and absurd walking along Michigan Avenue in his vest with the satin back, belted in like a woman's waist, and his white shirtsleeves and the collar button showing on his collar. He looked like a stranger.

Henry stared down the street ahead of him. He could see Liz sitting there at the meeting, hearing it that way! She would never feel that it had been right to use the microcydin on Nancy. She would never feel sure that Nancy wouldn't be living without it. Perhaps it would have been better to tell Liz when he first suspected it was causing the deafness. . . . If he had known more about it. With a smaller dose the deafness might not have been permanent. But he had seen microcydin work wonders on Lester Small and Walsh and the others, and there had been no auditory disturbance in them to warn him. He had such faith in its harmlessness. That had been his trouble from the beginning: he had had too much faith in himself. He had been so sure that he would be able to find the mold that would work in TB. He supposed he had mixed himself up with a myth and thought he was another Louis. It wouldn't have mattered if he'd been alone in it. But he'd dragged Liz with him up to Pomeroy and let her in for twelve years of drudgery . . . for nothing.

He would go right on working with the molds if there were only himself to consider. Up in Paul's room, telling those young fellows about the stuff, he had almost forgotten the disappointment over the Stockton mold. What the woman from Hopkins knew about Stockton's work was interesting. If he had only himself to think of for the next three years, . . . but there was Liz, Liz and Nancy.

They couldn't go on at Pomeroy. But he didn't have any plans. He had been too absorbed in the day's work; he was a fool. "Little man, what now?" applied to him. What other bright idea will you find, only to discover that it has been better done before you, he sneered at himself.

He would go some place where Liz would be happy. He could dig in and make enough to live decently, wherever she wanted to go . . . couldn't he? Liz wanted things for Nancy. She was so afraid Nancy wouldn't have friends like other girls. He'd see that she did. . . .

"It seems as though we tried so hard, and all we have to show for the years since we left Woodstock is Nancy's deafness," Liz said in a low voice, as though she had been in his mind, Henry thought.

Henry looked at her quickly. Her face in the light from the store window was resentful, almost the face of a stranger. Liz didn't mean that. It was hearing that the microcydin had made Nancy deaf that made her say it. This noon, before his paper, she had said, "There was nothing wrong with our way. If we had found the most effective mold, it would have been remarkable and fine. Well, it still is."

"Liz, we wouldn't have Nancy at all if it hadn't been for that work we did up there," he said again.

He said that, but he couldn't be sure. "Here, Henry, put on your coat. You can't go into the hotel like that." She held his coat out to him. They were at the corner across from the hotel.

When the lights changed, they walked across the street and up the steps into the lobby. Liz held the torn skirt in one hand. The banquet must have just ended. Couples in evening dress stood talking in the lobby or passed by on their way to the bar or elevator. She and Henry looked as though they had just come from the banquet too, Liz thought, seeing themselves in the mirror as they passed. She felt as though they had been so far away.

"Everyone's just coming out," Henry said. "It wasn't very long; we should have gone."

"You could have gone. I couldn't have sat through any more speeches. I'm going on upstairs. Why don't you stay and talk? She turned away from him. She wanted the refuge of her own room where she could rip off Hester's dress and be herself again.

"Liz." Kay came hurrying toward her. "We tried to save seats for you at our table, but evidently you sat on the other side of the room. That was such a shame."

"We were so late in coming, . . ." Liz began.

"The speaker was dull, didn't you think?" Kay asked. "But mercifully brief." So there was no need to explain. Kay turned to speak to someone else and Paul came up to Liz.

"We missed you, Liz," Paul said. He looked at her so intently that her eyes flicked away.

"I can see that I've lost Henry," she said lightly. Henry and Sam and the woman doctor were talking to some other man. Henry was smiling as though he were having the best time in the world. She watched him go off with the stranger.

"That's your friend, Stockton," Paul said. "You won't see Henry for hours now. Let's go and sit down over there, Liz. It's a long time since we've had a chance to talk."

They walked over to the thin façade of a Southern mansion that was really a cocktail room and sat at a table on the make-believe veranda.

All through the banquet Paul had been thinking about Liz and Henry. He hadn't seen them there. Kay thought they must be over on the other side of the room, but he didn't think so. After that outburst of Liz's they must have had things to say to each other. He wondered why Henry told her the stuff caused the deafness.

"Liz, I don't know whether you and Hen realize it, but you two stand for something to the rest of us, I mean, to our particular little group at Woodstock—the way you two did the thing we all talked of." He couldn't tell what she was thinking from her face; it would be better if he could get her talking about the way she felt.

"I thought of taking a job pioneering in psychiatric work out West where they didn't have any program at all, but I didn't. I took a more congenial, safer thing. I'm not at all sure that I haven't been more useful where I am, you understand, but it was a safer bet and I've made a lot more money at it." Liz was fiddling with a coaster on the table, but he felt she was listening. He groped his way. "I mean, we all had some idealistic notion of not thinking of the money but doing something for mankind, and only Henry really went ahead with it. It's just a damnable piece of bad luck that someone else had to find a mold that overshadows Henry's, but it doesn't lessen the magnitude of his accomplishment . . . yours and Henry's, together."

"Except that we paid too much for it. We haven't done much else but work all these years. Henry hasn't thought of anything but his mold." She turned the coaster in her fingers and bent the edge of it back until the cardboard circle broke. "And that made Nancy deaf."

Paul was aghast. She was so blunt and bitter. "Henry told me about Nancy this morning, Liz." He hesitated.

"He never told me that the microcydin caused it," she said. "I went to the meeting and heard."

Paul laid his hand over hers on the table. For a moment he could think of nothing to say; he could see so clearly how it had been. "But it must have been a relief to him to have you know that," he said finally.

"It was hard for Henry, of course," Liz went on slowly, as though she were making an effort to be fair to him. "But there is never any doubt in his mind that he did the right thing. He would do it again if he had it to do over. That comforts him."

"It should. It saved her life, Liz." He was shocked that Liz of all people could take such an attitude. Kay should hear her; she thought they were so close.

"Perhaps," Liz said stubbornly. "Oh, I know he had to do what he thought was right, Paul, but he's always so sure. He was so sure that he had to give up any idea of practice until he had found a mold to cure tuberculosis. And then he was so sure he had found it—the right one, I mean. He doesn't ever stop to think that he could be wrong. After all, he *was* wrong about the mold."

In spite of his experience in listening to women talk about their husbands, Paul was uncomfortable, and his discomfort raised himself in his own estimation. He said earnestly, "Liz, don't talk that way. His very sureness is

143

part of Henry's strength. He couldn't go ahead if he didn't have that. I . . . I've envied him that. But if you lose faith in him, he'll lose that sureness in himself. This is a bad time for him; he needs you to believe in him. Remember the wife in *Arrowsmith;* what was her name? The four of us went to the movie together and picked flaws in their laboratory technique, but I know we were pretty thrilled too. The thing I remember best was that wife. . . ."

"She died, you remember, fairly early in his life," Liz said. "She might have grown tired of his working and working and not having anything to show for it eventually."

"It's pretty hard to know what any of us have to show for the years," he temporized cautiously. "And very uncomfortable to try," he added, thinking of Kay and himself. Then he saw Bill. "Look at Bill there, going into the bar. 'Member what a dapper, earnest young fellow Bill used to be? Now he's a paunchy little man with thinning hair who drinks too much. And Alice hovers over him like a worried mother. What have they to show for the years?"

They sat a few minutes without talking. He passed Liz a cigarette, but she shook her head; her chin rested on her hand and her face was tranquil in the subdued light, but when she turned toward him again, her eyes held his with a deep intensity. They were blue tonight rather than gray.

"I think doctors and their wives are more pathetic than other people," Liz said, dropping the personal, moving out with maddening irrelevance to generalities. Kay did that too. But it was a good sign Liz could.

He asked patiently, "Why? They don't seem much different from the rest of the human race to me."

"Oh, because they start out with such ideals, most of them: the doctor healing the sick, searching for truth, sacrificing personal considerations. . . . They can't help it; everyone exalts the role of the doctor—books, movies, the radio, even advertising. You know, Stevenson's calling it the noblest profession. And that's partly what draws them to it in the first place and girls to marry them. Then they turn out like Bill or John . . . or Henry," she said.

"Good Lord, Liz, how can you say Henry?"

"Because he hasn't spent all these years trying to find a mold just to cure tuberculosis," she said quietly, looking down at the table, turning the untouched glass in front of her. "Or he wouldn't feel so badly now, as long as some-one has found a better one. Whether he admitted it to himself or not, he's wanted to 'make his mark in the world,' to be famous," she said, mouthing the word quickly, al-most scornfully.

"Well," he began.

"Oh, I wanted him to too. I don't say I'm any better than he is, but I'm saying we're not particularly noble, and we're a long way from where we were when we left Woodstock. I wanted to see him succeed; I kept thinking how, once he'd done this, he'd be through, and we'd go some place where it was delightful to live, and we'd have enough money and time for friends. . . ."

"Motives are always mixed, noble and ignoble," he in-terrupted. "Liz, I want to say something to you that isn't going to be easy to take, maybe, but I think you'll under-stand because you are so honest." He moved aside his glass and leaned a little forward. "You want to be sure that you aren't blaming Henry for Nancy's deafness and attributing these motives to him just because you're let down and disappointed about the result of all those years of work. It's easy to do. Kay, for example, hasn't been particularly happy this winter; she's finding that middle age isn't quite what she bargained for, and she blames me for things that, with all my faults, I am not guilty of."

He had meant to make it easier for her to accept the fact that she was being unjust to Henry by showing that same mechanism in Kay, but instead he seemed to lose her. He felt the change in her attitude, as though she pushed a door shut with all her might. He saw her looking around the room.

Liz stood up. "Thank you, Paul. You've been a dear to listen to me. You're probably right and we're all 'utterly vile'; at least we all talk too much. I seem to be tired, and I think I'll go on up without waiting for Henry." She managed to smile at him, but he could see that he hadn't helped her.

He walked with her back across the lobby to the elevators.

"It helps to talk sometimes," he protested a little feebly.

"Tell Kay I'll see her tomorrow. Thanks, Paul." She stepped swiftly into the crowded elevator.

The sound of her feet seemed stealthy to Liz as she went swiftly along the corridor to their room. She felt furtive and unclean. Perhaps she had left Paul too quickly for politeness, but she had to get away.

"It helps to talk sometimes," Paul had said. He had meant well, but it didn't help. You said more than you had any right to say; you spoiled something. It was Paul's talking about Kay to illustrate his point that had shocked her. How could he? Henry would never talk about her like that. And then she had become suddenly aware of herself talking about Henry.

She had meant what she said about him. She felt as though she and Henry had been tied tight all these years to Henry's work, like balls on two separate strings, and now when the work was taken away, finished, unimportant, they flew off in opposite directions. She was far enough from Henry to look at him clearly, even to look at herself. But she had no right to tell Paul what she saw. She should have protected Henry. Marriage ought to make a room where you were safe.

It didn't matter about Paul. He was used to hearing people's troubles; he would only think that she was hysterical or overwrought. He was so sure that he understood her, as he did Kay. But he would remember all she had said, and it would be in his mind when he saw them tomorrow.

A woman's voice came over an open transom: "I said to him, well, if you think . . ." Light ran from the wide crack under the door as though nothing was safely held in that room. Liz hurried past, stepping over the streak of light.

As she opened her own door, she glanced quickly, almost fearfully around the room, not wanting to see but seeing first Hester's flowers. Perhaps Henry was attracted to Hester; she understood him so well. And he always enjoyed hearing about the medical men who were friends of Hester's father. Perhaps he talked to Hester about her . . . the way she had talked about him to Paul. Perhaps he said, "Liz doesn't understand why I keep working at this."

Henry had forgotten to take the Scotch with him. He might as well take it back to Carl since there was nothing to celebrate.

The desk was still covered with Henry's papers. Liz put them together in his new brief case. She took Nancy's letter out of her bag and laid it on the bedside table so she could read it again before she went to sleep, but the round handwriting reproached her. She had hurt Nancy tonight, telling everyone in Kay's room that Nancy was deaf, letting them pity her. She hated people pitying Nancy, people whose children could hear.

Liz pulled the curtains against the windows across the court and turned on the bed lights, but the room remained hostile. There was no way of making it personal or friendly.

She undressed quickly and hung Hester's dress up without looking at the tear. There was nothing to do about it until she got home. She reached up and turned off the light. It would be easier to pretend to be asleep than to talk to Henry tonight.

PANEL DISCUSSIONS

WHEN Sam and Dr. Walters introduced Henry to Dr. Stockton in the lobby after the banquet, Dr. Stockton had been very cordial but quite casual.

"I didn't hear your paper this afternoon, but one of my men did. He said it was most interesting. Curious how closely these molds resemble each other and yet differ!"

"Curious"; the word jarred a little.

"Wasn't it amazing that you both should happen to report your findings at this same meeting!" Dr. Walters said. Amazing and curious. And tragic? Only to him and Liz. "I thought you might have some points you might like to discuss together," Dr. Walters said. She and Sam made some excuse for leaving. Henry hardly heard them.

"I certainly would be interested in, . . ." Henry began.

"Well, I . . ." Dr. Stockton looked at his watch. "It's getting a little late. They never start these banquets until half the evening's gone."

But he couldn't leave like that. Henry ignored his remark and said quickly, "There are some points I would like to ask you about, Dr. Stockton. I've eaten and drunk and slept this work for the last few years, and I haven't had any opportunity to talk with anyone else working in the same field."

"Yes, of course," Dr. Stockton said.

But they couldn't talk standing here. "Could we find some place to talk?" Henry asked. "Or perhaps sometime tomorrow?" That would be better, when there was more time.

"I'm leaving in the morning," Dr. Stockton said. "As a matter of fact, I'm going to see one of the drug houses about producing bacteromycin in quantity. We've been in correspondence for some time."

That was what he had hoped. Henry had visualized it, standing in front of the Mason jars in their little laboratory.

"So perhaps we better talk right now. I'll tell you, come up to my room," Dr. Stockton said. "I'll call Fenton and Grayson and have them come over."

He felt like a boy being allowed to go into the museum after hours. He tried to marshal his questions.

While they were waiting for the others, Dr. Stockton sketched the history of their work. "After the penicillin discoveries . . . then the work of those two Russians. . . ." Henry hadn't heard of their work. They had begun later than he had; if it were only a question of priority, but it wasn't.

"I got started earlier than that," Henry said. "A Dr. Perth at the State Agriculture School had read Fleming's article when it first came out. . . ."

"Is that so?" Dr. Stockton was more interested as Henry went on talking. "There are so many thousands of molds," Dr. Stockton murmured. "You say you set up your own laboratory?" His eyes had a way of darting out at him and then returning again under their lids.

And then Dr. Fenton came in. He was a "bright young man" who had been working in Stockton's laboratory. When they had been introduced, Stockton said, "I told him that you had heard his report."

"No, Grayson did. I didn't, I'm sorry to say," the young man said politely. "I left a note for Grayson to come down if he got back in time. Where did you do your work, Dr. Baker?"

"In a little laboratory set up in my home. I'm assistant at the tuberculosis sanitarium in Pomeroy, New York."

"Oh, yes," Fenton said still politely, but patronizingly. "You must have found many difficulties; the complications in a process like ours were considerable."

"We did," Henry admitted. "Plenty."

"Tell him what you've just told me," Stockton said.

Henry told him briefly, minimizing the difficulties and the false starts, but when he came to the recital of the first human test of microcydin, his excitement crept in.

"We tried it on a case, Lester Small," he said, and then realized how idiotic it sounded. No one was interested in the name, but he saw Lester as he talked, a small man with graying red hair and a drooping mustache and warm brown eyes.

"What do you call your mold?" Fenton asked.

"Microcydin," he said distinctly.

"You must have thought you were the first in the field," Fenton said. Stockton frowned at his lack of tact.

"Yes, I did," Henry answered.

The young man shook his head. "I know we thought of getting out a preliminary report last year, but we hadn't tried it on enough human cases."

"Naturally it was a blow," Henry allowed himself to say, smiling to take away any dramatic tinge.

"Quite naturally," Dr. Stockton said. That was all. Henry wanted to burst out at them, as Liz might, they took it so calmly, but he took a cigarette, leaned over a little for the light young Fenton offered, and sat back, inhaling with the tobacco a deep breath of envy and frustration. It was definite and final . . . "quite naturally." Even today, after his paper, he had not quite believed it could be over like that. He had felt something must come of it; but nothing could.

"We were careful not to be overly enthusiastic in our preliminary report, but the results are going to be far better than we indicated," the young man said.

"You were chiefly interested in its effectiveness in tuberculous conditions, but we're beginning to think that bacteromycin's greatest usefulness may be in other fields. Bacterial endocarditis, for example."

"Have you tried it on brucellosis?" Henry asked.

"We haven't directly. There is a man who's been working with brucellosis who has tried bacteromycin." He said it as though the name was still new to him, the way he and Liz said microcydin. "So far, it hasn't proved at all effective."

"What was the man's name?" he asked and wrote it down: "Dr. Hanna." He wouldn't mention Nancy's case yet. Instead he asked, "Have you had any permanent deafness as a result of the use of bacteromycin? Your paper mentioned auditory disturbance."

"Yes, two cases," young Fenton said. "One case of spinal meningitis, but, of course, that could have been the result of the disease itself. The other was a case of pneumonia, and the deafness must have been due to the drug. It may be partly dosage."

"Yes," Henry agreed, remembering the dose Nancy had had that Tuesday morning. If only he had stopped with the Monday dosage!

"It's so much less dangerous than the sulfas," Fenton said.

"Yes, so is microcydin."

"Of course, we feel we've only just started with bacteromycin," Dr. Stockton said. That was what he had said to Liz and, instead, he was finished now.

"I can't get out of my head the cases that the microcydin cured, yet I suppose bacteromycin would have been more effective in the same instances," he said ruefully, yet it was a question.

"I would think so," Stockton said gently, as though he were reluctant to say it.

"Definitely!" young Fenton said. "You can see here. . . ." He picked up a chart from the folder on the table and pointed to the last column with the end of his pencil. For a minute the little figures blurred for Henry. He focused his eyes on the slender black pencil in the young man's hand.

"I should like to have a reprint of your article to go over your cases," Stockton said.

"As a matter of fact, I have the paper in my pocket," Henry said, feeling naïve. He had slipped it in his pocket when Liz was hanging things in the closet. There was no reason for it, but he had wanted it with him, as though it were a part of him. He smoothed out the folds and spread it on the desk. Dr. Fenton leaned over Dr. Stockton's shoulder. Henry had a great desire to lean over his shoulder too, to explain and amplify as they read, but lighting another cigarette, he picked up one of their charts and sat down in the chair under the lamp. But he wasn't reading it; his ears strained to any comment. Now they had turned to his data columns.

"Dr. Baker, why did you . . . ? Oh, here it is, I see."

They had come to the case records. He knew the paper so well he could keep pace with their reading.

"You cured a fulminating case of brucellosis?"

"Yes, but there was residual deafness."

"That's exceedingly interesting."

"He had already given sulfonamides," Fenton noted, with his pencil pointing to the fact.

"You mean the combined effect might have something to do with it," Stockton said. "I must mention that to Hanna."

It was his, Henry thought rebelliously. He would talk to Hanna himself. He took another cigarette. He had reported the case; it was anybody's right to draw any inference and use it as he chose.

"I thought I might look up Dr. Hanna if he's here at the meeting and talk to him about my experience with micro-cydin in that case," he said. He felt they got his meaning. Then he was chagrined; that was lock and key stuff. That wasn't science. He flushed a little.

They had come to the end of the paper before Stockton's other young man, the B. H. Grayson of the paper, came in. He was older than Henry, a queer-looking duck, tall and stooped as though from looking through microscopes for too long a time.

"Oh, yes, Dr. Baker, I was interested in your paper," he said in a flat, colorless voice. "A very complete piece of work." He hesitated, coughed, straightened his glasses, and said in the same flat tone, "I worked on one of the early sulfonamide drugs that tested out experimentally but proved to be impractical to produce. We had to discard it."

He stated it so casually Henry didn't get the significance for a second. Then he saw. "You know what it's like then," Henry said. But already Dr. Grayson had become a disinterested observer.

"This is a most extraordinary accomplishment of yours," Dr. Stockton said warmly, handing back the paper.

"Thank you," Henry said. "It's turned out to be a little futile but . . ." But what? No one finished the sentence. It was time to go. Henry had a sense of leaving something besides the sentence unfinished. "Thank you for going over my data. It's been a pleasure to talk with you."

"If you get over to Philadelphia any time, I'd like to have you stop in."

Henry's excitement lasted all the way down the corridor to the elevator. They had been interested but not concerned about microcydin and its fate. Bacteromycin was established. He thought warmly for an instant of Grayson who had worked with the sulfonamide that wasn't practical to produce.

The elevator came to a stop. Henry discovered he had taken the down elevator to the lobby. "Lobby floor, sir," the attendant said as he hesitated. In his embarrassment, Henry got out and bought a package of cigarettes before taking the elevator up.

This time he got off at the twelfth floor, but halfway down the corridor he stopped. He had left Liz down in the lobby hours ago. She would have no idea where he had gone, but by this time she would have come back to their room. Now the earlier part of the evening came back to him: their walk down the avenue, Liz brooding over Nancy's deafness, blaming him for it.

"It seems as though all we have to show for the years since Woodstock is Nancy's deafness," Liz had said.

He turned the key in the lock and opened the door on the dark room. Enough light came in around the shades and from the hall to show him that Liz was in bed. Usually she was sitting up in bed reading, waiting for him. He went into the bathroom to undress so the light wouldn't bother her.

"Liz!" he said softly as he got into his bed. "Liz!" He felt sure she was awake; her breathing came too regularly, too heavily, but he was thankful not to talk any more tonight. He was too tired to talk about the paper or Nancy or what they would do. His mind went back to the morning, before Stockton's paper, as though it were a long time ago. "Friday afternoon I give the paper," he had said to Liz and Hester and Carl and they had all been excited. As he shaved this morning, he had gone over his cases in his mind. . . . Why did he keep going back over the thing? It was over and done with.

He heard a clock somewhere in the neighborhood strike two. He must have talked to Stockton till after one.

"What did Dr. Stockton say to you?" Liz asked from the other side of the bed table. Her voice startled him.

"Liz, I'm sorry I went off and left you like that. Sam introduced me to Stockton, and he asked me up, and I, well, I stayed till just now." Against the silence he went on. "He hadn't heard the paper and he was just politely interested at first, but he warmed up. He couldn't have been more cordial."

Liz tested the word; it didn't mean much.

"Did he tell you he was sorry about your mold?"

"No. That's the kind of things your friends say. He couldn't, and mean it. He said it was 'an extraordinary accomplishment.'" Henry brought the words to her as a gift, such a small gift beside the one he had hoped to bring. "Liz, it was amazing how many things we did that they did too. And they even made some of our mistakes."

Liz made no comment. He ran out of things to say.

"I don't suppose he offered you a position working with his stuff?"

He didn't quite get the tone of her voice. Was it eager or sarcastic?

"No. He has his staff, of course. They don't pay very well for jobs like that or I suppose I would have taken one instead of going to Pomeroy. We can't go on at a pittance. You've done that long enough." He put assurance into his tone, but it sounded hollow to him. A strangeness, a kind of chasm, lay between them. It was so deep, anything he said dropped into it and made no sound as it touched bottom.

"Are you really through with it, Henry? We'll go back and get rid of the guinea pigs and close the lab?" Disbelief was in her tone.

"I guess that's the size of it." He hadn't thought that far. "There isn't any use going any farther with it," he added to reinforce his indecisive answer.

"It brings you to a complete stop, doesn't it?" she said in a dry voice.

"Yes, it does, Liz. I know it's tough on you to have it all come to nothing."

"Why me? It's hard on both of us," she said. She didn't sound angry, but she seemed separated from him so that he couldn't reach her.

After a while she said, "I don't believe I could stand to have you start any more research."

"I'm not thinking of it, Liz."

"What do you think of doing?"

"I haven't decided. I might go into private practice wherever you want to live. I believe I could swing it; it might be a little slim at first, but if I worked half as long hours as I have these last twelve years, I ought to be able to do all right. Where do you want to live?" His tone was forced, the tone of an adult who has other things to think of but humors a child. "We might go to Buffalo after all. You liked it there, remember?"

"That was twelve years ago."

Oh, Lord, how long could he keep this up? "It's probably even better there now."

"I don't care where we live. If Nancy has to be away at a school, it won't matter."

"She won't have to. With her lip-reading and her instrument she'll be able to live anywhere."

Liz gave a little cry. She hated the thought of a hearing aid.

Anger flared into his tone. "Liz, you're going to drive yourself crazy if you keep brooding about Nancy's deafness or about my causing it with microcydin. By God, Liz, it saved her life, and you ought to be thankful. You'll ruin Nancy's life if you act as though it were a tragedy. We've been over and over that before, and we agreed that it wasn't a tragedy. You only have to look at her to see that, or read one of her letters. Your harping on that all evening hasn't helped any, I can tell you." He knew he sounded petulant, but he was baffled by her mood. "You used to see things so clearly. What's happened to you?"

"That's just it. I am seeing things clearly," Liz said. "I'm seeing us."

Henry turned over in bed. "I'm afraid I've had enough for one day, Liz, do you mind?"

Then a forced stillness lay on the room. Through it came noises from the street, the sound of the clock striking three, footsteps going down the corridor past their door.

He couldn't leave it like that. He had sounded like a calf. Liz had had enough too. They were both more drained by this day than any of their twenty-four-hour stretches at the lab.

Liz raised herself on one elbow and thought that Henry was asleep, he lay so flat in bed, one hand close to his side. She could go over and wake him. She didn't want to be left alone with her thoughts. When she had tried to tell him how she felt, he had stopped her. What if he were going to be like that, so she couldn't talk to him? What if disappointment and brooding should change him as they had other men. She wanted Henry to laugh at such a fear the way he did her fear of death.

"Henry?" she whispered.

"Liz." Henry slipped into bed beside her and gathered her into his arms. Words were hard and accusing and without comfort. They were past words.

Her body had known his in weariness and discouragement before now. Often the more tired they were after a long night's work in the laboratory, the more drawn they were to each other, as though their bodies were intended to comfort and renew their minds.

But tonight, when they most needed to ease this day's anguish and frustration, their bodies too knew only frustration, and they lay tense and hopelessly alone.

"Liz, I'm sorry," he said.

"Never mind," she whispered, but she was frightened. He went back to his own bed.

After a long time Liz said, "Are you all right, Henry?"

"Just tired, I guess." His voice was flat.

CHARLOTTE HOLMES finished cold-creaming her face and hands and climbed into bed with a new novel. John probably wouldn't be up for a long time. She turned on the radio by the bed. This was the best part of going along with John; she really got a rest. Of course, John didn't, poor dear. He was busier than any politician in election year. It was so important to be on the executive committees of the right medical societies. Important for the University too. John was good at it.

Charlotte reached over on the table for her emery board and applied it carefully to her nails. She had never known John would be, he was such a boy when they were married. But then, she never expected him to be head of surgery, either. He had done so well! Satisfaction spread along the pores of her mind like the cold cream on her skin.

Then she thought of Liz and Henry, poor things. He had seemed so bright and promising back at Woodstock. But you never could tell. He'd certainly put in an awfully long time on one thing. They ought to have realized that they were taking an awful chance. Charlotte took up her novel and read until she fell asleep.

She woke suddenly, hearing the door open.

"John?"

"Hello, dear."

"What time is it?" she asked sleepily.

"Around four. I had a good time though. I was up in Hensley's room. Morton was there and Babcock and Hobart."

"Oh, Hobart was the one you wanted to see." Charlotte kept her mind on John's affairs.

"Yeah," John said, yawning. "I didn't talk to him about anything in particular tonight. You don't do it that way. I'll see him tomorrow." He snapped his suspenders over his shoulders. "If I'm still interested. I've got enough to keep me busy as it is."

The note in John's voice woke her up completely. "What's the matter, John?"

"Nothing. Oh, I don't know. That business of Henry's paper kind of got me. I didn't hear it. I was in a committee meeting, but when Paul told us about it up there tonight . . . good Lord, do you realize what he's done off there by himself, Charlotte? He actually isolated a mold and raised a culture from it and extracted stuff that cured certain types of tuberculosis."

"I thought Paul said it wasn't as good as the other man's."

"Yes, that's the devil of it, but anyway Henry did it, don't you see? It gave me a regular itch to do something myself."

"Why, John, you do a lot all the time. Dr. Cole told me just today that no one in the country did a neater pancreatectomy than you."

"Oh, sure. But I mean, I've been going to collect my series of pancreatic tumors and write a paper. But I get so darned busy with medical politics and trying to see every private patient I can see that I have to let the younger men do it for me and stick my name on it."

"John, did you know that their child was deaf, before Liz said that tonight?"

"No. I guess Liz didn't know what caused it until today. Paul said she heard it at the meeting; she went in and heard Henry's paper."

"How ghastly! Can't we do something for them? Let's take them to dinner tomorrow night."

"Sure," John said absent-mindedly. "If you think they'll want to go." He was thinking about what Paul said to him.

"Couldn't you work Henry in on an appointment at the University, John?" Paul had said. "He deserves something better than going back to that assistant's job at that sanitarium. I imagine he and Liz would love getting back to Woodstock."

"Just because I'd like to, Paul, doesn't mean that I can. Besides, I'm on surgery," he had stalled.

"Well, you can cause a lot of things to come to pass, old boy, as I've noticed from a close perusal of the bulletin. I often see your fine hand in what goes on at Woodstock," Paul had insisted.

As he got into his pajamas, he wondered how easy Henry would be to work with. He must be pretty much of a lone wolf after all those years up there. And, of course, he wouldn't get any prizes for that work he'd done even though it was amazing. All that work, and then phooey!

He went in to brush his teeth vigorously.

ALICE HAMILTON finished her fourth letter: "Dad is very busy with meetings. He is still at one now so I am going on to bed. He sends his love with mine, Mother."

She addressed the envelope to Dicky, the youngest. "Master Richard Hamilton, Rainslee Road, Pittsburgh, Pa."

Then she took the four letters, one to each child, and went along the hall to drop them down the mail chute. It was so late no one passed her as she went swiftly in her dark negligee. A hotel corridor was depressing late at night. Cold drafts came through open transoms and the sound of someone snoring.

She got into bed, but she never really slept before Bill came in. She leafed through her new magazine. None of the stories held her interest; none of the women in the magazine had anything real to worry about, it seemed to her, glancing at their smooth faces in the illustrations: whether they could win the man they were in love with or hold him once they were married; that was all. Bill loved her; she had no fears there. Bill's troubles were all with himself; he couldn't help it, she thought sometimes. Of course, everyone did drink now, almost, that is, and Bill was as fine in every other way as you could want. There was no use in fretting about him, she often told herself. But seeing the old crowd together, seeing Liz and Hen Baker had sort of upset her. It brought back the old days; the boys didn't do much drinking then. Oh, beer and sometimes Scotch for a celebration after exams or something like that, but not real drinking.

Dr. Alston had wanted Bill to stay on at Woodstock in ophthalmology. She remembered the reception when Dr. Alston had talked to her about him and she had been proud. "He has the right touch for an eye man," he had said. She had wanted Bill to stay on; she liked nursing, and the baby was all right in the nursery school. And then she was pregnant when she hadn't meant to be, and Bill had the offer to go as assistant to Dr. Hobbs who was in general practice in Pittsburgh. Alice looked quickly over her shoulder at the years.

One thing had led to another. Dr. Hobbs had a wealthy practice and then he had retired in four years. "How wonderful for such a young man," everyone said.

Bill had gone to Boston to do some special work the spring before Dr. Hobbs had retired, and she had been going to join him as soon as the children were out of school. But he had called up one night only a month after he had gone and said he was coming home.

"But why, Bill? You want to get all that."

"Hell," he had said, and she had known he was drunk. "Hell, honey, I know enough now. I might as well get paid for learning back home."

"Bill, don't talk that way," she said sharply.

"Whatsa matter, don't you want me home?"

He had come home, and he had been successful. Five years ago he had limited his cases to geriatrics, the specialty of old age. He was good. All their friends took their old people to him. He had gone back for refresher courses, and as soon as they let years of practice count for specialized training, he had taken his Boards, hadn't he? Sometimes she thought of old Dr. Alston, but he had died. Bill didn't know the new head of the department. Perhaps Bill was happier as he was, only . . .

Charlotte had pretended not to see them tonight in the hall outside the banquet room. She and John went in to dinner with that doctor from Boston who was up in Paul's room tonight. And Kay had smiled and said she and Paul were waiting for Liz and Henry. Bill had said, "We'll save places for you."

"No, don't bother. Paul has it all arranged," Kay had said.

Bill didn't feel it. Bill never expected to be hurt, but she did. She had smiled quickly and hurried Bill along. It was plain enough; they didn't want them. They were afraid Bill would get drunk, and they didn't want to be with them.

"Over there, Bill. There are two places," she had murmured protectively, glancing at the older couple sitting next to the vacant chairs, unimportant people who had come to the banquet alone.

"Who's that? No, we want to be with some of the old crowd," Bill had protested so the people coming behind them could hear.

"Everyone's mixed up. We better just sit down, Bill," she had lied. Then she had seen the Swartzes from home. "There's Mel Swartz, Bill."

"Hi, Mel. Any places over there?" Bill had asked.

"Yea, sure, there's two here, Bill," Mel had said, not too eagerly, but cordially enough. Mel had offices in the same building with Bill, and they all belonged to the same country club. Barby Jean had had Donny Swartz to her Christmas party. They were closer to them than the old Woodstock crowd after all.

"Well, hello," she said with enthusiasm to Lucile Swartz. "This is wonderful to find you in all this crowd," as though they had been hunting them, as though they couldn't have called from their room if they had wanted to meet them. Lucile Swartz was president of the Junior League last year. Well, Barby Jean would be in the League too, when she graduated from college.

"We were at a cocktail party with some friends we used to know at the University and nobody thought of the time. We were just lucky that we didn't miss out on this altogether and have to go out somewhere to eat." She made it sound hilarious, as though they had been so busy with friends. She wondered if the Swartzes had had a cocktail party and whom they had invited; she knew how to handle that. "We were going to call you and Mel, and then these people we hadn't seen since Bill's intern days landed here and I tell you . . ." Let her see that they were so busy themselves that they were unaware of being omitted.

The banquet had seemed interminable, from the grapefruit with the wizened cherry to the tepid coffee in afterdinner cups. She had hoped for a big cup of hot black coffee for Bill. It always helped him. He had dozed off during the speech, and she had pretended to get her compact out of his pocket and waked him. She wished he had heard the speech, all about the future of medicine. She always liked the noble phrases, sort of like a speech at capping ceremony or graduation, but everyone around her looked politely bored and she made her own face blank too, like Lucile Swartz's.

Afterwards, as they all gravitated out into the lobby, she and Lucile had said the usual things—about shopping and what plays there were in town and who was staying with the children.

"Goodness, you're lucky. How long have you had that woman?" Lucile said with genuine envy.

"Ten years. Isn't it amazing? But you know Bill saved

her daughter's life, and she'll do anything for him." There, let Lucile repeat that to Mel, and it was true. Bill's patients loved him.

"See you," they both murmured at each other and separated in the lobby.

"Bill," she had said, letting her eyes plead, keeping her tone casual. "Let's go on up."

"You go ahead, honey. I'm going to see some of the fellows first. We'll have a nightcap and then I'll be along. Chuck Holden is here. 'Member Chuck?"

"I should say so. Is Althea here too?" Althea was Chuck's wife. Maybe they could make it a foursome. That was always safer.

"Don't think so. Chuck didn't say anything about her."

She had stood a minute in front of the newsstand and looked to see whom she knew. She saw Kay talking to Peder, and Paul and Liz going off together, and Sam and that woman doctor he had at the cocktail party. Women doctors always made her uncomfortable; they always used to be so superior with the nurses in the old days. Charlotte was talking to someone she didn't know; she had grown so self-important since John became head of surgery. Alice bought a *Good Housekeeping* this time and came on up to the room.

But now she dropped it on the floor. The others were in bed and asleep by now. They had nothing to worry about, not even Liz.

"It scares me to think what this will do to them," Paul had said. Why should he be scared? Liz and Henry were disappointed, of course. Their future wasn't very rosy, maybe. They would have to start out all over again, but what wouldn't she give to be starting again! If she had it to do over, she would never let Bill go as assistant to a doctor with a wealthy practice. They would stay on at the

University and manage somehow. She would work, doing the washing at night or the baking and getting up at five to be over at the hospital by seven, and Bill working his head off with no time or money for drinking. . . . They had been much happier then. Liz and Henry were lucky if they only knew it.

"I'd take it all," she said aloud to her own image in the mirror across the room. "No money, deaf child, and all."

And then she heard Bill coming along the hall, stepping lightly the way he did when he was drunk, unlocking the door without trouble, not like the funny-paper drunks at all, but quite as drunk.

PAUL, how does Liz feel?" Kay asked, lying on top of the bed, smoking a cigarette.

"A little bitter. You can't blame her. She didn't know that this stuff Henry developed caused Nancy's deafness until she heard his paper. Naturally she blamed Henry."

"How could she, Paul?"

"Quite understandably, I should think. I tried to make her see that he saved Nancy's life and, of course, she knows that, really, but this disappointment has been as hard on her as on Henry and she's overwrought." Then he added, "I imagine Henry has been so immersed in this research of his that he's taken Liz a bit for granted. She resents that."

Kay shook her head. "They're as much in love as ever."

"I'm not so sure," Paul said.

"Why do you say that, Paul?" Kay asked.

"Because of what Liz said."

"What *did* Liz say?" Kay insisted.

"Well, she feels that Henry's work hasn't been entirely selfless. She has enough insight to see that he wanted to make his mark in the world too."

"Doesn't every man? Don't you?"

"But you see Henry put his work on a different basis. I imagine he himself believed that he was sacrificing everything to his work for humanity, even Liz."

Kay smiled at him. He hated that smile of hers. "Well, that makes *you* feel better."

He said, "You can be pretty unpleasant when you put

your mind to it." Then he was irritated with himself for showing his annoyance.

Kay put out her cigarette and leaned her head back against her arms. Her tone of voice remained quiet, almost sweet. "You are so busy helping other people see into the dark places of their souls that you have no time to do it for yourself. I'm just helping."

Paul was quiet for several minutes. Then he said, "Thanks."

Kay turned her face into the pillow and lay still. Even now, with Kay in this disagreeable mood, he took pleasure in her long, lithe body, her straight shoulders, the curved line of her arm against her head. He could almost forget her mood in his delight in looking at her. The very clash of their moods was an aphrodisiac: matching her anger, her sneering tone with sarcasm, his superiority of knowledge, cool indifference. They quarreled, not vulgarly like a workingman and his woman, but skillfully—rapiers not fists, knowing where to penetrate the armor and turn the point in the tender secret pride. Kay knew so well how to get to him, and her thrusts stirred him into an awareness that was exhilarating. He came back at her; he knew how too: just a word about her painting would do it, a suggestion that she was a dilettante. Or a mention of Paisley. Kay didn't get along well with Paisley. Paisley was his child.

He waited, choosing his words as he might select his weapon, feeling the slender blade, the sharpness of the point. These quarrels followed a pattern: Kay would sit up, facing him, flinging her dark hair back out of her face. Her eyes would narrow, and she would forget to be cool and detached and answer angrily. He would go over to the bed and lay his hand on her, telling her not to be childish. That would really send her. She would beat at him with her fists. He liked the feeling of the blows. If he held her down, she would struggle, trying to throw him off. She was strong, and it took all his strength to hold her until she was tired. Slowly the strength would go out of her and she would lie still. When he put his mouth on hers, he could feel her lips and teeth moving savagely, trying to form the words "I hate you," until he stopped them with the pressure of his own, and they gave up, parted a little, quiescent, while he lifted his mouth to form the words "I love you." From hate to love, the complete catharsis.

Kay turned around, leaning on her elbow. She spoke very quietly. "I'd give anything to be in Liz's place."

"Think so? You always were attracted to Henry."

"It isn't Henry. It's that their life has some meaning. They've done something with their lives. They've tried anyway. When you're young, it's enough to be in love; you don't see each other very clearly, but after a while you look at each other, maybe not wanting to see, but seeing all the same just what you are. You even try to hide from yourself the other person's faults and lacks because he is willing to hide yours from himself. I suppose it's the only way people can stand to go on together, but they make a horrible compromise with what they meant to be. And why should they? I should insist on your being what you could be. You should insist on my being what I could be. Something might happen to people if they did."

"You sound like a girl in her teens, Kay, being dramatic."

He saw her mouth tighten, her anger creep beautifully up into her face. He watched her eyes, but they moved away from him.

As though she hadn't heard him, she said, "I tried to tell Liz tonight how lucky she was."

"Hardly the time, I should think."

Kay swung her feet to the floor and sat on the side of

the bed. "I mean it though, Paul. They've both worked hard at something, so hard they've forgotten themselves. Remember when you had the chance to go out to North Dakota and take over that sanitarium and start a psychiatric program for the whole state?"

"Mmm." It was queer Kay's remembering that tonight, just as he had.

"If you had gone, maybe things would have been different; perhaps we would have been different."

"How long would you have stood living off in some little town like that?"

"You didn't give me a chance, remember. I would have gone."

"It would certainly have been different from the way you were brought up. You don't know anything about life in a place like that, the kind of women you would have known, the things they talk about. They wouldn't be exactly your type, Kay."

"Sometimes I think you married me because you liked my background, the people I knew, the schools and places I had been to, my type. Maybe I wanted to change my type."

"I'll see what I can do. They need psychiatrists in China, I hear."

"Paul, do you mind if I ask you a question?"

"Not at all."

"Why did you go into Medicine?"

He looked at her, twisting the corner of his mouth a little. "Would you like a passionate declaration of ideals, my dear? Something from *Men in White*, or Gottlieb's prayer, or the Hippocratic Oath?"

"Don't bother. I'll tell you. You were a bright boy and you had a charming personality and you liked the idea of a profession. I fitted into your picture so you asked me to marry you. You haven't ever lost yourself completely in your work any more than you've ever cared for me more than yourself."

He went over to the dresser for a cigarette. As he lit it, he glanced in the mirror at himself. Then he saw Kay's face in the mirror watching him. She smiled.

"You see what I mean, Paul? Even now you're interested in seeing how you look. Seeing Liz and Henry again, knowing the way their life has been, made me positive that I'm not going on as we are any longer."

"Kay," he began patiently, in the warm understanding tone he used with patients.

"There's no use talking to me about it, Paul. We've talked too much. I mean it this time."

Something about Kay's voice . . . it was so quiet, so empty of feeling . . . made him think of Henry's voice after his paper.

"All right, Kay, if you feel that way," he said, taking care to show no concern. Kay didn't meant it. They had had so many wrangles; there was the time Kay went to the Cape for the whole summer, and the winter she stayed in Florida. Kay was in one of her moods. She grew bored and needed a feeling of crisis every now and then. There was no use in talking any more tonight. But he couldn't throw off his sense of depression.

"Want a nightcap?" he asked.

"No, thanks," Kay said, without looking up from her magazine.

He started to make one for himself and then poured the Scotch back in the bottle.

"I don't believe I do either," he said to no one in particular.

PEDER wasn't ready to go up to bed yet, but he felt a little foolish standing alone in the lobby. The evening had been a waste: American banquets were not very good. It was not for that he had paid eight-fifty American money, for a plate of overcooked roast beef and a mix-up of fruit in a sauce on a limp lettuce leaf and a cup of lukewarm coffee. He was hungry already. The speaker at the banquet had talked about the dangers of socialized medicine when he knew so little about it. He could have told them more about it himself, from the way it worked in Norway.

Peder looked once more around the lobby and consulted his program to see what meetings would be held the next day. Somewhere, right now, there must be groups of doctors talking about things he wanted to talk about. He had wanted to talk to Henry about his mold, but Henry had gone off with that other doctor. Then he saw John coming across the lobby.

"John!" He hurried over to intercept him.

"Oh, hello, Peder."

"John, I wondered . . . I saw you talking just after the banquet to the man who gave the paper on the effects of plasma on cases of infectious hepatitis. We had a good deal of catarrhal jaundice in our camps. I would like very much to talk with him."

"Hensley his name is, A. G. Hensley. Sure, I know him. He's on the executive committee of the Eastern Society with me. As a matter of fact, Peder, when you saw me talking to him, he was asking me to come up to his room. I've got the room number here somewhere." John felt in his pocket and pulled out the day's program with a number scribbled on it. "Here it is, 821A. We'll drop up there right now, Peder. Of course, they'll all be relaxing a bit," John said with a smile. "Boys like Hensley, you know, the really important fellows, don't get a chance except when they're away."

Peder nodded happily. This was what he had come to the meeting for, to the United States for that matter: a chance to talk to the men whose articles he read in the journals and ask them questions.

"These men you'll meet up here are really tops in their field," John told him as they stepped out of the elevator. And then as an afterthought he added, "They'll have some real stuff to drink up here too."

Room 821A was separated from the main corridor by a little vestibule. As they turned into it, a roar of laughter came out to them. John knocked and a young man opened the door.

"Come in, Dr. Holmes. The professors are hard at it!" the young man said with a grin. "Tibbs and Bailey and I are bartenders. What'll you have?"

Peder followed John into the big room at the right. The room seemed as large as the drawing room of an apartment. Eight men were gathered at the far end of the room around a big table covered over with a hotel blanket. He looked a little closer to make sure; they were shooting craps. All of them were in vests or shirts. Two of them had taken off the collars of their dress shirts.

"They're shooting craps," John explained.

"I don't play the game myself," Peder murmured. "But some of our soldiers in the camps picked it up from soldiers in England. They used to . . ." But John walked on over to the group. He clapped one man on the shoulder.

"Are you hot, A.G.?" he asked.

The man turned only for a second, and Peder saw that he was the one who had given the excellent paper on hepatitis that morning. Peder stepped closer to be introduced to him, but Hensley was already back in his game. He had the dice in his hands, rubbing them lightly back and forth, leaning over to blow on them. "I'm coming out."

It seemed to Peder that everyone threw out green bills on a heap at one side of the blanket. He tried to follow, but their comments were incomprehensible to him. "Twenty says he's right," someone shouted. "Twenty he's wrong," someone else answered.

The dice rolled out on the blanket top.

"Natural!" Hensley's voice was a shout of triumph. A roar rose around him. "Better cover it, gentlemen, I'm hot!" he boasted, leaving the money on the blanket.

"I'll take ten," one man said.

"Fifteen to me." Another counted out his bills.

"I said we oughta move this table up against the wall. I don't like the way he handles those dice," someone joked. Peder gazed in amazement at the denominations of the bills. Then he noticed the money sticking loosely out of the vest pocket of the man next to Hensley.

"Careful now, A.G. You're going to crap. I'm betting on it."

Peder looked incredulously at the black hair streaked with gray, the intelligent face he had noticed with respect this morning at the meeting.

Hensley shook again. "Eighter from Decatur!" he announced. "Come on dice, let's hit 'em again." The moment was tense. The dice fell out on the blanket, five black dots on one, two on the other.

"He did! He did!" Hobart sprang up from his seat, yelling like a boy. John had pointed him out to Peder when they first came in as the head of surgery in one of the New York schools.

Hands snatched up the money on the table.

"You hexed me!" Hensley protested. "What I need is a drink," and he passed the dice.

"Coming right up, Dr. Hensley." The boy named Tibbs picked up his glass on the floor by his foot and started over to the other end of the room. Someone brought Peder a glass. He wondered if this was the time to speak to Dr. Hensley. Peder glanced at John, but he was laying a ten-dollar bill on the pile in the center of the blanket.

"Remember the *Maine,* John!" someone called out.

"Yeah, remember the game at the Atlantic City meeting, John. Lady Luck didn't do you any good."

They all knew each other so well. Peder felt like an intruder. They must play together at every meeting. He thought of the men in the concentration camp shooting dice made of wood with spots burned on that were always a little pale. The younger men played; he hadn't. For money they used rocks and redeemed them in chocolate or cigarettes when they had them. After a while, of course, there wasn't anything, not even the energy to play. Peder went up to Hensley as he stood there with his drink.

"How do you do, Dr. Hensley. My name is Hansen; I am from Norway."

"Oh, yes, how do you do." Hensley's manner was cordial as he shook hands.

"I heard your paper this morning." Peder spoke quickly because he had the feeling that Dr. Hensley was about to go back to the game. "We had a good deal of hepatitis in the concentration camps. I wanted to ask you: the poor diet, anxiety, exhaustion . . . they have much to do with the intensity of the disease?"

Hensley nodded. "Exposure, undernourishment, worry.

We touch on the etiology more fully in the paper. It's in press now, and all the studies from which the slides were made, of course. I imagine you will be interested in seeing that data." His tone dismissed the matter.

"I wondered," Peder said doggedly, "if you felt that . . ."

Loud outcries came from the crap game. Dr. Hensley nodded at Peder. "Excuse me, Doctor, there's a little matter here that needs my attention." His smile was gracious but final. Peder was embarrassed at being dismissed so summarily. He walked slowly back to watch the game.

Tibbs came over to him. "Can I fill your glass?" Peder shook his head. The young fellow lingered. "I heard you trying to talk to A.G. about hepatitis."

"Yes," Peder said apologetically, "I didn't mean to interrupt him, but I thought he was through."

"Did I hear you say you had a lot of it in the concentration camps?"

"That was one of our greatest troubles. That was why I asked Dr. Holmes to bring me up here," Peder said, glad to have a chance to explain his presence. "I wanted to ask Dr. Hensley some questions but . . ."

Tibbs grinned. "You won't get anything out of the old man tonight." He nodded toward the crap game. "A.G. doesn't know too much about the statistics anyway. Kiefer and I did the studies on the rats. Look, why don't you come up to my room? The fellow that ran all the tests on the prisoners in the Jap camps will be there. Come along and we'll all pick each other's brains."

"Thank you, I should like very much to come," Peder said. He glanced over at the game. "Dr. Holmes brought me here. I should . . ."

"Don't bother. Chances are he won't know you left. I've

been along at these meetings often. This bunch always has a crap game."

"Don't you play?" Peder asked.

The boy laughed. "Not me. I haven't got enough money to stick out of my vest pocket. Besides, you have to be pretty important to get in on that lil game."

"Can you leave? You've been pretty busy here."

"Bartending? Sure, sure. They know how to mix 'em themselves. Kiefer and Bailey and I were just up here at the beginning. There was a crowd here before the regulars settled down to their game. We've met everybody; that's the main thing."

Kiefer and Bailey and Tibbs escorted Peder down the corridor to the elevator. They had a room together on the same floor with Peder—one like his, looking out on the court. Besides the twin beds there were two cots, one made up, the other laid on top of it, sandwich style with bedding for filling.

"It's a little crowded here after the ballroom upstairs, and there isn't any Black Label or Old Crow, but we have beer." Tibbs swung open the bathroom door and waved a hand at the beer bottles standing in the tub with a diminishing chunk of ice.

"This is what I like," Peder said. "After almost six years of no chance to talk medicine, I . . . This is better than bourbon," he said and was uncomfortable again for fear his remark would sound too emotional. He felt grateful to the point of moisture in his eyes.

"Swell," Kiefer said briskly. "Here, take the one good chair and move it up to the bed. We'll spread the charts out here. Hey, Tibbs, get a sheet of white paper to put under the slides."

"What's the matter with the sheet, you dope!" Tibbs answered back.

"Of course, what's the matter with me?" Kiefer ripped back the spread and blanket and spread out his slides.

Someone outside kicked the door.

"That would be Shields. Come in," roared Tibbs. "And bring your manners; we have a guest."

The newcomer couldn't have been out of his twenties, Peder decided. He was short and dark and puffed at a pipe that from the side seemed absurdly to take the same curve as his ear. He carried a paper bag under his arm which he shifted to his left so he could shake Peder's hand. They had all been in their twenties back at Woodstock, Peder reminded himself.

"You see, here we have . . ." This was it, Peder thought, even as he listened. This was the sort of thing he had craved.

"Hey, wait a sec before you get started." Shields brought some hamburgers. "None of us made the banquet at eight-fifty per," Tibbs explained. "Will you have one, Doctor?"

"Thank you, I will, if you will let me order another round," Peder said. He felt at home as he hadn't since the first evening. He turned back to Kiefer. "Of course, in the concentration camp we had no quinidine. . . ."

LONG-DISTANCE CALLS

HENRY heard the phone ringing almost at once and reached for it, but it was in a different position on the bedside table at home. His arm flailed the air. Then he was awake enough to realize where he was and turned on the light.

"Henry, the phone!" Liz said, waking suddenly.

"I've got it."

"Dr. Henry Baker?" the voice of the operator asked, rolling the *r*.

"Yes." Henry glanced at his watch. It was six-thirty.

"Pomeroy, New York, is calling Dr. Henry Baker."

"Is it Nancy, Henry?" Liz asked, her face twisted in sudden, frightened lines.

He shook his head. "The sanitarium, I guess."

"Henry? Oh, it's good to hear your voice. This is Hester. Henry, Carl had a bad heart attack this evening after dinner. Much worse than that other time. Dr. Noble says he must be in bed for three months anyway. I talked to Mr. Cooper. He said to call you and ask you to fly right home. Your paper is over, isn't it?"

"Yes, yes, it's over. Of course, Hester. I'll come at once. I'm so sorry about Carl. Perhaps I shouldn't have left him with the whole load."

"No, I think it would have come anyway, but he's very sick, Henry. It scares me."

"We'll see that he rests now. We won't let him come

back until he's really ready," Henry said reassuringly.

"He's not going back, ever. He's resigning. As soon as he can be moved, I'm taking him to California." Hester's voice had almost a triumphant note, Henry thought. "They want you to take his position, Henry. Cooper said so."

"I'll have to look up planes. I ought to get to Binghamton by midnight, Hester. Tell Carl not to worry about anything."

"I will. Henry?"

"Yes, Hester."

"I'm terribly sorry about this, spoiling your trip this way."

"You're not spoiling it. We were leaving tonight anyway. Don't think of anything but Carl."

"Your paper. . . . Was it exciting?"

He had been waiting for this. "Well, it wasn't so good, Hester."

"What did you say, Henry?"

"We'll tell you all about it. I better hang up now and get on the phone about reservations. Good-by, Hester. Liz sends her love."

He put the receiver in its hook before the sound of her "Good-by, Henry" was quite gone. He threw back the covers and slipped into his dressing gown without looking at Liz.

"You heard, Liz? Carl's had a heart attack. We'll have to take the first plane back."

"Yes," she said. "Is Carl terribly sick?"

"He doesn't sound good." Henry lit a cigarette and picked up the phone book. "Airlines." He leafed the yellow pages of the classified directory. "Hester says she's taking him to California as soon as he can travel. She says he's going to resign."

Liz lay back against her pillow. "And they want you to

take the superintendent's job?" Liz jumped to conclusions.

"That's what Hester says. I don't know." He couldn't tell how Liz felt. He tried to test the sound of her voice, but she said so little. Some distance, some awkwardness from last night lay between them, or did he just imagine it?

"And then they'll get another assistant?" Liz asked.

"In time, certainly. There has to be more than one doctor there."

"That would be funny, wouldn't it—living in Hester's house and someone else, some young couple, in our house."

Henry found the number and picked up the phone. All the time he was getting the airport he thought of what Liz had said. He thought of himself in Carl's office. He couldn't quite see himself. . . . This time they ought to get a young man who had had more surgery than he had had. If the fellow weren't busy with research, he would have time to . . .

Liz tried to think of Henry in Carl's place, but she kept seeing him in the laboratory instead. She thought of Henry talking to Mr. Cooper over the phone, forgetting to be tactful in his anger over Mr. Cooper's interference. She wondered if he were diplomatic enough to manage the Board that Carl always spoke of with such deference. And Carl was always talking about the budget. She paid the bills and kept the accounts because Henry was too busy at the hospital; how would he like that sort of thing? When a patient was very sick, Henry let everything else go while he worked with that patient. And when he was busy in the lab with the molds . . . but there wouldn't be any more molds. She kept forgetting that. Henry was going to *have* to make a different sort of life for himself.

"The plane leaves the airport at six-ten?" Henry was asking someone over the phone. "And gets into Binghamton at two-thirty. Then to get to Pomeroy, we'll have to take a train at . . ."

Liz pushed her pillow up higher and sat up in bed. If Henry did take Carl's place, they would live in the superintendent's house. If he were superintendent and there were none of that endless drudgery over the molds, everything would be very different. Henry would have an assistant so they could get away once in a while—someone like the young doctor she had met at the cocktail party, only it made her feel old to think of someone younger living in their house.

She tried to see herself in Hester's place. She had never thought of herself there. . . .

Henry turned away from the phone. "We'll have to be ready to go, Liz, at five-fifteen. We weigh in here at the office in the arcade and take the limousine out to the airport." Henry's voice had changed. It was brisk. "I'm sorry about leaving early. We'll miss the final jamboree with the bunch tonight."

"It doesn't matter," she said quickly. It didn't. She was ready to leave.

"I'll go down and have breakfast. Why don't you take your time and have breakfast when you get ready?"

He wanted to go alone. She could see. He didn't want to wait for her this morning.

"I guess I will." She slid farther down in bed, pulling the cover over her shoulder.

"But there won't be too much time, Liz. If you'll get us packed up, I think I'll try to take in some of the session. Then there's a man named Hanna who's done quite a little work on brucellosis; I thought maybe I could catch him around noon."

How could Henry still be interested in brucellosis? She never wanted to hear of it again. He had said he was through with research. He wouldn't have time for it if he were running the sanitarium. Carl had to be away often; he had to go all around the state holding clinics. That would be good for Henry. Maybe she could go with him. . . .

Henry was dressed now. She watched him packing his pockets: the pen and pencil in his vest pocket, the program of the meetings in the side pocket of his coat where he had carried Hester's letter. His pipe made one pocket stick out a little. His tobacco pouch went in the hip pocket and the clean handkerchief in the upper coat pocket.

"I'll try to get back here about four o'clock at the latest." He came over to her and leaned down to kiss her. "Liz, I'm sorry about last night. I don't know what was wrong with me. I don't think I'm that ancient yet." His tone was light, but she could feel the hurt underneath it.

"It was no wonder, Henry. You had quite a day. Having the microcydin turn out to be nothing was enough to make anyone feel flat," she comforted, but as she would Nancy: "Of course, it's hard to be deaf, but there's so much that you can do. . . ." Knowing all the time that her words didn't help, that she didn't really know how it felt to be deaf, or impotent.

"Well." He shook his head the way he did when he was baffled by something in the lab.

"What do you think you'll do, Henry?" She changed the subject.

"About Carl's job? I'll have to take it for now, while Carl is so sick anyway. I suppose it's the thing to do. I imagine Carl gets about six thousand a year. That has its points after . . ."

"Twenty-three hundred," Liz put in. "The superintendent's house goes with it too, doesn't it?"

"Oh, yes, and most of his living. It's not a bad proposition. And there's this about it: it comes at the right time for us, just now. I've got to go. We can talk about it on the plane. By, Liz."

"Henry, can I call Nancy? Let's tell her to come home. She could be there Sunday night. She wants to so."

Henry's hand was on the door knob. He wanted to go. She held him there with her question about Nancy. She felt his thoughts so clearly that she looked away across to the window. He was thinking about her hearing at the meeting that the microcydin had caused Nancy's deafness. He was remembering that she blamed him. He couldn't say no.

"It wouldn't be a good idea now, Liz, with Carl sick and Hester upset. It's going to be a little difficult just at first. If they leave right away, we may be moving. . . ." But his tone wasn't firm.

She pressed her advantage. "It won't make any difference. Nancy will be with me. She's done so well, and you promised her she could come home early. I want to see her, Henry."

"Look, Liz, why don't you call Nancy and talk to her? But let her finish the term. This wouldn't be a good time to have her come; it wouldn't be good for her either. Give her my love. I've got to go, Liz." He closed the door firmly behind him.

She listened to the sound of his feet going down the corridor as long as she could hear it. He was glad to get away from her as he never had been before. He was uncomfortable with her. He didn't want Nancy home now. Her deafness made the failure of the microcydin more tragic. Liz lay still in bed in the strange impersonal room. She felt cut off from Henry.

She had always felt she knew how Henry felt about things. Sometimes, working late in the laboratory, not talking for a couple of hours, Henry would suddenly say something and she would be startled to have it so close to her own thoughts, as though their minds converged. But ever since the paper their minds had been separate, as though each of them were hiding certain thoughts from the other. And when they had tried to lose that separateness in lying together, they couldn't. She wondered if their loving, that had always been such a natural thing, could ever be the same again. They would be uncertain and concerned, like the pathetic people that surreptitiously bought those textbooks on sex, the sort of books she had only touched with the fingertips of her mind before.

Henry hadn't gone to sleep last night for a long time, but she had been almost afraid to speak to him because of the strangeness that stretched between them. That sort of thing happened to people when they were old. But they weren't old and, surely, when you were old the desire must die too, so it wasn't just pathetic. Henry was pathetic last night; they both were.

It wasn't important; it didn't matter, and yet it did. It had been an odd thing to discover that she could love with passion. Her mind curled shyly around the thought. That she could like Henry's possession of her body with his, could even want it. "We're lucky, Liz," Henry had said, and she had taken that to her heart and let herself know the joy of naked closeness to each other that could pertain to the mind as well as the body, but not so completely without the body.

So much was written about passion out of marriage, so little about passion in marriage—about the way it grew and changed and became a part of your life. If that was over, their whole living would be different. They could never lose themselves in each other or forget to think for an instant. She wondered if they would ever be so close even in their minds.

Liz stepped out of bed and went over to the dresser. She picked up her brush and then laid it down again and stood looking at herself. With both hands she smoothed back her hair, and her face seemed strange to her. It looked frightened and ugly. A trace of last night's lipstick sat falsely on her lips. Her gown hung over one shoulder and fell limply from her breasts. Not since she had stood in front of the mirror when she was pregnant had she looked at herself with such distaste. Her bare feet that were light and strongly arched felt flat against the never quite clean carpet of the hotel room. She dropped her hands and her hair hung around her face. Always, when she looked at herself, she had known she was lovely in Henry's eyes. Henry loved her face and her shoulder and breast and thigh.

But this morning she saw herself through her own eyes, like an unretouched photograph. She moved her mouth and the mouth in the mirror moved grotesquely. She turned away quickly and went over to the phone to put in a call for Nancy.

It was cold sitting on the edge of the bed in her nightgown, and the call might take quite a while to get, but she waited, holding the phone in her hands.

When the phone rang, she picked up the receiver with a loud beating of her heart. What if Nancy couldn't hear her? What if she cried and didn't want to stay out the term?

"Nancy?"

"Yes, Mother. Oh, you're calling from Chicago!" Nancy's voice was clear and high and happy. It was happy, wasn't it? "Is Daddy there?"

"He had to go to a meeting. He said to give you his love." She swallowed to clear her voice. "I just called to tell you, dear, that Daddy's going to be the superintendent at the San. He's going to take Uncle Carl's place." That wasn't really what she had called for; she had wanted to feel close to Nancy. She had needed her.

"Oh, Mother!" Nancy squealed. "How super."

Liz laughed. "We'll have to move, and we think you better wait till the end of the term to come home." She said it tentatively, waiting to see how Nancy took the idea.

"O.K.," Nancy said cheerfully. "We'll have so much room in Uncle Carl's house. And I can sleep on the sleeping porch, can't I? Won't it be fun?"

"Of course you can. It will be lots of fun, Nancy. We won't have to work with the molds any more or the guinea pigs, Nance, and we'll have so much time to do things with you. We'll take a real vacation every summer."

"Is Dad all through with his molds?" Nancy's voice was disbelieving.

"Yes, all through, dear. He wouldn't have time as superintendent." How well Nancy was hearing. She hadn't asked over once.

"Mother, I'm getting wonderful at lip-reading."

"Good, dear."

"You'll be surprised when I get home. And I'm wearing a hearing aid now. You know, Dad had Miss Carter order one for me. I wear a velvet band around my head and you can't even see it."

"That's fine. Do you like it?" Liz asked weakly, shrinking from the thought of Nancy with the paraphernalia of batteries and wires. She hadn't known that Henry had really ordered one. She had resisted the idea so, he had ordered it without telling her.

"Ever so much. I can hear everything." There was a little pause. Liz couldn't speak for a moment. "Mother, are you and Dad having fun in Chicago?" Nancy asked.

"Yes, dear. We've seen lots of old friends."

"Did Dad's paper go all right?"

"It went very well," Liz said quickly. "We must stop now. We love you, dear."

"Guess what, Mother? I love you too."

Liz continued to sit on the side of the bed after she had put the phone back. She wasn't helping Nancy any by minding her deafness more than Nancy did herself, or by blaming Henry. Nancy was Henry's child too. Whatever she suffered over Nancy, Henry suffered as well. Maybe he needed to talk to Nancy as much as she had.

"You want to be sure that you aren't blaming Henry for Nancy's deafness because you're disappointed about the result of all those years of work," Paul had said.

That wasn't it. She had minded Henry's not telling her about Nancy; minded finding out that way. No, that was little and childish and mean-minded. Henry had wanted to save her from suffering. Of course, she had been shocked and angry that the microcydin had caused Nancy's deafness; who wouldn't be? But Henry had to try it, she saw that. She didn't blame him any more. He must go on believing that the microcydin had saved Nancy's life. Whether it had or not, she must make him feel that she believed it too. He couldn't stand it the other way.

Liz put on her dressing gown and started packing to go home. She tried the old trick of keeping her mind on something they could do for Nance: now that Henry would take Carl's place, they could do so much more for her; this summer Nancy would have the best time she had ever had, but it didn't lift her spirit as it sometimes did. She had turned to Nancy because she felt separated from Henry. Women were always turning to their children for comfort, but it wasn't the same.

BREAKFAST MEETING

H ENRY met John as he came into the cafeteria.

"Hi, Henry. We have a table over there by the window. Paul just came down too."

Sam joined them there.

"Well, good morning," Paul said, looking at Henry a little closely, wondering what he and Liz had said to each other.

"Look at the breakfast he eats. Holy smoke, Hen, you order a breakfast for a twenty-year-old. If I ate hot cakes and sausage every morning, I'd have a waistline like old Doc Whipple!" John jibed at him.

"Good for him. He's just a boy; he isn't afflicted with the terrors of middle age yet," Sam said.

"Oh, yes, I am," Henry said, laughing, but his mind twisted wryly. How did the ads read: "Men—40, 50, 60! Have you lost your pep?" The kind of an ad you joked about in Medical School. It didn't apply to you yourself. But it did after all.

"Did you ever get your call, Sam?" Paul asked. "They paged you in the lobby."

"Yes," Sam said. "I told Rachel all the old guard were here. She said she wished she could see you all, sent her best. Tell Liz and Kay and Alice, will you?"

"You bet," they said.

"How is Rachel?" Henry asked.

"Oh, she's fine. She looks younger than ever," he added.

His lips moved as though he were going to say something more, but instead he drank his coffee.

"I'm glad I ran into you at breakfast," Henry said. "I had a call early this morning from the wife of the superintendent at the sanitarium. Dr. Dalton's had a bad heart attack, the second one, and he's pretty well knocked out, I gather. Liz and I will have to catch the six-ten plane back."

"Will you get his job, Henry?" John asked.

"Well, they want me to take it," Henry said, glad to be able to say this to John.

"Good," John grunted. "The superintendency ought to carry a pretty good salary."

"Not too bad. Maybe not to you plutocrats, but . . ." Some of the old Henry was coming back. He seemed less tense, Paul thought.

"Do you have an assistant?" Sam asked.

Henry nodded. "Yes, that was my job."

"How is Pomeroy?" John asked.

"It's a beautiful little place, really," Henry said. "A bit cold in winter, but we don't mind that, and the sanitarium has lovely grounds." He sounded to himself like someone else, someone with a button in his lapel that said "Boost Pomeroy." "The buildings and the superintendent's house are all built of gray fieldstone, . . ." the someone else went on. "You know, it's not so far from New York. You'll have to drive up and see us. We'll have plenty of room now."

"That's fine, Henry. I'm so glad," Paul said. He wondered how glad Liz would be to go on living in Pomeroy. He couldn't just see Henry as the administrative, executive type, but maybe. Coming just now, after the disappointment over the mold, was a lucky break. It gave him an easy out on the research work. But he had to ask: "Will you have time to go on with your research work, Hen?"

"Well, I don't know, Paul," Henry answered slowly. "It depends a little on the sort of young fellow I have as assistant." He crumpled his paper napkin into a ball and kneaded it in his fingers. Then he looked up and his eyes met Paul's. "Right now, I'm washed up. The bacteromycin did that pretty completely, wouldn't you say?"

His direct gaze was disconcerting to Paul. He was back in their room in the Interns' Quarters and Henry was looking at him with the same direct gaze, saying: "I'm not going to do research for research's sake, Paul. I'm not one of those birds. I'm going to see if I can find a mold that'll work on TB germs. There's a difference, if you can understand it with that thick head of yours." Henry had been angry when he said it.

"Everything really works out pretty well for you then," Sam said to Henry. Rachel's words were still in his ears from last night: "Sam, it would never work out for us; it just wouldn't. You'd always go on believing it would and wanting to try it again, and we'd go through all that hell again. I know, Sam, I've thought it all out. I just don't want to live that way. I'm not the type for a doctor's wife. Sam, don't make me go all over that. I called to tell you, I'm married again. I married Justin Bardwell, yesterday. . . ."

The waitress came by with a coffee pot. "More coffee, sir?"

"Please," Sam said.

"Cream and sugar, sir?"

"No, thank you, black."

Peder paused at the doorway of the cafeteria and then came over to them.

"Hello, Peder. I lost you last night," John said.

"Yes, you were busy so I went along. How did you come out?"

"All right! I found I had a latent talent for the game."
Then to the others he said, "A. G. Hensley and Babcock
and Morton got me into a little game of craps with them.
I guess there were about eight of us all together. We really
took Hensley to the cleaners." He brandished the names
about a little self-consciously.

"That the Morton of the Morton-Peck operation?" Sam
asked.

"Yes," John said. "He's editor of the *Journal of Surgery,*
you know. Well, look who's here."

Bill was coming toward them, his face a little florid but
firm and shining from the skin lotion he used. The pads
under his eyes as well as the slightly rheumy look of the
eyes themselves were hidden by his glasses.

"Morning, boys!" Bill said cheerfully. "I thought of
course you'd all be at the meeting. You know it started
about fifteen minutes ago. I counted on having a cup of
coffee with my newspaper in peace here."

"You certainly believe that old one about the best de-
fense is offense, don't you, Bill?" John remarked.

"You look pretty spry, fella, considering everything,"
Sam said.

"Henry, you won't be here tonight then for dinner, will
you?" John asked. "Charlotte and I wanted you and Liz to
be our guests."

"No, our plane leaves at six-ten, John. I'm sorry."

"Why are you leaving so soon, Hen?" Bill asked.

Henry explained again. Suddenly, he was glad to be
going, glad of the urgency, something to do next without
having to make any decision. But it was a decision; if he
took the position as superintendent, he would stay for
years probably. There was nothing binding, but that was
the way those things worked out. Look at Carl Dalton.

"Hen's going to be the new superintendent," John explained. He was glad that Henry's problem was solved without involving him. Henry had changed in the years since Woodstock. He was more serious. You had to learn to mix well if you wanted to get ahead in the top brackets in the University. As he told Charlotte, it was a revelation to see Morton and Hensley and the top men, you might say, in their shirtsleeves in a little crap game. Morton must have dropped two hundred dollars last night without turning a hair. He had lost a bit himself, but it was worth it to get to know those men, really know them.

"Say, I heard a good one last night," John began. "Hensley was telling it." As he recounted the story, it didn't seem so funny as it had last night. "I thought Morton would die laughing at it." He tried to bolster up the effect of the story.

The men at the table laughed politely.

"John, who did you say you were with last night?" Paul inquired, raising one eyebrow in mock reproach. He thought how thoroughly Kay disliked John. "He has an overcompensated inferiority complex if I ever met one. And Charlotte simply adores him; she thinks John can do no wrong," Kay had said. It would be a comfortable thing to feel your wife thought you could do no wrong. He looked at John in a new light.

"Paul, you are going to hear Dr. Timmons at eleven, aren't you?" Peder asked.

"No, Peder, I don't believe so," Paul said slowly. "I want to visit a bit with Henry. I think I'll skip the meetings this morning."

"What about you, Henry?" Peder asked.

"I guess I better use what time I have left, Peder, to look at some equipment we ought to have for the sanitarium. They have a nice display of that stuff here." What was he doing with equipment? Carl had liked all that: a

195

better bed, a more convenient sputum cup, devices for keeping dishes warm. He used to bring samples into the office to show him proudly. "What do you think of that, Henry? Pretty slick little trick, eh?" But that wasn't what he himself was interested in. He cared about the chart findings, the pulse and temperature graphs, the history; and always a piece of his mind was on the molds. He thought suddenly of work at the sanitarium without the little lab to go to.

"Well, if we should not meet again, Henry, it has been very, very good to see you." Peder held out his hand.

"It's been fine seeing you, Peder. We were worried about you. We're so glad you came through safely."

"I wanted to say to you," Peder said, "but there was never the right time; somebody else finds a better mold, that is no matter." Peder talked more brokenly when he felt deeply. "You must keep on in your research to see what else it can do. That is important."

They were all standing, ready to go. The waitress was picking up their dishes, but Peder's solemn, formal way of talking held them an instant longer.

"Well, I . . . I don't know, Peder," Henry laughed. "I don't know how important it is."

Peder nodded vigorously. "In the camp we learned that the men who survived best had something their minds worked on, an idea, a problem, something to work on besides just how to survive." Peder shook hands again. "You remember," he said. He was still in high spirits from last night's talk. The others were a little embarrassed.

"Hen, old boy," Bill clapped his hand on Henry's back. "It's been swell seeing you and Liz. But, say, I've got something I want to show you before you go, something I'd like your opinion on. How about meeting me in the lobby sometime between meetings?"

"Sure, Bill, only I've got to get around pretty fast if I leave this evening." He hesitated; he didn't want to have Bill on his mind. "What've you got? A rare case of pelvic nystagmus?" Bill always used to get steamed up over some good case in the old days.

"Something just as good," Bill said. "How about . . . ? I'll tell you, I'll have to go up to the room and get it. I'll meet you in a couple of minutes by the elevators."

"Fine. I'll be right there," Henry said.

"Wonderful how he perks up the next morning as fresh as a daisy," John said. "Say, Hen, I'm mighty glad things have turned out so well for you. You've done a nice piece of work regardless. Babcock mentioned it to me: said it was like the early days, when a man had to work by himself."

"Thanks, John. Say good-by to Charlotte if I don't see her," Henry said a little hurriedly. John was too patronizing to take easily.

Sam waved to him over the heads of people going out the door of the cafeteria. "See you both at the airlines office," he said and disappeared in the crowd.

Henry and Paul walked up the stairs to the lobby instead of taking the elevator. The wall facing the head of the stairs was sheeted with mirrors that gave back their reflection. Each of them looked at himself a little self-consciously. Paul's appearance had always given him a certain pleasure. He liked his height, his well-shaped head and strong profile, even the look of his hands. Sometimes, looking at them, he thought it was a pity he hadn't gone on with surgery. His glance moved to the reflection of Henry. Henry looked too thin in that tweed suit. His hair, receding from his forehead, made him seem older, but there was something about him that made you look at him. They came to the top of the stairs.

"You feel pretty good about taking this position, Hen?"

"Well, I hadn't ever hankered after running a sanitarium," Henry said, "but there's nothing else to do right now. I'm obligated, of course."

"You'll do a beautiful job of it," Paul said.

"I don't think the executive end is exactly my forte."

"No, I always think of you as doing research," Paul said.

The word "research" flicked against a raw spot. "I'll enjoy the patients, of course. We have two hundred and fifty beds," Henry said, ignoring the mention of research.

"If you and Liz ever get fed up with Pomeroy or institutional life, or if you'd like Nancy to get a taste of the city, just drop us a line and come on down. You know how much Kay and I would love to have you." And if Kay did leave. . . . He had a sudden impulse to talk to Henry about Kay. It wouldn't be the first time. Back in their room at the fraternity house he had asked Henry's advice about marrying Kay. Henry had said: "You're in love with her, you nut. Why don't you tell her so?"

"But do you think we're good for each other?" he had worried. He remembered Henry's blank look. "Why, Paul, I don't know why not. I never thought about it that way. I don't know whether Liz and I are *good* for each other."

"Thanks, Paul," Henry said. There were a lot of things to say, more to Paul than the others. He and Paul went back so far, but none of the things to say came handily to mind. There was one thing, though, that he wanted to get straight with Paul—that part about the identification with the myth. If he and Liz had ever had any idea that they were like the Curies because of the similarity between their difficulties and drudgery and sacrifices, they had no such idea now. He wanted to have Paul know that, to laugh at himself before Paul.

"Now that my late mistress has turned out to be a hussy,

I can get back to normal living," he said. "By the way, there's a convention of sanitarium heads in New York sometime in February that Carl Dalton usually goes to. I imagine I'll be there this year. I'll bring Liz along and we'll drop in on you and Kay."

Paul frowned a little, listening to him. "Good. We'll be looking forward to seeing you." He wondered if he shouldn't talk to Henry about Liz, help him to see that the motivation for Liz's resentment wasn't really personal, that it was disappointment over the reception of their work, referred to Nancy. It might help Hen, but Henry kept him off at arm's length.

"Bill has something he wants to show me. I guess I better gravitate over toward the elevators," Henry said. "It's been grand to see you and Kay, Paul."

"Seeing you both was our chief reason for coming." Paul took hold of Henry's arm, but as his fingers touched the coat sleeve, he felt self-conscious. He and Henry shook hands. This was going to be all there was to it.

Paul tried again. "Good luck, fella." Why would he say "fella"? He never had before. He had heard other men say it, and it had an affectionate, intimate sound, but it grated on his ears when he said it himself.

"You too, Paul," Henry said.

"We'll be there to see you off." Paul said it more to carry himself off across the lobby, an exit speech, walk off right. He looked at his watch. He had just time to hear a paper on psychosomatics. He walked briskly up the stairs to the mezzanine. It was all just as it had been yesterday: men lobbying outside the closed doors, some talking earnestly, some smoking.

"I've had dozens of those cases in my own practice," one man said as he passed. "Just a rehash for the sake of giving a paper and being on the program."

". . . If we'd had a change of party and a little more time to work out our own program, but this way we'll have the government running every hospital in the country. . . ."

"Marvin's never been psychoanalyzed himself, has he?"

The snatches of conversation were like fragments from radio programs when you moved the pointer rapidly across the dial, and they irritated him just as badly. He hadn't said anything to Henry, anything real. He didn't have a gift for friendship. Hen was the closest he had ever come to it. All these years he had thought of Henry as his most intimate friend.

Too many years had gone between them. He couldn't get back. Henry was absorbed in his own problems. He didn't want to take that job; you could see that. He was unhappy. There should have been something he could say to show him that he understood how he felt. But they hadn't really got together. Now they never would.

He didn't want to hear any papers after all. He had heard enough. He'd go on up to the room. Perhaps Kay was still there. He would ignore what she had said last night. Kay was always interested in hearing about Henry and Liz. Maybe it would help if he could make her see that they weren't perfect.

"You could see that Henry would rather be hung than take that job, but I imagine he's doing it for Liz, and maybe a little economic security to boot. They haven't anything tremendous to lose themselves in just now, Kay. I'd say they're thinking pretty much about their own futures, like everybody else," he would tell her.

Kay was closer to him than Henry. Kay understood him, too well for comfort often, but her very knowledge was better than his own loneliness. She was good for him;

even her sharp lashings out at him, her cunning interpretations of his motives, her anger, made him feel alive.

He waited eagerly for the elevator going up; one hand toyed with his AOA key that swung from his watch chain. He just happened to remember: he had had that undergraduate honor the year before Henry.

CLINIC

HENRY saw Bill almost as soon as he reached the bank of elevators. Bill was hurrying across the lobby with an X-ray plate under his arm.

"There you are!" Bill said. "Hen, I wanted you to take a look at this plate of a friend of mine, a doctor. He brought it to me and, of course, it isn't in my line, but he didn't want someone locally to see it; you know how it is. He had the X-ray taken in his own office."

"Sure, but . . . well, Bill, we can't see it here," he said reluctantly. Any one of the others who weren't leaving so soon could give him an opinion on it.

"I'd take you up to the room, but Allie's still in bed. She likes to sleep in at these meetings. I suppose it's the same thing with Liz."

"Yes, I imagine so," Henry said. "I wonder about some room off the mezzanine where the meetings are. There must be some place up there with good light."

They went up the stairs together, and Henry realized that Bill was still a little shaky from the night before. His brisk air and manner cost him considerable effort.

At the other end from the ballroom where the meetings were going on they found an empty room where the banquet had been held the night before. Soiled tablecloths were still on the tables, and the hundreds of little gilt chairs stood just as people had left them. The windows were closely curtained over leaded glass. Henry pushed one open and sudden, bright daylight flooded in over the heavy carpeting. It struck full on Bill's face as he stood there. Henry was about to say, "You feel pretty bum, don't you, Bill?" Then he realized that Bill might not enjoy any reference to his health after his state last night so he said instead, "It's all your life's worth to get to some honest daylight in a place like this. Let's see your prize case."

"It isn't exactly that," Bill corrected. "It's a friend."

"Oh, yes, I remember."

Bill sat down on one of the foolish-looking little gilt chairs. Henry took the X-ray plate and walked over to the windows so the bright light came through the big chest plate. The white column of spine stood out of the soft liquid gray of the film, as striking a landmark, he used to think as a student, as the white chalk cliffs of England. The heart showed white and large, a little larger than normal, against the gray shadow of the lungs. The right diaphragm was lifted by the shrinkage of the right lung. The dense white rounded mass to the right of the mid-line was there for anyone to see. He followed the ruthless lines and shadows closely for a minute, then he glanced at Bill.

Bill's eyes shifted quickly away from him, and he took out a cigarette and his lighter.

"Well, Bill, this is the way it looks to me." Henry took out his pencil. "The plate shows clearly a rounded mass in the right superior mediastinum in the position of the bronchus to the right upper lobe. The minor fissure on the right is elevated and is convex upward. . . . I can see that you'd feel it's a textbook picture of a cancer of the bronchus, originating in the right upper lobe and with spread to the paratrachial lymph nodes," he finished.

"That's about the way I had it sized up," Bill said, "but I didn't like to pass sentence on this guy till I had someone else's say-so."

Henry noticed how pale Bill was; he ought to ease up on the drinking. He waited a second, not liking to rush Bill.

"You don't think removing the lung would offer him a chance?"

"No, Bill. That bunch of glands up there means extensive spread, and you couldn't get them, even with a total pneumonectomy."

Bill was quiet so long that Henry said, "I suppose you've got to be the one that tells the poor devil?"

"Yes," Bill said. "Oh, I gave him a pretty good idea about it. I haven't told him how long he could look forward to. I suppose about nine months, wouldn't you say?"

"Or less, possibly six," Henry said, looking at the plate again. "What sort of a temperament has he?" he asked, more because Bill continued to sit there on the little gilt chair, absorbed in his friend's fate.

"Oh, he's an easygoing sort, in his early forties. He never thought of anything like this, of course. He's pretty active usually—plays golf, fishes, hunts. Drinks too much. . . . Works hard though." Then he added, "You know, like the rest of us."

Henry made a sympathetic sound in his throat. "Pretty tough. Wife and children, I suppose?"

"Yeah, wife and four children."

"That makes it nice," Henry said.

"You're right, that makes it just too sweet," Bill said.

"Has he any fever, Bill?" Henry asked, slipping the plate back in the large green envelope.

"No. A little blood in the sputum though."

"Any pain in the chest, Bill?"

"No, I haven't really had any pain, just . . ."

Henry's hand tightened on the envelope. He didn't look at Bill, but he was aware of the gilt chair squeaking under Bill's weight. The bright sun came in too glaringly, and he went over and closed the window. The room was gloomy again but more endurable. The sounds from the street were muted.

Henry was used to telling patients that they had advanced tuberculosis, that they wouldn't live, but not Bill, somebody he had gone through Medical School with. He wanted to go over to him, but he stood by the window fitting the bolt into place.

Bill spoke first. "I'm sorry, Hen. That was a stupid trick. I didn't mean to let you know."

"Gosh, Bill, I'm . . . that just can't be." He looked at Bill. He had lost the crisp, freshly shaved look he had at breakfast. His eyes were veiled behind the glasses. He had a fresh cigarette in his mouth.

"Well, I guess that's it," Bill said. He stood up. "You've got to get going, Hen. I just somehow thought I could take it better from you. You haven't had such a damned picnic, either.

"I'm not going to tell Allie yet or the older kids. I'll wait as long as I can. I thought we might go on a trip together, have a hell of a big time. We haven't had time for much of that. I don't know; maybe we'll send the kids all to camps, and just Allie and I'll go off."

They stood together in the long banquet room. Henry touched Bill's arm without knowing he did it. "Bill, I don't know whether I could take it like that." They walked across the room.

"I'm sort of glad you know about it, Henry. You get to feeling so, well, lonely with a thing like this." He smiled. "You're not, of course. Plenty of people in the same boat, all over the world. It's really no worse than being killed in the war. I might have been, you know. Why is it so damn much harder to die in ordinary living?"

"I don't know, but it seems that way," Henry said.

They opened the doors on the mezzanine. The doors of the ballroom were still closed. Men with badges still loitered outside.

"If you and Allie have the time, come and see us in Pomeroy, Bill," Henry said and wished he hadn't used the word time.

"We might just do that little thing, Hen. Allie thinks a lot of Liz. And thanks, Hen."

"I wish you would," Henry said.

"Say, Hen, there's one good thing about it: when I'm dead, all the good souls who ever sneered at my drinking will be ashamed of themselves. They'll think I drank to drown my sufferings." He laughed. "Of course, I didn't suspect this thing until two months ago, but it will make a good story."

"Bill, how'd you ever have the guts to go through with your Boards when you knew this?" Henry asked.

"Oh, I had been notified that I had qualified for the final oral exam, and I didn't want Alice to wonder why I didn't take it. Maybe the certificate will give her a little satisfaction, or the boys if they ever go into Medicine."

"Jesus Christ!" Henry said as though to himself.

"Well, good-by, Henry. Here, you don't want that." Bill took the X-ray plate Henry was still carrying under his arm and walked briskly down the corridor.

Henry was too much upset to go about his own business. He lit a cigarette and stood against the wall, smoking.

WOMEN'S LUNCHEON

"VICHY SOISSE," Kay said to the waitress. "And chicken livers on toast, the watercress salad, and coffee." She prided herself on ordering quickly and never haggling over the menu.

"Dear, so many things I'd like," Alice said, hesitating. "I guess I'll have cream of fresh mushroom. It is fresh, isn't it?" The waitress assured her that it was. "And frogs' legs and French fries and a fruit salad. Oh, yes, and coffee."

"Consommé and combination salad and tea," Charlotte said with a pained expression. "I know I've gained on this trip; I can tell by this suit."

"I'd like the Vichy soisse too, please," Liz said, choosing it because of the name that had no relation to her usual meals. "And a vegetable salad and rolls and coffee."

Women at luncheon gave to their ordering that concentration demanded of all creative expression. Then they sat back, waiting with ill-concealed eagerness to see the result of their selection.

"We might as well have something to drink while we're waiting," Charlotte suggested as the waiter with the beverage list paused by her chair. But there was a hint of indecision in her voice.

"Well," Alice deliberated. "I could stand an Old-fashioned. It does pick you up in the middle of the day." She really only liked the cherry, still, since Charlotte had suggested it, she wouldn't be less sophisticated than Charlotte. Lucile Swartz always ordered a cocktail at lunch.

"I'll have a Martini," Kay said.

"Sherry," Liz said.

"And I'll have a Martini," Charlotte told the waiter.

The drinks appeared almost immediately. Liz had the same sense of make-believe and yet familiarity she had had at lunch yesterday, but now she remembered: she was a little girl again, playing tea party in the willow tree, sipping a concoction of left-over tea and root beer and water from the brook, but out of a tiny chipped wine glass the neighbor next door had given her, instead of a teacup. "That's a wine glass," her mother had said disapprovingly. "You don't want a wine glass." But she did. She had felt very grown up. She felt so now.

"This is a terrible Martini, isn't it?" Charlotte said to Kay. "You really have to order a double to get anything in it."

"Mine's not bad," Kay said, and managed to make the words a rebuke.

"You're always safe with sherry," Charlotte said to Liz. "But it doesn't agree with me."

They were doing the "safe" thing now, taking Carl's position, Liz thought. It would mean a very good living. The sherry tasted exactly like the cold tea and root beer drink, thinned down with brook water.

"It spoils everything to have you and Henry leave early, Liz," Charlotte said. "I was just counting on tonight. Honestly, I don't know when I've had so much fun as the other night. You have friends now, but, I don't know, they're always different from the crowd you interned with."

Kay looked at her morosely. Had she really had such a good time last night? How could she with that oaf of a husband?

"John says Henry's all fixed in a splendid position," Charlotte said. "My, I'm so glad for you, Liz."

"Fixed." The word stuck unpleasantly in Liz's mind, like the moths she used to pin on a card in high school for General Science. She always hated pushing the pin down through the soft furry center of the moth, even after the drop of chloroform had made it quite dead. The moth kept its color but lost all its glow. It dulled. The bright bulging eye became just another spot. She only got "C" on her collection because it contained only four moths and three butterflies. "Surely, if you tried, Elizabeth, you could have found some more," Miss Hatcher said. But she didn't want to find any more. Was Henry fixed now?

"Tell us about it, Liz," Kay said. Interest softened her and dispelled the air of remoteness.

"Well, it's an institutional job, of course, but we have our own home and garden, and Nancy and I have very little contact with the sanitarium. The superintendent's house is very attractive." She stood outside and heard herself.

"Is the house furnished?" Charlotte asked.

"No, I don't believe so. I'm sure the furnishings all belong to Mrs. Dalton." Mrs. Dalton . . . Hester. She had never though of taking Hester's place.

"How big is the house?" Alice asked.

Mentally she walked through the house: the time Hester was ill and she had gone up to see her in the big front bedroom with the fireplace; the time Hester had given one of her rare dinners and the women had laid their coats in the east bedroom that opened on the porch, the one Nancy would have. Carl's bedroom down the hall had always reeked of tobacco. Then there was the guest room. They must have her mother to visit after they had moved. . . .

"And you mean to say that's all supplied to the superintendent?" Charlotte asked.

"Yes," Liz said. "And there's a car for Henry so I'll have our old coupe myself." She had just thought of that. She wanted to have them see what a fine proposition it was. There had been a hint of pity in their voices yesterday, all but Kay's. The Vichy soisse tasted differently from the canned soups she heated for lunch at home, very smooth with a taste of herbs.

"I can certainly see the point of an institutional job," Charlotte said. Liz noticed the perfect grooming of her hands, the soft cuticle and polished perfection of her nails, and was conscious of her own that were dry and red from the solutions in the laboratory. There would be no more of that.

"It's really amazing the way it turned out and your problems are solved overnight. I don't know where we got the idea, but Bill thought Henry was thinking of moving from there," Alice said.

"We did intend to, but we had made no definite plans because we'd been spending every minute working." Already that seemed long ago. The big jars with the growing molds . . . Henry should have wired Jake not to go on growing the cultures.

The new assistant would probably turn their little laboratory into a nursery. It would take a while to get the smell of the molds out of that room. They would have to repaint it. If the new assistant and his wife were sporty young people, they could make a rumpus room out of it. The counter would make a good bar and the stools would be fine painted a bright color. Still, she might take the stools with her; she had spent so many hours with her feet wrapped around the rungs of those stools.

"Are there interesting people in Pomeroy?" Kay asked.

"We were always so busy and Henry was so tied down we never did anything with anybody in town. Hester, the superintendent's wife, had friends. In summer there's quite a colony of summer people."

In the tree house she had had to make up her callers because there were no children there. "This is Mrs. Mortimer Hall from Boston and this is Mrs. Ashley Randolph from the Deep South." They were two of the persons she made up, talking aloud in a grown-up voice. She had had no idea as to what the Deep South was like, but it had a mysterious sound and made the state of Connecticut seem thin and rather shallow. She had no idea of the inhabitants of Pomeroy either. She hadn't had time to play house.

"I know they have a University Women's Club there and a country club," she added.

"Be careful, Liz, you'll be just like the rest of us," Kay said.

One day in the tree house Liz had been frightened by a storm. The brook turned dark and the wind shook the boughs of the tree and broke off a big branch that left the crotch she called her upstairs bedroom all exposed. A cold wind went through her sweater and middy blouse and made goose pimples on her legs and arms. She climbed down out of the tree so fast she knocked the little chipped wine glass off of her shelf and it broke on the stones below. She had left all her play dishes and her mirror and the old alarm clock with one leg without putting them away in the box underneath the tree. She only wanted to get home to the fire. She never played in the tree house again. The next summer she was away and after that she was too old. Kay's words made the same cold wind go through her.

"These frogs' legs are wonderful. I wish you'd had them, Kay," Alice said. "Liz, what did you order? Oh, vegetable salad is so uninteresting."

"I suppose I ordered vegetable salad because I make it so often at home for Henry and me," she said, paying no attention to the wind.

"You won't have to help Henry any more, will you?" Kay asked.

She hadn't thought of that. "No, I guess not," she said.

"I've envied you that," Kay said too quietly for anyone across the table to hear. "Working together would hold you together. I'm going to find a job this summer. I've been working part time, copying books in Braille, you know." But perhaps she wouldn't take a job; perhaps she would take painting lessons instead, and work at it, really work. Paul would see whether she could paint or not.

"Why, Kay, how splendid." She had to make a new picture of Kay.

Kay drank her coffee and wondered if she should tell Liz that she was leaving Paul. Liz seemed different from the way she had the other day. She seemed so busy with the idea of the superintendent's house. But Henry wouldn't change. It was Henry that she would really like to talk to about Paul.

"Do you think Henry will like his new work?" Kay asked abruptly.

"I think so," Liz said slowly. "He'll miss the work with the molds for a while; he's lived with them so long, of course." The cold wind still crept in around her thoughts. Henry wouldn't take it if he didn't want to. She certainly hadn't said anything to influence him—just that about not wanting to see him start out on some problem and have it come to nothing and have him disappointed again. She had said that before they had any idea about Carl's being sick. Kay seemed waiting for her to say more. "Henry couldn't stand another experience like that with the microcydin," she said.

"Yes, I can see that," Kay said. "But it wasn't a failure."

"Well, in a way it was," Liz insisted. "I think Henry feels it was."

"But how could he?"

"Bill just floored me," Alice's voice broke in. She was smiling as though she were pleased. "He came up to the room just before lunch and lay down on the bed while I finished dressing. 'What would you think, Allie, of our running away to Bermuda next month?' he said. I was so surprised I nearly died. 'You aren't serious, Bill?' I said. He said, 'I was never more serious in my life.' 'But what about the practice and the children?' You know that isn't like Bill. He never goes away except like this to a Medical Meeting. He said, 'Oh, the practice will keep, and your mother would love to come and stay with the children.' Just like that!"

"Take him up on it quick. You'll love Bermuda," Charlotte said.

"I guess I'm going to because Bill's mind seemed so set on it," Alice said. "I'm terribly thrilled. I thought I'd look for a couple of summery-looking things while I'm here."

"You'll have a second honeymoon," Kay said a little dryly.

"Yes." Alice colored faintly on her plump cheeks and below the gold choker at the base of her throat.

"I hope we can get to the Cape for a month this summer. The Archie Belknaps have a place down there; he's brain surgery, took Willard Murray's place, and they always ask us down," Charlotte said. "What are you doing this summer, Kay?"

"I'm going to stay right in New York. I don't like running away in the worst weather." Kay saw herself clearly now, in an apartment somewhere, just a modest one but with northern light where she could paint. She would work so hard she would be worn out at the end of a day and have the good feeling that she had worked. After a while she would make some friends, her own friends who weren't charmed by Paul.

"Well, I wish you joy. I loathe the city in summer. Ugh!" Charlotte said.

This summer they would have a screened-in porch of their own, Liz thought, and Nancy would be home. Henry would have time to do things with them and they could take a vacation. It wouldn't be like the other summers when they couldn't leave the molds.

They came out of the dining room and stood irresolutely in the lobby, about to break away but held a moment by the piece of their youth that they had had together. At first, two days ago, they had seemed hardly changed at all, but now there was little resemblance to their younger selves. We are women, Liz thought. No one could call us girls any longer. We look even older dressed in our best clothes and hats and gloves—Charlotte with that veil, and Alice looks so much heavier in that short squirrel jacket. She could see herself too in the same glass at the top of the stairs that had reflected the images of Paul and Henry this morning, but she looked away quickly.

She saw suddenly, with painful clarity, that she and the other women had all come to this meeting wanting something from it, hoping that seeing each other after all these years would do something for them, but it hadn't and they hadn't really expected that it would. They were grown up enough to know that.

"Thank you so much, Kay," Liz said, since she had been Kay's guest.

"Paul and I'll be there to see you off, Liz," Kay said.

Alice lifted her face to kiss Liz and, for an instant, Liz

was engulfed by perfume and soft fur and the rough thread of the veil against Alice's cheek.

"Good-by, Liz. I've loved every moment of it," Alice said.

"If you ever come back to Woodstock, come up and stay with us, Liz," Charlotte said, not kissing her, but putting her arm inside Liz's and squeezing it.

It was so long since Liz had been with girls, women rather, that these demonstrative woman ways discomfited her.

Alice and Charlotte left her then to go shopping, and Liz went back to the room to finish packing.

FINAL CONFERENCE

Henry walked slowly through the lobby over to the desk. He might as well pay his bill now as later, and then he would see if they couldn't keep the room until five. A sign above the mailboxes said plainly "CHECKING-OUT TIME 3 PM." Hotels had to make a deadline, of course, but they didn't really enforce it.

As he waited in line in front of the cashier's desk, he thought about Bill. Bill must have felt that the X-ray plate didn't really mean what it said. He must have still hoped when he brought the plate to show him, even though it was there plain as day.

"I wanted to pay my bill. We're checking out, but I'd like to have the use of the room until we leave for that five o'clock plane," he explained to the impassive face behind the brass bars of the cashier's desk, so impassive it seemed to belong neither to male nor female. The light blue eyes showed no interest; the dry curled blond hair was no real color. The flat chest under the navy blue dress gave no indication of a bosom, compassionate or otherwise.

"Checking-out time is three o'clock," the colorless voice told him. "People waiting for rooms. Can't make exceptions."

Slight irritation turned to anger in Henry, a deep unreasoning rage that made it hard for him to keep from retorting as he picked up his change and the receipted bill and crumpled them all into his pocket. There was nothing to do about the checking-out time: no other tribunal, no exceptions. It was like Bill's dying.

He looked in the pigeonhole under 1214 to see if Liz's key was there. The key was gone, but there was a note. He unfolded it and stepped away from the desk to read it.

Dear Dr. Baker:

Dr. Grayson has told me about your work with a mold similar to bacteromycin and the success you had in treating a case of brucellosis.

We have been working on brucellosis and would like very much to talk to you. You were out when I called. Would you call me, Room 1422, before you leave?

John Hanna.

Henry folded the paper carefully, bringing the corners together with great exactness, then he slipped it into his vest pocket. He walked with new purpose over to the line of house phones against the wall.

"Give me Dr. John Hanna's room, 1422, please," he said, and his voice was not quite his own.

"Dr. Hanna? This is Henry Baker. I just got your note. Yes, I should like to. I'll . . . well, I have to leave here at five-ten for the plane. I'll be right up."

Then he called his own room.

"Liz? We have to be ready to check out at three o'clock. Good. I hoped you were. If I shouldn't be able to get up there then, would you call a boy for the bags and bring them down here to the lobby? I'll look for you here. Oh, anywhere in sight. I have to talk with a Dr. Hanna. Thank you, Liz. No, do I sound excited? I'm fine. I've been hurrying around, that's all."

But he was excited. There wasn't any reason, of course, but after feeling that microcydin had dropped into complete oblivion, it was a relief to have someone, anyone,

217

want at least to talk to him about it. "That case of yours interests me greatly," Dr. Hanna had said. Grayson had told him about it, that queer duck of a man who had understood how he felt. He would call Grayson before he left.

Dr. Hanna's room was so neat it looked hardly used. No slides lay on the desk or dresser, no papers spread out untidily over the bed. Only a bright satin tie in a geometrical design lay on a chair, and a handkerchief that matched flowered out of the pocket of the coat over the back of the chair.

Dr. Hanna was younger than Henry, a slight, dark young man wearing an immaculate white shirt under his Roman-striped braces. He looked as like a hundred other young doctors attending the meetings as this hotel room resembled a hundred other rooms. His face was very freshly shaven and an aroma of shaving soap still clung to him. There was no distinguishing characteristic except for his bright inquisitive eyes behind his glasses.

"Sit down over here," he said after he had shaken hands. He himself brought up a straight chair and sat down in front of him. "I'm sorry I missed your paper. I didn't arrive here until last evening, but Grayson told me about it."

"I should have brought the charts and slides with me," Henry said. "It will just take me a moment."

"No, Grayson told me about it in some detail. I don't need to see that now. Just tell me about your one case. Everything about it," he added.

"Well, as a matter of fact, it was my daughter," Henry began. Dr. Hanna sat completely still, listening to every word. He interrupted to ask about the dosage and the reaction.

"But she is permanently deaf," Henry finished.

"On the other hand, she recovered completely from any symptoms of brucellosis. Tell me how to your mind micro-cydin differs from bacteromycin?" Dr. Hanna asked. He did not say "your mold" or "your microcydin"; he spoke of it as though it had an existence of its own and by so doing gave it reality.

"And you have never had another case of brucellosis to try it on?"

"No, I don't come in contact with such cases often in the sanitarium."

"I suppose not."

Dr. Hanna was silent and Henry had nothing more to say. He looked at his watch and found it was ten of four. Liz would be down in the lobby with the bags. He should go. He had told Dr. Hanna everything there was to tell. There was no point in lingering, but some expectant quality of the silence held him.

"You're going on with your research with the micro-cydin, of course?"

Everyone else had assumed he was through. Hanna didn't say "with your research" as though it were a hobby of his. He asked it as though he expected the answer to be in the affirmative. A warmth stole through Henry's mind. It made it possible to answer easily, without bitterness.

"I'm afraid not. Bacteromycin does so much more; I doubt if it would be . . ." "Practicable" was the word Grayson had used; it was true. ". . . Practicable," he finished. "You see, what investigations I have made, my wife and I have carried out by ourselves. Naturally it has taken a great deal of time. It was possible only because I had a position as assistant in a tuberculosis sanitarium. Now the superintendent has been taken ill, and the Board wants me to take his place." He stopped feeling a little foolish that he had gone into so much detail. He took pains to make his tone casual as he asked, "It would be wasted energy to go on raising the microcydin, don't you think? Aside from other drawbacks."

"I don't know," Hanna said slowly. "If it can cure fulminating brucellosis, it's a pretty important mold. You must find out why it worked when the bacteromycin has not, at least as far as we have tried it."

Hope, terrible in its intensity, seized Henry. Quietly, like a man who cannot hear his own voice, he said, "How could I go about that?"

"We have a certain amount of money from the Hooper Foundation at the University. We have all the cases we need, of course. If you wanted to come there, I think it could be arranged to give you an appointment." Hanna was looking directly at him.

"I can't think of anything I would like better," Henry said.

"You wouldn't be working with tuberculosis."

"It would be with disease. I would like to satisfy myself that it was responsible for curing the brucellosis in that case."

"I feel sure we are on the right track," Dr. Hanna said. "With the bacteromycin we have had some partial results as we did with sulfonamides earlier. But why your antibiotic should have worked so completely interests me; it excites me. You gave it in the same way?"

Henry hesitated, not wanting to diminish the mystery of microcydin's effectiveness and yet feeling that Grayson might have put his finger on the reason.

"It may be," Henry said. "It's just possible . . ." his tongue moved reluctantly over the words ". . . that the combined effect of the sulfonamides which I was also giving and the microcydin was the answer. Dr. Grayson thought there might be something in the combination of the two."

"Tell me again how much sulfonamide you had given." He listened intently, nodding his head. "In that case, the bacteromycin used with sulfonamides might work also?"

Henry nodded. "I think it might." He could see no reason, except a personal one, why they should not. There was no apparent virtue in microcydin that bacteromycin did not have too, according to Stockton's report.

Dr. Hanna plunged his hand deep in his trouser pocket a minute and jingled the contents. Then he brought out a patent nail clipper which he held between his thumb and third finger. He took it in the right hand and reversed it before returning it again to the left. He had sat so still before when he listened that the business with the nail clipper disconcerted Henry.

"Perhaps, but it needs to be worked out, not speculated about. Bacteromycin acts differently from penicillin, and microcydin may act differently on brucellosis from the way bacteromycin acts. Do you think you might be interested in working with us on this problem, Dr. Baker? The stipend isn't large. . . ." He left it up in the air.

"What does it amount to?" Henry asked.

"We'd get you in on a fellowship, I believe. Twenty-four hundred would be the best that we could do. Are you married? Of course, your child."

"Yes." Henry hesitated. "That's it. If there were just myself to consider I wouldn't hesitate. But my wife has given up a good deal these last years so I could do this work."

"We might possibly be able to give you three thousand the second year."

Henry shook his head. "I've about made up my mind to take the superintendency of the sanitarium; it carries a salary of six thousand and a good living. I suppose I've had enough experience so that I'm fairly well fitted for it."

"I see your point, of course. But I can't get any more money. We already have two men and one woman working on our brucellosis program. I just thought that we will be trying bacteromycin with the sulfonamides and would want to try microcydin too. Your case has suggested the combination. We can get anything we want in the way of facilities, of course.

"You think it over. I'll write you a letter when I get back, making you a formal proposition. We'd like to have you with us if you should see your way clear to coming. It seems too bad for you to give up research work altogether."

"Thank you. I will certainly think about it," Henry said. His voice felt tight. Dr. Hanna would go ahead with the idea of the combined effect anyway. It was just a courtesy to ask him. "But I'm afraid it's out of the question he added. Of course, I'll be glad to send you some of the microcydin cultures when I get back."

Part Three

"... *you always knew when you made a decision against life. When you denied life you were warned. The cock crowed, always, somewhere inside of you.*"

ANNE LINDBERGH

H<small>E</small> COULD tell that Liz was annoyed the minute he saw her. The bags were beside her and she sat in a tall-backed chair across from the front desk. Sam was there with her. Henry glanced at the clock. It was quarter of five.

"Liz, I'm so sorry to keep you waiting like this. I couldn't help it."

"It's all right, only I could have checked the bags and done something until time to go to the airport, but I thought you'd come any minute," Liz said. "Sam came along and kept me company."

"We decided you were captured by some salesman for sanitarium equipment," Sam said. "In another five minutes we were going to go through all the exhibits and rescue you."

"You two had a good visit so I won't feel sorry for you," Henry said.

"We might have a drink before you go," Sam suggested.

"No," Liz said. "Not and fly."

"Why, that's the best thing to take before a plane trip," Sam insisted.

"Maybe for you but not for us," Liz said and wondered if she had been too short. Sam was trying to send them off well. They moved across the lobby, Sam and Henry carrying the bags. The lobby looked differently now in the late afternoon from the morning they arrived. Then everything had looked so shining and fresh; now it seemed tired and a little subdued, Liz thought. There was a sign saying "out-of-order" on the first elevator.

"I know one thing we will do: we'll stop in here and buy the lady a flower," Sam said.

"Oh, no, Sam," Liz said. She didn't want a flower. There was nothing to celebrate. But they stopped in the florist shop anyway. After the heavy, smoke-filled air of the lobby the air was fresh and softly fragrant. Water dripped into a stone fountain in the wall. Flame-colored flowers that looked like tropical birds filled a gray stone urn. Roses and tulips and daffodils crowded the glass cases. Sam followed the clerk toward the rear of the shop and Henry and Liz were left alone.

"I felt guilty leaving you to get the stuff down," Henry said.

"I didn't mind," she answered, walking away toward the case of roses.

"You packed the slides carefully and put in all those papers that were on the desk, Liz?"

"Of course," she said.

"Thanks. I'll go on and pay for the tickets. You can wait for Sam. The airlines' office is the third door down the arcade."

"I know where it is," she said. She had loitered past it that first afternoon that seemed so long ago now. Perversely she continued to study the roses without looking up. He was almost out of sight when she crossed the florist's shop quickly and stood in the doorway watching him.

"Here you are, Liz." Sam brought an orchid to her in its cellophane bag.

"Oh, Sam, it's beautiful, but you shouldn't have bought it."

"But I wanted to. It gives me great pleasure. I can't buy flowers for Rachel any more, so . . ." She looked up at him quickly. He shrugged and smiled so ruefully at her, she pinned the orchid on her coat without any questions.

"Feel loved?" he asked.

"Yes," she answered, laughing.

"That's important," he said lightly.

Kay and Paul were talking to Henry outside the airlines' office. Most of the passengers had already taken their places in the long limousine by the curb. Liz was glad there wouldn't be any wait.

"I guess we better get in," Henry said. "It was good of you to come and see us off."

"It won't hurt you any, Henry, to take it a little easier," Paul said. "Liz, make him play a little."

"If I can, Paul," she promised.

"Good-by, Liz," Kay said quietly. Seeing Liz and Henry again had helped her make up her mind. She wondered if Liz would tell Henry what she had said about Paul. She wished she had had a chance to talk to Henry.

"Good-by, Kay." Had Kay really meant what she said about not mattering terribly to Paul? She felt that Kay had wanted to talk more the night of the cocktail party, but there wasn't any time.

"Good-by, Liz," Paul said, putting his arm around her. "It's been wonderful seeing you and Henry."

It had been, of course, only Liz wished she hadn't said so much to Paul about Henry. She could feel Paul remembering that in the warmth of his glance.

"Good-by, Paul," she said a little briefly and turned to say good-by to Sam.

Then the doors of the limousine were closed and they could only wave and smile through the windows. Something was finished that had been unfinished when they left Woodstock, Liz thought. They had been so eager to see Paul and Kay and Bill and Alice and the others, but, somehow, they didn't seem to know them so well after seeing them again as they had before. It was strange and sad in a way. She wondered if the others felt as she did. They looked very gay, standing bareheaded on the curb in front of the hotel. Sam took out his handkerchief and waved, Kay pantomimed grief, Paul made a gesture to show that both Sam and Kay were crazy. Liz and Henry laughed and waved again.

"Well, there they go," Sam said.

"Liz looked very young, didn't she?" Kay said. "You must have given her the orchid, Sam. I thought of flowers, but Paul and I were involved in an argument that ran on too long."

"Come with me and I'll buy you one." Sam took her arm. "I'm in an orchid-buying mood."

"I love men in orchid-buying moods. So long, Paul." Sam and Kay walked off down the arcade to the florist's. Paul followed at a slower pace. Halfway there they met Charlotte hurrying toward the street.

"Kay, don't tell me they've gone."

"About five minutes ago."

" 'Too late y-war quod Beautee whan it paste,' " Sam quoted but no one heard him.

"Oh, I'm so disappointed," Charlotte said. "I wanted to see them off. I see you had the same idea."

"Only we got here," Kay said, starting on again.

"That's just a shame. The time went so fast, didn't it?"

"How about an orchid for Charlotte, Sam?" Kay suggested when they were passed.

"Let's let John buy her one. She isn't one of my favorite women."

Paul joined them in the florist's and they walked back into the hotel together.

"This Medical Meeting was a tragic thing for Henry," Paul said.

"You mean for Henry's mold," Sam tried to strike a lighter note.

"No, I mean for Henry. I know he 'consumes his own smoke,' but that doesn't mean that the smoke doesn't do a good deal of damage inside."

"I think he'll manage, Paul," Sam said. "He and Liz look pretty solid to me. That's what counts."

"That's what Kay thinks," Paul said. "I wonder if Hen can just give up his research after so many years and turn entirely to clinical and executive work and be content."

"Oh, Paul, stop it!" Kay said sharply. "Come on up, Sam, and have a drink with us."

"Kind of fun to fly again," Henry said when they were settled in the plane. "I haven't since the time I flew with that patient from Woodstock to Canada."

"I haven't since before we were married," Liz said. "Remember, I was going to fly back to meet Mother and it was too expensive."

"I remember," he said. No one could buy airplane tickets on twenty-four hundred a year either, he thought.

"Henry, I talked to Nancy." She felt guilty keeping it to herself so long.

"How was she?"

"She sounded just fine. She could hear perfectly."

"Was it all right about finishing the term?"

"She didn't seem to mind. I think she was too excited about your being superintendent and moving into the Daltons' house."

"Oh, you told her!"

"Yes. I thought she would enjoy thinking about it."

Liz felt the whole thing was settled then. She was counting on it. Nancy was too. Well, he'd told Hanna he couldn't accept his offer. It wouldn't be fair to Nancy and Liz. He had had his chance. Henry shifted in his seat. Still, it couldn't hurt to tell Liz about Hanna's offer, about the work he was doing. But he hesitated.

"Gum, sir?" The stewardess was passing a box of gum.

"Thank you," Henry said, and unwrapping the gum, he chewed it slowly, meditatively.

Liz looked over at Henry. He was so deep in his own thoughts that he didn't notice her turning. Was he going over the whole miserable outcome of the meeting again? He looked tired in the gray white light. It was good for Henry that he had Carl's position to step right into.

She was tired too and glad to sit still without talking. There was something familiar about this, as though she had done it before. Then she knew: they were like children coming home from an excursion, tired and a little disappointed. Children always spent too much and the prize in the Cracker Jack box was never worth the price and they quarreled and got separated and were glad to get home. It was true of them too.

"Henry, how long a wait do we have in Binghamton?" Liz asked.

"We get in at two-thirty in the morning and have to wait two hours for that milk train. I thought we might see about a bus. It's less than a hundred miles."

"Sounds grim. Anyway, we'll get there too early for a Sunday afternoon dinner with Hester."

Henry said, "I wonder how Carl is." If he were better, perhaps Carl wouldn't retire. Then he could take the job with Hanna for a year perhaps. . . .

This was like that other time when he went to Buffalo to see about a practice. He had signed up for the apartment and seen the gas company and the electric company and applied for the school clinic job, and then he had thought about it all the way home on the train and known he didn't want to do it. He had hurried back to Liz and told her so. And Liz had said, "Then we won't do it, Henry."

But that was twelve years ago. You couldn't always run away from the thing you didn't want to do. Liz had been young then. She hadn't known what it would mean. She did now, and she wanted a different kind of life for Nancy. He glanced at Liz and saw her profile against the window of the plane. Her face in repose was sad. She grieved so over Nancy. And the disappointment over the mold had been hard on her.

He settled farther down in his seat. Some things you couldn't do and live with yourself. He closed his eyes and leaned his head against the back of the seat.

I FEEL as though we were fleeing from something," Liz said as they walked across to the terminal from the plane.

"If we get to the border, we're safe," Henry said. "It's a good night for an escape. Turn your collar up and we'll run for it."

A cold wind blew at them from the dark, and water splashed up on Liz's ankles as they ran. His brief case bumped his legs. The word "escape" hit him unpleasantly.

A few people waited behind the wire fencing. The rain made a lively sound on their umbrellas.

"You can't help but feel a little superior when you get off a plane, can you?" Liz said, slowing to a walk. "All those people waiting there are mere creatures of earth and we were airborne five minutes ago."

"I'm not sure that they're so impressed," Henry objected.

"Oh, I'm sure they are, underneath," Liz insisted.

"Henry! Liz. I'm so thankful to see you." Hester stepped out of the little group under the umbrellas. She was wrapped in a white raincoat and her head was tied up in a dark scarf. Caesar was with her, walking beside her with long sinuous strides. "I couldn't let you come on that poky old train so I drove over for you."

"You shouldn't have come way over here at this time of night," Liz said. She had a swift sense of disappointment. She didn't want to see Hester yet. The picture was so changed by Carl's illness, by the letter Hester had written Henry, even by the evening dress she had borrowed and torn.

"How is Carl, Hester?" Henry asked.

"He's a little better, the doctor says. He can talk and he eats a little, but he's so weak! You know what a hearty-looking man Carl is, Henry, and he looks positively fragile." Hester's voice sounded worried.

"After an attack like that, it takes time, of course," Henry said.

"Carl seemed worried about the sanitarium. He'll be better now that he knows you're here to run it." Hester said it so finally, Henry thought. But, then, why shouldn't she?

"You both wait in the car and I'll get the bags," Henry said.

"Liz, why don't you curl up in back and sleep on the way home? There are blankets on the seat. You won't mind Caesar, will you? Lie down, Caesar."

"I couldn't sleep, but I'll get in back," Liz said, feeling the old irritation with Hester's way of managing everyone. Now, while Henry was getting the bags, Hester would ask about the paper.

Hester passed her a cigarette and lighter. When Hester lit her own cigarette, Liz was startled by the shadows under her eyes and her lips without lipstick.

"You've had a bad time, Hester," she said gently.

"A hellish time, Liz. I thought Carl was going to die. You can't imagine what it was like. He had the attack the night before I called you; that was Friday night. He was in the most terrible pain and so cold I got him a hot pad and extra blankets, and I wanted to call Dr. Noble out from Pomeroy, but he didn't want me to and kept saying he'd be all right. He was in bed all that next day, but he had Miss Harper come over and tell him about the San, and he fretted about not being able to get there.

"And then that afternoon I couldn't stand it and I

called Dr. Noble anyway. When Dr. Noble told him he'd have to be in the hospital, Carl said he'd go over to that empty room in the San in the morning." Hester was so different, so busy with each detail.

"And that night I was lying in bed trying to read when I heard an awful thud and knew Carl had tried to get up and fallen."

Liz could see it all as Hester talked. She could feel Hester's terror at the thought of death. Doctors' wives were, after all, more sheltered from the fear of illness than other women. All they had to do was keep dinner hot while their husbands settled with such things as disease and death. When their own husbands were sick, they were terror-stricken.

"I couldn't sleep all night, and as soon as it began to be light, I put in a call for Henry. After I talked to him, I sat by the phone and just cried like a baby." Liz couldn't picture Hester crying. She must care greatly about Carl, more than they had thought. Liz was silent, trying to reconcile her ideas about Hester.

They both watched Henry coming back with the bags. "Don't you want to ride up in front too, Liz?" he asked.

"No, this is fine," Liz said, but she was absurdly pleased that Henry had asked her.

"Can I drive for you, Hester?" Henry asked.

"No, thanks. I'd rather drive," Hester said. "Since Carl's been sick, it makes me nervous not to be doing something." Hester turned the car around in one large circle, impatient of small backings and turnings, and drove rapidly down the curving road from the airport.

"Now tell me about Carl," Henry said and listened intently while Hester went back over Carl's attack.

"And it's so cruel, Henry!" Hester broke out. "Carl's

had such a humdrum, dull sort of life, really, and now he's struck down like this."

"He may get over this, Hester, just like the other time, and live a completely normal life, if he just . . ."

She took the sentence away from him. "If he watches his salt and rests and never gets excited or does anything strenuous. That's no way to live!" Liz thought of Hester's note: "I was suffocated with dear, easygoing Carl. Living is meant to be more strenuous than that."

"It's a way to live though, Hester. Carl likes his life. It has all sorts of compensations," Henry said slowly. It was going to be important to think of those for himself.

"You mean the jelly one patient's wife sent and the bag of oranges and the hen someone brought one time without even drawing it, and now the phone calls from people who've heard he's sick." Hester's eyes flashed as she turned to look at him.

"I mean the devotion he has from all those people. He means a great deal to the community."

Would he, himself, come in time to take Carl's place here? Henry wondered. He and Liz had lived so much alone. They couldn't have done as much work any other way. He hardly knew anyone besides the patients. He tried to think of himself joining a service club, playing golf and poker. Carl was so jovial; he, Henry, was naturally serious.

"What does it matter now?" Hester said impatiently. "He's a terribly sick man."

The car swerved suddenly and Hester drove in beside an oil truck parked in front of a squat wooden building. Over the door the word PETE's in bright red letters seemed to hang suspended in the darkness. "That's the first place I've seen open. You must be ready for breakfast."

Two men from the truck sat at the counter eating pie. A heavy-set man with a dish towel tied around his waist leaned against the wall by the coffee urn, chewing a toothpick. Everything in the room that could be painted was a bright orange color: counter, stools, window frames, shelves, and the two wooden booths. The orange paint had a thick, wet look of never having dried. Two naked electric light bulbs filled the room with glaring light.

Hester slid into the booth on one side of the table, Liz and Henry on the other. Hester took off her scarf and pushed back her hair. The bright light searched out every gray hair in her dark head and the thin places over her temples. It made her face haggard.

"Quarter of four," Hester said. "It was time to stop."

The restaurant owner called from his position by the coffee urn, "We ain't got no menus. You c'n have ham an' eggs, hamburgers, coffee an' pie."

Liz thought how different this was from the way they had planned to come home: Carl meeting them at the station and driving them to the sanitarium; Mrs. Plew serving dinner in Hester's sunny dining room, sparkling with silver and glass. They had expected to tell about the triumphant reception of the paper.

"Could we have our coffee while we're waiting?" Henry asked the proprietor. He went over to the counter and carried the three cups back himself.

"This was a hard trip for you to make, Hester. You were up most of last night too," Henry said.

"No, it's a relief. Mr. Cooper offered to drive over for you; he's very anxious to see you."

As chairman of the Board of the sanitarium, Cooper would ask him to take Carl's position. There it would be in front of him.

Hester put out her cigarette. "You haven't told me a word about the meeting or your paper, Henry." Weariness seemed to drop from her. She leaned on the table.

Henry lit his cigarette before he spoke. He hated telling Hester, Liz could see. Perhaps it would be easier for him if she weren't there. She glanced around for a woman's room, but there was none. She looked away from them at a calendar on the back wall, trying to remove herself.

"As I told you over the phone, Hester, the home team didn't come off so well," Henry said. "There was another paper given that morning, before I gave mine, on an antibiotic called bacteromycin. It was a dirt mold very similar to microcydin but more effective. It about knocked my paper into a cocked hat."

Hester sat up very straight. Her eyes narrowed. "What do you mean, Henry?"

"Just that the other mold is better than mine, so much so that there isn't any possibility of interesting anyone in producing microcydin commercially."

"And all that work you've done goes for nothing?"

"I'm afraid so."

Hester banged her fist suddenly on the table so the spoons clattered against the thick cups and the men at the counter looked around. "Why, I never heard anything so terrible. But you cured patients with it. Did you tell them? Can their stuff cure people as sick as Lester Small?"

Her indignation and anger must comfort Henry a little, Liz thought.

"I'm afraid it can. They've had quite a staff working and they've tried it out pretty thoroughly. There are thousands of different but similar molds, you know, Hester."

Hester was silent a moment, her mouth set. "Wouldn't you know we couldn't do anything here that would really amount to something," she burst out. She took another cigarette and Henry leaned over to light it for her. Liz saw how pale his face was. You mustn't say that, Hester.

Tell Henry . . . tell him anything else, Liz's mind cried out.

"Who had the ham an' two eggs?" The man with the apron set down their plates. They picked up their forks and began eating. Hester buttered a piece of the pale toast.

"You must have felt foolish giving your paper after that," Hester said.

"No," Henry said. "I didn't feel foolish." The color had come back into his face. "The similarity in our results was amazing, obtained so independently. In a field as little known as this, all the knowledge obtained is important." His voice had a cold edge to it.

"But you won't get any credit for it," Hester said.

"No, I won't get any credit for it. I wonder if we could have some more coffee?" he called over to the proprietor.

"Carl wrote Dr. Higgins, Father's old friend in Baltimore, just the other day and told him we were doing great things here. He told him we had a new cure for some kinds of tuberculosis. And I invited Mary Forbes who does free-lance articles for women's magazines to come up and write up your work from the human angle," Hester said almost accusingly.

"There is plenty of human angle in it at that," Henry said dryly.

Liz sat frowning at her plate, cutting her ham into tiny pieces. She looked over at Hester, trying to catch her eye.

"Well, I'll write Mary about Carl's illness and tell her not to come now. That will cover that."

"You don't need to cover anything, Hester."

Couldn't Hester see what she was doing? She sounded as though Henry could have helped it, as though it were something to be ashamed of. "I can imagine what Hester will say," Henry had said that noon after he heard the other paper. He cared about the way Hester felt. Liz opened her bag nervously, to be doing something, and saw the edge of the glass cup plate.

"Hester, I was in an antique shop and saw one of those little plates that looked like yours. I'm afraid it's an imitation of the old ones, but I thought maybe you could use it somewhere." She didn't care what Hester said about it, how scornful she was, if she would just stop talking about the microcydin. She took it out of her bag and found it had broken where the crack had been.

"How stupid of me. It must have broken against my compact. Well, you can see I meant well." Like Henry's paper, she thought, and tried to laugh as she held the two pieces across the table to Hester. They looked absurdly delicate above the thick mugs and plates.

Hester took the pieces in her long, thin hands and fitted them together. "They copy them awfully well, don't they? Just to glance at it you'd think it was exactly like the ones I have at home, but you can see that the glass is much thicker." She held the larger piece between her forefinger and thumb and snapped the edge. A small perfect sound rang out distinctly, a little louder at first, and tapering down like a pear. She snapped it again as though the perfection of the sound were a mistake. They bent closer to hear it.

"Why, it rings true, Liz!"

"That's strange. I snapped it when I bought it and it didn't. Maybe it was the way I did it. When I got out of the shop, I discovered there was a crack through it and I was sorry I had bought it. It must have broken right through the crack."

"Let me try it," Henry said. His voice was natural again. The plate looked smaller in his big hand. He held it as he did the plates for the culture media.

239

"It looks like a fancy petri plate, Henry," Liz said and then was sorry she had mentioned anything connected with the molds. But it was hard to keep away from them.

Henry snapped the larger fragment and evoked the same perfect drawn-out ring.

"It can't be imitation, Liz," Hester said. "Not and have that genuine ring."

Liz felt absurdly triumphant. It was important that this should be genuine, almost as though it proved that the work Henry had done was genuine too.

"But I should think the antique dealer would have known," Hester said with a shade of annoyance in her tone.

"He didn't. He said it was glass, that was all he could tell about it. Do you suppose that it rings now because there's no crack in the broken piece?"

"I suppose that could be it," Henry said.

"There isn't any point in keeping it now that it's broken," Liz said, but she picked up the two pieces and put them in her bag, knowing that she would keep them always.

"Thank you anyway," Hester said. "It was thoughtful of you to look for it."

When they came out of Pete's Place, the dark was wearing thin. The word PETE's no longer sprang out of space but was tied to the shack by strings of neon tubing running from each letter.

"Let me drive the rest of the way, Hester," Henry said.

"All right. I guess I will get in back and sleep a little," Hester agreed with sudden docility.

Liz sat in front. They drove without talking for fear of disturbing Hester. She wondered how much Henry minded Hester's attitude. His face was stern and his mouth was a tight line. But Hester had written, "I want you to know how much you have meant to me." Then how could she be so unfeeling now? Had she forgotten what she had written him? Now that the microcydin work would be lost and Henry wouldn't make any great mark in the world, Hester was angry, as though Henry had let her down personally. Hester was like Fame, Liz thought with sudden satisfaction. Sometime she would tell Henry that. Hester had flattered him and he had been pleased with the flattery. That was natural enough. She had hurt him too. Fame wasn't reliable. There was a satisfaction in understanding things, in seeing clearly. If you understood them you weren't so easily hurt by them . . . or were you?

Slowly the sky lightened. The little towns along the way came to life. They met cars and early morning trucks coming out from town. Then they came to Pomeroy and took the turn at the corner of Main Street where the sign read "STATE SANITARIUM, 3 miles."

"It's too early for Lester Small to be out," Liz said very softly as they drove across the tracks.

"Yes," Henry murmured. "Nice that plate turned out to be the real thing," he said irrelevantly.

Liz smiled to herself. "Very nice."

POMEROY SENTINEL

Dr. and Mrs. Henry Baker have returned from a Medical Meeting in Chicago where Dr. Baker presented a paper.

Henry went right to the sanitarium with Hester to see Carl. Liz walked over to their cottage. Wednesday night they had left; they had been away Thursday, Friday, Saturday, only three days, and yet it surprised her that nothing had changed.

She came around the Women's Building and noticed how the corner of the two-storied porch kept the early morning sun from reaching their house. The curtainless windows of the room they used for a laboratory gave that side of the house a deserted appearance.

Liz unlocked the door that opened so abruptly into the small living room and went in almost timidly. On the couch lay her gray gloves where she had thrown them when she decided to wear the new ones instead. The card table that they had worked at until so late the night before they left was still set up. The half-used box of typewriter paper lay on it, and a slide that Henry had decided not to use. She took off her coat and hat and threw them over a chair, trying to act as though this were any day and she were completely at home.

She went briskly out to the kitchen and filled the tea-kettle. When Henry came, they would have another cup of coffee. She heard the faint squealing of the guinea pigs in the cellar. Jake had fed them all right. "What if he forgets and they die?" she had said to Henry.

She walked through their bedroom that was always a little dark because of the pine trees outside, and looked in the narrow room that was Nancy's. Nancy would love her new room.

Then Liz crossed the passageway from the kitchen and opened the door to the homemade laboratory. The smell of the molds teased at the membrane of her nose, and she sniffed and felt in her pocket for a handkerchief. She turned the switch and the ten-by-twelve room was bright with light. Automatically she glanced at the thermostat by the door. The molds had to be kept at an even temperature. The indicator of the centigrade thermometer stood at 30 degrees, just as it had when they left, not deviating at all through those days that had changed everything else. By the thermostat hung the pad on which Henry wrote notes and directions for her, but it was blank today. The other rooms in the house needed dusting and straightening, but the lab was still in order. She had mopped the floor herself the afternoon before they left. "Do you suppose doctors will want to come here, Henry, and see the molds?" she had asked the night they left. "They might," Henry had said. "I know I would, once I'd heard about something like this."

She glanced at the rickety autoclave that Henry had bought secondhand with their own money. They called it "The Beast." It was old and hard to open and close, and hissed when the steam was coming up. It gave off a sweetish hot smell that crept out through the whole house and sickened her. Henry had typed out the directions for using it and fastened them on its copper belly with tape so long ago that the paper was discolored and stiff. She read them every time, but she never used The Beast without a little fear. The time she had put a sealed fruit jar filled with liquid in The Beast, the glass had exploded with a horrible noise that shook the whole house. Henry didn't say so, but she knew he couldn't understand why she wouldn't *know* the glass had to be pyrex.

By the sink were the piles of brown paper squares to be tied on the washed bottles before they were sterilized and the lengths of string hanging over a nail. There was the five-gallon earthen jar marked TSP, only she had to say to herself, "tri-sodium phosphate," because the initials looked so smugly secretive. They could sell it back to the sanitarium lab since they wouldn't have any more use for it.

Her glance moved past Henry's microscope and his stool.

"Look here, Liz. Move that screw there till you get it focused for yourself. See the section of guinea pig lung? See how clear it is? Not a sign of tubercles!" Henry had been so excited.

"Henry, that means, . . ." she had said tentatively, pretty excited herself.

"Darn right! That's just what it means," he had answered before she could finish her question. His voice was very quiet. But it hadn't meant anything after all. She looked away from the microscope to the other side of the room where the twenty-five big jars of molds were ranged on shelves.

Liz picked up one of the jars and walked over to hold it against the light. The liquid was cloudy, and grayish-green filaments reached out from the downy surface of the mold itself. Out of habit she grasped the jar tightly at top and bottom and shook it—"agitated it" was the way Henry had put it in his paper—until the contents looked like a strange submarine world where the light threaded through greenish-yellow waves and caught on the tangled fibers of some deep-sea plant. When Nancy was small, she had held the jars down for her to see, only then they had contained the molds Dr. Perth had given Henry.

"Look, Nancy, see Daddy's molds. See how they grow, just like plants in the garden." And later, only a year ago, she had said, "These molds saved your life, Nancy."

She set the jar down sharply on the counter. The noise of the guinea pigs began again, penetrating easily through the floor of the lab. Now that she had been away from them for a while, she heard them every time they squealed.

It was going to be strange not to work in this room any more. She had minded it sometimes. Henry didn't always realize how much time it took to keep the lab spotless and wash and sterilize the plates and jars and pipettes and test tubes. Henry did as much of it as he could, and Miss Symes helped, but only an hour at a time. She had grown tired of being tied down to it, but now that they had been away, she wouldn't mind working here again. They had to keep the door of the lab closed and it was always quiet. She had come to like the order and routine. There was a kind of urgency about the work they did. Everything had to be done at the right time. She had liked working with Henry here.

"Working together holds you together," Kay had said. "I've envied you that." She had never thought about it before, but many husbands and wives didn't work together on anything.

Would it make a difference now if they didn't have this? They worked so well together. Henry was so patient with her lack of knowledge; they had so many jokes over her mistakes. "You're no natural-born bacteriologist, Liz, that's for sure, but you've made yourself into a pretty darn good one," he had said. "Oh, even a moron learns a little after the first ten years of slave labor," she had answered. Over against the wall hung their two lab coats, Henry's a foot longer than hers. The sight of them bothered her this morning. She went over and rummaged for a cigarette in a crumpled pack in the pocket of Henry's coat.

It would hurt Henry to come in here and know there wasn't any use in going on with the molds, that all of it had been pointless. The sight of the molds in their jars would bother him. She wished she had wired Jake or Miss Symes to get rid of them before they came home. It would be so hard for Henry to do. She reached for Henry's ash tray on the ledge back of the microscope and saw the deep burn where he had left his cigarette and been so preoccupied he had forgotten it. The dark brown scar in the wood held her eyes a moment. Then she put out her own cigarette in the ash tray and went quickly to the jars of molds.

She unscrewed the top, sniffing at the strong moldy odor. Under the counter stood the big covered vat where they dumped the refuse, but instead she carried the jar across the hall through the back door to the little garden behind the cottage. Microcydin was a dirt mold, and she would pour it out on the ground and let it go back to the earth. When she held the jar upside down, the liquid came out with an explosive gurgle, carrying with it the soft greenish mold. The liquid ran off into the spring earth, softened by the rain, and left a thin mat of filaments on top of the ground that quickly lost all color and contour.

She went back and got two more jars and carried them out, pouring them on the same spot, adding a few more thread-like filaments to the others. A nurse looked out the window on the second story of the Women's Building and watched Dr. Baker's wife, wondering if she was housecleaning.

Once she had started, Liz didn't stop but went back and forth. There were twenty-five jars. Sixteen, eighteen . . .

She turned the empty jars upside down in the sink and on the counter. . . . Twenty. They had always made her think of her mother's dill pickle jars and the greenish-yellow liquid was like the dill pickle juice. She looked down curiously at the soft, slimy-looking mold and touched it with her finger as it lay like a wet spider's web on the ground. There was hardly enough to fill a single jar when she was through.

The shelves were empty. There was no need now to keep the temperature of the room constant. She leaned on the counter and opened the windows wide to let out the mold smell. The jars were yellowed at the bottom; some of them showed a water mark where the level of the liquid had been. Liz drew hot water and ladled a generous table-spoon of the TSP into the chipped and stained old sink and washed them vigorously with a bottle brush. There was no need to autoclave them.

The bottles more than filled the clothes basket, and she made three trips to the basement, storing them in the fruit closet that never had fruit in it because she had had no time to do any canning.

She went into the heated room of the basement where the guinea pigs were caged. She had always loathed them, in spite of their bright beady eyes and soft clean fur, in spite of Nancy's calling them bunnies. Henry shouldn't have to hear them squeaking either. There were eight of them; you never knew how many there would be. She piled them into the clothes basket, covered them with a blanket, and carried them over to the back door of the sanitarium. They kept guinea pigs in the lab over there too.

"Dr. Baker doesn't need them any more," Liz told Jake, who raised the laboratory animals at the hospital.

247

"I'll fill out a slip, Mrs. Baker; the lab usually pays a dollar a pair."

"We don't want anything for them, Jake. I'm grateful to get rid of them."

Liz went back into the lab and drew the shades halfway and put the microscope in the cupboard out of sight and pushed the stools under the counter. She felt as though someone had died, a child, almost, and she had disposed of its belongings to save Henry the anguish. Now there was nothing more to do. The fresh, rainy air made the room chilly, but she left the windows wide open. Henry would be relieved that he wouldn't have to throw out the molds himself. It would make it a little easier for him. She ripped the sheet of instructions off The Beast for good measure, then she closed the door and went back into the kitchen.

The water had boiled down, but there was enough for a pot of coffee. She poured herself a cup and took it in the other room, but she only drank a few swallows.

The card table would remind Henry of his paper so she folded it up and put it behind the coats in the closet. The wastebasket was full of old papers. One that Henry had crumpled and aimed at the basket had landed under a chair. Liz picked it up and smoothed it out.

"This slide of Lester Small shows amazing recovery in spite of extensive miliary tuberculosis." Later, Henry used only initials. Her eye moved down the page. "The success of this case encouraged us to select a group of cases. . . ." She crumpled the sheet suddenly in her fist and held it against her mouth. Tears ran out from under her tightly closed eyelids.

HERE'S Henry, Carl. I drove over and met them at Binghamton this morning," Hester said as she and Henry came into Carl's room. Caesar followed them and laid his muzzle on the bed, his ears very black against the white spread.

Carl's face was an unhealthy gray color; one side had lost all expression, but his eyes brightened at seeing Henry and he held out his hand.

"Well, Henry, I'm glad you're back."

"Hello, Carl. You didn't behave very well while I was gone," Henry said. He felt the weakness of Carl's grip.

"I should say he didn't, scaring me to pieces!" Hester said.

"I'm not too proud of myself. I'd hoped if I was going to have a heart go bad, it would go the whole way, but you can see I had to have a clot thrown off," Carl said a little more slowly than usual. "Only dispensation I got was that the damned thing missed my speech center, and I can talk with you and keep Hester in order. You can see how things are. Now let's forget about it and talk about you, Henry." It was a long speech. Carl seemed tired.

"Carl, haven't you had your breakfast yet?" Hester interrupted. "It's almost half-past seven."

"No, Hester, I'm in no hurry. I told 'em to take care of the patients on the floor first and I'd sleep a little late."

"But you never do sleep late. You haven't even had any coffee. Honestly, I'm going to tell Dr. Noble that you'd be better off at home where I can take care of you."

"I'll tell you, Hester, you might see if you can find Miss

Hurley. Tell her I'm raising the old Ned down here and I need some coffee." Hester went off in a hurry, relieved to have something to do.

Carl smiled. "It's hard on Hester. She just can't get used to my being laid up for a little. I thought I'd send her on an errand so we could have a few minutes. How did it go, Henry?"

Henry shook his head. "It didn't, Carl. A man by the name of Stockton presented a paper on a dirt mold he called bacteromycin. It's similar to ours but more effective. It worked on the same kind of cases, but it seemed to work in twice as many. They even had better results with their TB cases than we did." Henry was amazed at the calmness with which he could tell it now.

"I'll be damned. I thought you had the field to yourself. I asked Hester last night if she'd seen anything in the papers, but you don't get much out here, of course."

"The bacteromycin made the headlines all right. You're going to see plenty about that." But he felt no bitterness talking with Carl. Already it had become a fact. He sat back in his chair. It was easy to talk to Carl. Carl had never done any original research of his own and had no aspirations along that line, but he understood why you had to carry through with an idea. Most people didn't understand that much.

"It's hard to believe you could find stuff that does as much as we've seen microcydin do and have it not count for anything. You wait a bit, Henry; there may be a place for it yet. You've only tried it on TB."

"No, Carl, I'm afraid not. It's just like the various sulfonamides. There are some of 'em that can cure certain conditions, but they're not practicable to manufacture because others are better. I met a man by the name of Grayson who'd worked on one they had to throw overboard in the end." He thought of telling Carl about the brucellosis and his chance to work with Hanna on it, then he decided not to. It might upset Carl to know he had any thought of leaving here.

"Did you have a chance to talk to this fellow?"

"Grayson?"

"No, the fellow that unearthed the other stuff. Unearthed, that's pretty good, isn't it, considering it's an earth mold?" Carl smiled.

"Stockton," Henry said. "Yes, I had a good talk with him. He went over my findings and showed me where we differed."

"It must have done you good to talk to someone who knew your problems too."

Henry saw Carl's hand go up to the empty pocket of his pajamas. He looked over on the bedside table and a sheepish smile came over his face. "I told Noble I wouldn't smoke right away. Darnedest fool thing I ever promised."

"By the way, Henry, could you get some of this bactero-what's-its-name for us to use here? Mrs. Bailey's still alive, and you remember she didn't respond to microcydin. Maybe we ought to try it on her."

Henry was startled. Carl was eager to try the other if it offered anything for his patients. He hadn't come that far just yet himself.

"Yes, I'm sure I could. I'll write Stockton. It should be an especially interesting test because the microcydin didn't touch her. We might as well throw out the microcydin."

"Not so fast, Henry, not so fast. At least keep your original cultures. You can't tell. You don't know enough about it yet. It's all a brand-new field."

Henry let himself be cheered by Carl's words. He knew that in his heart he had never really accepted the idea of throwing everything overboard. Oh, eventually he probably would, but there was no hurry. He had to send the cultures to Hanna first and hear from him about them. If he left here, of course, he could take them with him. He was suddenly anxious to get over to the lab to see the microcydin. He had been away a long time.

"Hester's set her heart on getting me out of here, Henry; has been for years, and I might as well go some place and lie low for the next three months. But I don't know how much she's going to like toting an invalid. At the end of three months, if I have any luck, my arm and leg ought to be pretty useful again." He was silent a few minutes, considering the other possibility, but he said cheerfully, "Anyway, Henry, I'm not going to think about this place any more. It's yours or will be as soon as the Board meets officially. That's one thing about it, if your microcydin had turned out to be the thing we felt it was, it would have likely taken you away, and you're needed here."

Before Henry had to answer, they heard Hester's voice outside the door.

"Couldn't it be arranged, Miss Hurley, so that Dr. Dalton gets his tray promptly? He's always awake by seven every morning, and I think it's very bad for him to have to wait." Her tone was irritated and imperious.

Miss Hurley's reply was not audible, but when she came in with the tray her cheeks were very pink.

"What were you trying to do, Hurley, starve me?" Carl asked with a wink.

"I'll be back a little later, Carl," Henry said. "I want to stop over at the house and get rehabilitated."

"I'll walk over with you," Hester said. "Good-by, darling, be good!" She patted Carl on the cheek. Carl glowered amiably. Miss Hurley looked down at the tray, but her lips tightened.

"How do you think he looks, Henry?" Hester asked, walking beside him.

"Pretty good for what he's been through," Henry answered cautiously. If he had had only the coronary occlusion, and not that cerebral embolus from it, he thought. "It's going to take quite a while, Hester, before he gets the use of his arm and leg back," he added. He wanted to be rid of Hester now. She had forgotten her anger this morning over the failure of microcydin, but she seemed to have forgotten that there ever was such a thing as microcydin too, and lost all interest in it. He thought how different her attitude was from Carl's.

"You know what I think I'll do, Henry, is to go down to California and find an apartment. Dr. Noble thinks California might be better for him than Baltimore. What do you think?"

"Really, Hester, I've never been either place, so I don't know."

"With you here to take care of Carl, there really isn't any reason why I shouldn't fly out there and have some place all ready for him."

When they came to the cottage, Hester went in with him. "I'll stop just a minute and see Liz," she said.

"Sit down and I'll look for her. She must be around." Henry went in the bedroom and out to the kitchen. "She's made some coffee anyway," he called back.

"Good." Hester came out to the kitchen.

"Liz must have gone in to the lab. I'll just have a look. Help yourself." He crossed the passageway and opened the door, closing it quickly behind him as he always did so the temperature of the room wouldn't be altered.

The cold, fresh air struck him in the face. He saw the windows wide open, the bare shelves where the jars of molds should be. He stood still, hardly breathing. His brain recorded what his eyes saw but made nothing of it: the microscope was gone, there was no sign of the jars, the temperature was down to 20 degrees, even the lab aprons were missing.

Liz must have . . . Liz could never do a thing like that. She had worked with the molds as hard as he had. He glanced hopefully at the pad hanging by the thermostat. It was blank. Then he remembered he had left Hester in the kitchen. He didn't want her in here. He stepped out quickly and closed the door behind him.

"I guess Liz went somewheres," he said vaguely. "Did you find the cream and sugar?"

"I like it clear," Hester said. "You look worse than Carl does, Henry. You better get some sleep."

Henry poured himself a cup of coffee.

"I'm a little tired, that's all. The meetings weren't exactly restful. It's a quarter after eight now; I'll just have time to get cleaned up before I make rounds with Miss Symes," he said, hardly thinking what he was saying.

"I wanted to tell Liz, I've invited the Coopers for dinner tonight. Mrs. Cooper said she didn't believe she had ever met Liz, and Mr. Cooper is anxious to see you, of course. I'll leave Liz a note and tell her to come over when she gets back. I really wish you and Liz would move over to the house right away. I'm going to leave it furnished. There are only a few things I want to take with me." Hester set her cup down on the table. "Where do you suppose Liz went to? Heaven knows, you can't go far in this place. Good-by now. I'm so thankful that you're home."

Henry closed the door after her and went back into the lab. It was true: all the jars of molds were gone. He opened the cupboard and found the microscope. He lifted the cover of the refuse vat. It was empty except for some wads of paper handkerchiefs, some wisps of cotton, and a pile of new squares of brown paper and short lengths of string Liz had cut before she left.

Liz had no right to touch the molds. How would she dare to throw them out?

"At least keep your original cultures," Carl had said. Of course, he had meant to keep them.

His eyes kept going back to the empty shelves as though this time he would see the jars there, the molds growing lustily. Sweat broke out on his forehead. A curious wave of nausea made him put his hand out for the door jamb.

There must be about ten sterile ampules of microcydin in the refrigerator at the sanitarium. They had been using it while he was gone on Mrs. Bailey and Jerry Pyle and those two cases on the men's ward. He remembered saying, "You'll have enough until I get back." But the end product could not reproduce itself. Then his mind came back again to Liz.

Could Liz hate the whole thing so? It couldn't be anybody but Liz. Nobody else would have been in here except Jake, and Jake only needed to go down in the basement and feed the guinea pigs. He listened intently. There was no sound.

He went down to the basement. The guinea pigs were gone. Only a faint smell remained behind. Liz meant to leave no least trace of the microcydin work. She had always hated the guinea pigs' squealing, and she wouldn't hang clothes down here because of the smell. Henry threw open the door of the basement closet. He could see the clean jars shining in the light from the outer room. He touched them and they were still faintly warm.

"I don't believe I could stand to have you start any more research," Liz had said. She was so fed up she couldn't wait to throw out the whole thing. But why wouldn't she tell him what she was going to do? Wouldn't it occur to her that the molds might mean something to him?

He came back upstairs and went again into the empty lab, as though there were no place else to go. Then he noticed some water marks on the floor and traced them to the back door. Liz must have taken the jars outside to empty them. He went outside and down the path, feeling a little hopeless about finding any trace of the molds. They would soon be lost when you poured them out on the ground. But he found them there at the end of the garden, on the tulip bed: an insignificant heap of matted filaments that looked like scum on the top of the ground. Liz must have felt pretty bitter to do a thing like this.

Henry went back into the lab for a clean petri plate and a wooden tongue blade. Kneeling on the ground, he carefully scraped a little of the mold onto the plate. He stopped in the lab only long enough to get a glass cover. Then he carried it over to the sanitarium lab. It would be safe here, he thought savagely. He would raise the microcydin over here. Liz need know nothing about it. If he was going to run the sanitarium, he could certainly do a little work of his own on the side. His fingers shook as he worked. It would take a month to purify a culture for Hanna.

"I'm going to need a corner of the lab over here, Miss Keeler," he told the laboratory technician firmly, "for some special work. I'd like you to see that nothing on these shelves is disturbed. I . . . I shall run some tests myself, from time to time," he added.

LIZ had gone over to the sanitarium for provisions; they had to go on living.

She took a pencil and made a list: bread, butter, eggs, some kind of meat. She wondered if Henry would have any appetite tonight. It would be better for him to come home while she was away, to go into the lab alone. When she saw him, she would be very casual about it, the way they were about Nancy's deafness. That would be easiest for him.

As the housekeeper checked her order, she said, "I guess your husband will be the head of the sanitarium now."

"For a time, while Dr. Dalton is sick," Liz said.

"It's too bad about Dr. Dalton. My, he's been a wonderful superintendent."

"Maybe he'll get well quickly."

The housekeeper shook her head. "No, he won't be back. But such a jolly man and so fair about the contracts; you know, eggs and milk and all that."

Liz wondered how Henry would be as superintendent. Would he like all the details of housekeeping? But he had seemed relieved about the opening. "It comes at the right time for us, just now," he had said.

She took the long way round instead of the short cut. The three units of the sanitarium looked a little like college buildings grouped around a campus, she told herself. In the summer they were covered with ivy. You saw a place differently when you thought of leaving it. She had

257

gone about all last week feeling that they were through with this place. Now they were going to live here and she must look at it in a new way.

She stepped off the walk onto the ground that was only faintly green and went as far as the beech tree. From there she could look across to the Daltons'. It would take a little while to make it theirs. After Hester and Carl had gone away and after Nancy was home, running in and out of the house, then it would belong to them. They would live pleasantly there. She would make an entirely different life, a more gracious life. There had never been time to have friends for dinner, to sit on the porch in the afternoon and talk and laugh. She had hardly known what to talk about with Alice and Charlotte and Kay.

She would lie in the swing under the awning and read. When Henry was through at the sanitarium . . . Carl used to finish around four in the afternoon . . . he would come walking across the lawn and sit on the porch too.

"Where's Nancy?" Henry would ask.

And she would say, "She's playing tennis at the country club. I thought we could drive over and have dinner there."

"Fine," Henry would say. "I'll just tell Brown"—or Smith, or Green, whatever the young assistant's name was—"that we'll be gone for a few hours." They would really have time to live, like other people.

The rain had stopped, but the air was still raw. The smell of the molds should be out of the lab by now. The earth in the big round flower beds on the sanitarium lawn was cracked and the tips of two red buds showed through the black dirt. What a tiny little heap the molds had made when she poured them out on the ground. They looked like nothing at all, yet they still seemed living. She wished she had covered them up so there would be no trace left.

Tomorrow she would spade the little heap into the earth and give them decent burial.

She wondered if Henry would be in the lab when she got back. He always went there before he did anything else. He would just stand and look at everything and think of all he had hoped would come out of it. He couldn't help but remember the day the mold had killed the germs on the agar plate. They had had that thrill anyway. They hadn't told anybody, not even Carl, for several days; they had had it all to themselves. That was what they had hoped and worked for, but when it really happened, it had seemed a miracle.

Liz stood outside the ordinary little bungalow and wondered that it could look unchanged in spite of all the living they had done there and the brave wild dream they had had there. Well, it was empty enough now. After they moved, she wouldn't pass it very often, she would go around the other way.

"Henry," she called as she opened the front door. She went as far as the kitchen and saw by the cups that he had been home. Hester must have come too. There was lipstick on one cup. She was glad she hadn't been here. The door of the lab was closed. She had never knocked before, but now she rapped on it with sudden hesitancy. Then she turned the knob and went in.

The room was just as she had left it. She was disappointed that Henry hadn't left any note on the pad by the thermostat saying when he would be back. She picked up the pencil that hung beside it and wrote *finis* and underlined it.

The smell of the molds wasn't gone. The dampness in the air seemed to make it linger more heavily than ever. She closed the door and went back through the house.

She found Hester's note on the table. It sounded like

Hester, Liz thought as she read it: "Come over when you get back. Plan to sleep there tonight, Hester." But she was in no hurry to go, and she certainly wouldn't sleep there tonight. Hester had been so stupid about the microcydin and she had hurt Henry. Fame was a good name for her: the strumpet Fame, the fickle jade. She amused herself thinking of epithets.

It was so late now Henry must be staying over at the sanitarium for lunch. He wouldn't be spending his noon hours working in the lab any more. Their days were going to be so different now. She would have time on her hands, like Alice and Charlotte and Kay.

The emptiness of the lab seemed to spread through the whole house and give it a lonely feeling. She sniffed and imagined that she still smelled the molds.

Henry had brought over the bags, and she carried them into the bedroom and opened one on a chair, but the wrinkled clothes that she had packed so carefully for the Medical Meeting repelled her. Maybe she would feel better if she slept awhile; she had had her clothes on since yesterday morning.

It was five o'clock before Henry left the sanitarium. There had been so much to do. Carl had been sick since Thursday, and Dr. Noble had only seen a couple of the very sick ones.

The patients had seemed glad to see him. He told Mrs. Bailey they might have something new to try on her. She did so much better when she had something to count on. When the microcydin hadn't worked, she had lost all appetite and turned her face to the wall. He had been glad about the bacteromycin while he was telling her about it. "Some doctors have found a new drug, Mrs. Bailey, that has given some wonderful results." Her eyes had brightened and she had sat up a little in bed. The nurse on Mrs. Bailey's wing told him that Mrs. Bailey played a record on the record player by her bed this afternoon.

Jerry Pyle showed marked improvement on microcydin. He hadn't put him in the paper because he had only started him the first of the week. It was a lucky thing that he had made up so many ampules before he left. When they were gone . . . It would take too long to make more from the spores he had rescued. The thing to do was to write Stockton. No, better wire him and ask for a supply of bacteromycin. A week ago he had thought others might be wiring him for microcydin.

He had to see two new patients who had been admitted. One was a child who had taken a good deal of time. She was frightened and clung to her mother, but she seemed happy before he left her. The other was a man, just his age: a teacher in high school. Perhaps he had given him more hope than he had any right to, but the poor fellow could do with it.

Seeing patients again had done him good. After all, it was trying to find something to help patients that had started him off in the first place, to prevent people dying as his own mother had died. If bacteromycin did it, it didn't matter about the microcydin, except for his own satisfaction, he told himself sternly.

There wasn't going to be much time to do anything but take care of patients and run the sanitarium, judging by today. Of course, the X-rays had piled up while he had been away; they had taken more time than they usually would. The X-rays had made him think of reading Bill's plate.

The desk work was going to be painful for him. He could never get anything done in that office of Carl's with Miss Connors running in with her memorandum pad.

"We're running low on history forms, Doctor. Would you just sign this order for the printer?"

"And Miss Siegel is getting married. I got out the applications that we have on file. We ought to get someone right away so she can work with Miss Siegel a couple of weeks."

And just as he was leaving, Miss Connors followed him out to the hall. "Dr. Baker, you won't forget that the bids for supplying coal next fall will have to be opened tomorrow."

"Yes, thank you, Miss Connors, I'll attend to that the first thing in the morning." Tomorrow at eight he had to see the housekeeper, and the dietitian at nine. The maintenance man was coming to see him at ten. He couldn't make rounds till eleven then. Carl often left the rounds to him and didn't make them at all. He had thought it was disinterest, that Carl was just easygoing. He hadn't realized all that Carl had to take care of. Hester ought to get an idea of one of Carl's days. She might be more impressed with what he accomplished.

Maybe it would look better tomorrow, but right now, coming back home, he wondered if he could stand it here, year in, year out. If he took this, and everyone assumed he would, then he was definitely committed to sanitarium work for the rest of his life. There wouldn't be another opportunity like the one with Hanna.

The three sanitarium buildings made a triangle on the grounds. The Men's Unit and the Women's Unit stood side by side, yet were as much apart as a convent and a monastery, and both knew as much or more of the renunciation of the flesh than many sacred orders. Next to the Women's Unit stood the Children's Unit. In summer the women lay on their beds and watched the children playing out in front. He had to move Mrs. Daniels to the other side of the building because the children upset her so badly.

After the rain the air was chilly, but a last edge of sun touched the brick buildings. They looked stark until the ivy leafed out. Some days, he went from building to building with his mind so occupied with his work that he never looked around him. He would have to train himself to see the physical aspects of the sanitarium and notice everything from the grounds to the gutters. He stood at the end of his walk before going in, looking across the slope of lawn at the three units and the laundry and power house behind them, and beyond these, to the fields owned by the sanitarium. This was going to be his world. It hadn't been before. He had merely lived here while he worked on the mold.

The house was quiet. Liz was asleep or over at Hester's. He stepped softly through the living room and went, for no reason at all, into the lab. There were a few things he would move over to the sanitarium lab tomorrow: his microscope and his dissecting set and his apron, if Liz hadn't thrown it out. They could sell The Beast. Liz would be glad to see it go. She had ripped off the sheet of directions, he noticed. But then, she would be glad to see it all go. What little work he had to do could be done in the sanitarium lab, he supposed, but he hated to give up this room.

There wasn't any sense of time in this room, or rather, there was all the time in the world. He never felt hurried here. He had worked till morning when he needed to, as though there were no niggardly limit to his time nor to his strength. Sometimes Liz was here, sometimes he was alone, with the microcydin. In this bare little room he had forgotten everything but the work. He had been as thoughtless of his wife and his financial welfare as though his microcydin had been a mistress, he thought grimly. In spite of all her loyal help, it had been too much to take for granted that Liz shared his feeling for the work. It was too separate a feeling to share with anyone. He glanced over at the empty shelves with an acute sensation of emptiness in himself. Then he saw the word on the pad in Liz's handwriting:

finis

It hit him between the eyes. Good God, she didn't need to rub it in. He tore the sheet off the pad because he couldn't bear to let it stand. Liz must have hated the lab, hated the whole thing, to dump out the molds and get rid of the guinea pigs so fast. She hated it because of Nancy's deafness. He would like to work with Hanna long enough to *prove* that microcydin, with or without the sulfas, had saved Nancy's life. This morning, driving home in the car, Liz had seemed all right; he had felt they were together again. But all that time she must have been brooding over what he had done to Nancy.

Henry stood with his hands in his pockets, staring out the window. Within his vision lay the part of the garden where Liz had dumped the molds, but he didn't see it. He was thinking about Liz. He thought of her with her sleeves rolled up and a lab coat on over her slacks, sniffing over the smell of the molds and singing some silly song. Or standing with her hands on her hips, sputtering at The Beast; or running to answer the phone from the sanitarium to give him time to finish transplanting a culture. And all of it she had done for him.

He remembered the time after they had given up Perth's molds, when he brought in the dirt mold. She had watched him separating the colonies under the microscope, not saying a word until he was through. Then she had said, "You're starting in all over again?"

"Well, yes," he had admitted. "I'd just like to see what I can get from this."

She had put her hands behind his head and brought his face very near to hers. "Henry Baker, I think you're crazy, utterly and stubbornly crazy, but I love you. I'll even help you with the pesky things."

An exclamation caught in his throat. He went out of the lab and closed the door. He didn't blame Liz. He didn't wonder that she had thrown the stuff out and written *finis*. He ought to be able to stand Carl's job, coal bids and order blanks and all. She had taken enough.

He went back through the house to find her. He saw the unpacked suitcase and her clothes heaped on a chair. She must have started to unpack and been too tired to finish. The thin spring twilight shadowed her face and darkened her hair against the pillow. One hand lay under her cheek. She looked worn out, almost ill.

"Liz," he said. "Liz!" He felt he had been calling to her all day, across his disappointment that was more acute now that he was back here again, across Hester's shrill yapping and his own indecision.

She stirred and turned away from the light. He lay down beside her, his body curved against hers. Her hair was against his face, and he smoothed it down and touched her head with his lips. For a little, it was comfort enough to feel her so close to him. Then he tightened his arm around her.

"Liz," he said softly.

She woke and turned toward him. He buried his head in the slight hollow of her shoulder, and his hands affirmed the curve of her breast and hip, the warm, live flesh that he knew so well yet always had to discover again. Then he raised his head and found her lips.

"I didn't know that you'd come, Henry, and I was so tired I went to sleep."

"I know. You looked tired out," he whispered. "Oh, Liz, you don't know how I love you."

They clung together as though they had been separated a long time.

Why had he ever imagined that he was through with this part of life? The throb of his blood was never stronger; it was so loud in his own ears that it blocked out his tortured thoughts, it was a rushing tide that carried him with it.

"Liz!" he said, but with a triumphant note that broke between laughter and a sob.

She reached up and held his head between her hands.

Why had she been frightened the other night when their bodies failed them, and stood coldly outside their trouble and called them both pathetic? She had been as foolish as she was in the beginning when she was afraid that the strange ways of love could be ugly or hurt. Now, for the understanding moment, she was any woman feeling a man's hands and his heart beating above hers, bearing his weight so lightly, answering and sharing his need.

There was a wind in her ears, but it wasn't a cold wind. It rocked her in the willow tree above the deep brown running water of the brook.

"Henry," she answered, and her voice had a lilt in it. The wind died and the tree was still. The water of the brook ran quietly in the sun.

He was almost asleep when Liz said softly, "Henry, you had to give the microcydin to Nancy. I knew it, really, but I didn't let myself admit it. I know it saved her life." She said it like a confession of faith.

"You're good to tell me that, Liz," Henry said humbly.

"No, I'm not. I'm not much without you."

"Nor I without you."

The phone woke them. Hester's voice was at the other end of the line. "Henry, the Coopers are here. Will you be over right away?"

"Oh, yes, Hester. We'll be there in a few minutes."

"Where, Henry? Do you have to go to the hospital?" Liz asked as she had a hundred times before.

Henry lay back on the pillow. His voice was young and laughter interlined it. "Hester's having the Coopers for dinner to meet us. In fact, they're there now, waiting for us."

"But, Henry!" Liz sat up in bed, pushing back her hair.

"As wife of the new head of the sanitarium, Mrs. Baker, it behooves you to step on it."

"Henry, I could shake you. Why didn't you tell me?" Liz was out of bed.

Henry still lay on his back, his arms behind his head. His first sense of well-being was slipping away from him. A sense of depression, of some lack, almost of impending calamity crept over him. He waited, testing it out.

"Henry, it's seven o'clock. You'll have to hurry."

THEY had gone up the front steps of the Daltons' house so many times in these years, but never like this, Liz thought, never thinking this will be our home. They might never ring the doorbell again since it would be their house and they would have the key.

"I'm sorry to be late, Hester," Henry said at once. "I had quite a bit to catch up on. There were some things I couldn't leave."

"Of course, Henry, I know." Hester touched his arm in understanding.

Liz took her coat off in the little room at the left of the hall and Hester came with her. "The Coopers are deadly," she murmured. Her face changed quickly, expressing how deadly by a rolling of the eyeballs, a dropping of the eyelids, a quick movement of the lips. "But, my dear, very important to you at the moment." Then, slipping her arm through Liz's as they went into the living room, she said, "Mrs. Cooper, you are meeting Liz Baker at just the right moment, with the sparkle of the city still on her. You've met Dr. Baker, already, I see."

Liz felt at once unsparkling, dull. She smiled at Mrs. Cooper, who was large and placid and imposing in a "good" black dress. A drift of powder grayed the edge of the V neck. Above a full face the hair was brushed into a roll that had the uncompromising firmness of a bolster. Mr. Cooper was, perhaps, the same height as his wife, but his sparse sandy hair lay flat on his round head so that he seemed shorter. His double-breasted blue serge suit fitted tightly over his plump form. He was busy now buttoning the jacket as he stood up. His quick, bright eyes looked at Liz very directly, suspecting at once, she felt, that she had been asleep in Henry's arms when the phone rang.

"Dr. Baker, you've come back to a big responsibility," he said to Henry.

"Yes," Henry said, "I realize that."

Liz sat down on the deep couch beside Mrs. Cooper and wished she had taken a chair instead. Mrs. Cooper seemed to loom over her. Caesar came up and smelled her skirt and shoes with great attention. Mrs. Cooper clearly did not care for dogs and pulled her feet in close to the couch.

"Don't you touch my stockings!" she said, shaking her finger at the dog.

Hester came back in with Old-fashioneds for all of them but Mrs. Cooper, whose untouched glass sat beside her on the table.

Liz found herself waiting for Hester to cross the room to the Savonarola chair at one side of the fireplace. She watched her settle herself with one knee over the other, her skirt falling gracefully to the ankle. Hester leaned on one elbow, listening to Mrs. Cooper but looking as though she would speak some lines from Shakespeare. Caesar left Liz and walked over to lie at Hester's feet as though to say, "I have smelled and drawn my own conclusions." Liz wondered if Hester would leave the throne chair in the house, if she could ever sit in it without feeling like Hester.

"How is your daughter, Mrs. Baker? I remember when she was so sick," Mrs. Cooper said.

"Oh, she's fine, thank you," Liz answered. "She's away at school just now and liking it so much."

"A school for the deaf? Of course, that makes a difference. I never wanted my children to go away until they had to go to college," Mrs. Cooper stated a little proudly.

"It is hard to let them go," Liz said, trying to keep her voice calm.

"Mrs. Cooper, you'll have to see that Liz makes some friends in Pomeroy. She's been so busy here that she hasn't had a chance to meet many people."

Why would Hester do that? Mrs. Cooper couldn't know anyone whom she would enjoy. Then Liz saw the gleam of amusement in Hester's eyes.

"How long have you been here at the sanitarium, Mrs. Baker? I've lost track, though I hear Mr. Cooper speak of your husband now and then."

Liz laughed a little. "We came twelve years ago this next summer" . . . "The groundwork of this study was begun twelve years ago" . . . "But, as Hester says, I have been quite busy." It sounded like no explanation at all.

"Dr. Dalton told me that you went to this Medical Meeting to present the results of your research, Dr. Baker?" Mr. Cooper asked.

"Yes," Henry answered and waited.

"Well, how did you get along? What did it amount to?" Mr. Cooper went right to the heart of the matter.

Liz looked down in her glass, waiting to hear what Henry said. What could he say that wouldn't put Mr. Cooper off? Why should he have to answer to him? He was so slow in answering.

Henry held back the frank answer that came to his lips. He thought of Carl saying, "You don't want to anger him, Henry. He's head of the Board, you know." Liz wanted to stay here. He had to have this position for her sake. Mr. Cooper wouldn't take kindly to failure.

"My work here added to the knowledge of antibiotics in combating disease," he said quietly. "Dr. Stockton, who is Allerbee Research Professor, expressed his amazement that a piece of original research like this was carried out at a state sanitarium. Of course, the work couldn't have been done if the Board hadn't been helpful, or if you, as chairman, had not been tolerant."

Mr. Cooper nodded. "Well, there have been some questions and criticisms. After all, it's the state's money, but as I told Dalton, I said, we've got to stretch a point now and then. Something worth while just might come of it and give some publicity to the sanitarium."

"I certainly appreciate that," Henry said, lighting his cigarette. He saw Hester's narrowed amused eyes, the tilt of her head. You might get good at this game eventually, he thought bitterly, telling the Coopers only as much of the whole truth as they would be pleased with. He glanced at Liz. She was smiling at him, as though she were pleased with him. She wanted him to do well with Mr. Cooper because he was head of the Board.

"Of course, Dr. Baker, the Board won't want you to go on with this research work now that you're superintendent," Mr. Cooper said. "They feel that you need to put in all your time on the sanitarium work. I might as well tell you frankly, that was the only question when the Board voted on your appointment."

"I imagined that would be the feeling," Henry said. Now that you are superintendent you must put away your childish toys, Mr. Cooper was saying.

Liz looked over at him quickly, but Henry's face told her nothing.

"Dr. Baker, I wonder if you could come and speak to our University Women's group in May? We had a speaker on penicillin and the women were just awfully interested; it really went over better than the review of a novel we had the week before. We would class your talk under Advances in Science."

Henry put out his cigarette before he answered. "I'm

sorry, Mrs. Cooper, but it is still too early to present this before a lay group. You and Mr. Cooper are among the very few who have heard of it." It was surprisingly easy, once you got the idea. Mrs. Cooper looked impressed and pleased. Mr. Cooper's face assumed a portentous expression.

"What did you say the name of the drug is, Doctor?" Mr. Cooper asked.

With hardly a pause Henry said, "Bacteromycin is the name of the drug the public will come to know. The substance we produced here was a different mold that we called microcydin." He had told the truth, and yet the inference was that they were part and parcel of each other. But weren't they? Weren't they both dirt molds, derived in the same way? Yes, but they were different, as different as his way of thinking from Mr. Cooper's.

"Ah, yes," Mr. Cooper said, as though already familiar with it.

"And this new drug will cure tuberculosis. I think that's just wonderful!" Mrs. Cooper exclaimed.

Liz looked at the wrinkle that hadn't shaken completely out of her dress. She smoothed it nervously without looking at Henry. Why did he try so hard? He sounded so careful, almost deferential. He had let them think . . . it wasn't like Henry.

"Unfortunately, we can't say that bacteromycin cures tuberculosis just like that, Mrs. Cooper," Henry said gently. The gentleness was ominous. "It is in an experimental stage. No one can say with finality just what it can and cannot do. It has cured certain kinds of tuberculosis, just as microcydin has."

Mrs. Plew appeared in the doorway and announced dinner. Hester nodded from her throne. Caesar rose at once and stood waiting, his long whip-tail waving slightly.

Liz wished they could go home without waiting for dinner. She glanced at Henry. His eyes were stormy. She couldn't understand why he bothered to please the Coopers if it meant being not quite frank. He must want this place so badly. On the way in to dinner she was beside him for a minute. He looked at her without smiling.

The dark green cloth was on the table just as it had been last Wednesday night, but there were yellow tulips instead of calla lilies. The genuine Henry Clay cup plates were at each place for ash trays. Liz noticed that Henry was looking at his. She had an insane desire to say, "Snap it, Henry. See if it rings true."

There was no wine tonight, and the meat was a pot roast with canned peas and canned peaches. Only the salad saved the meal from dullness.

"Now this is all furnished by the sanitarium?" Mrs. Cooper asked, chewing a morsel of the beef. "The reason I ask is that so many women tell me the patients complain about the food at the sanitarium, and I like to tell them that I've eaten here and you have the very same food and I've always thought it was delicious."

"Yes," Hester said, "good wholesome food, isn't it?"

"It really is," Mrs. Cooper agreed. "Well, it should be. Mr. Cooper says the Board approves only contracts with the best concerns in town."

Hester let her glance reach Liz before she dropped her eyelids and quirked her mouth for an almost imperceptible instant.

Again the cold wind blew in on Liz. She had run away from the cold wind to the fire, but not this fire. She wouldn't like this life of pretending pleasure with anything the Board gave. How free she had been from all this over in the cottage. They hadn't had to bother with dinners with Board members. How much fun it had been to eat quickly at the kitchen table so Henry could get to work in the lab. He was so near, just across the hall from her, while she did the dishes and picked up the kitchen. They had had their own fire and it had warmed them through.

"Mr. Whitney, who is on our Board, has a nephew who is finishing his internship in July and would like to come here as assistant. I told him I thought there was a good possibility that it could be arranged. If, of course, his qualifications seem satisfactory," Mr. Cooper added, seeing the slight frown on Henry's face.

"I think that we should consider more than one applicant," Henry said. "And decide entirely on the basis of qualifications and recommendations."

This is what it would be like, Henry thought, always having to consider the Board and explain every move. He wondered if he could do a really good piece of work here. He would hate it. It might be better to go out into private practice. Liz might have to take a job for a year or so to help out. She had substituted in the grade school in Woodstock.

"Let's see, you're forty, aren't you, Dr. Baker?" Mr. Cooper asked, pushing his plate a little ways from him to make room for his salad.

"Yes," Henry said. Yes, he was. Forty was a little old to start into private practice. He didn't have his Boards. His only specialty was tuberculosis. Henry Baker, M.D. Practice limited to diseases of the lungs. That meant a city, a pretty good-sized city. With living as it was . . . Liz and Nancy could go to her family for a year. But Liz wouldn't like that. He wouldn't either.

"Then I should say that this nephew of Whitney's would be about right for an assistant; he's twenty-seven," Mr. Cooper continued.

274

Henry glanced at Liz. The light shone on her hair and her color was high in her face. She looked as though she were happy. She and Nancy would enjoy living here. He couldn't snatch it away from them.

The telephone rang, and Caesar started up from the floor, his toenails clacking like shell against the hard wood. Mrs. Plew put her head around the swing door to say, "Dr. Baker, you're wanted."

Henry went gratefully to the phone in the pantry. He was glad to get out of the dining room.

"A wire; yes." Automatically he took out his pencil and wrote the message on the pad.

> Necessary to know at once if you are interested in work on project. Begin July first. Can offer three thousand. Reply requested.
>
> J. C. Hanna.

Henry stood leaning against the counter after he had hung up. Mrs. Plew going back and forth with the dessert looked at him curiously. He stood with his head on one hand, staring down at the pad.

"The dessert's on," she told him, the last time she came by.

"Thank you. I have to answer this message first. Ask them not to wait for me, please, Mrs. Plew."

Mrs. Plew nodded, wondering if he were liverish, he looked so sallow.

The Curies, Laennec, Koch, any of them would take it in a minute, he told himself. "Identification with the myth, that's called in my lingo," Paul had said. There may have been a time when it was true, but he was so far beyond that now. All he cared about now was the chance to go on working with some of these things, finding out. . . . Henry made a series of sharp black lines on the pad, one under the other. He would get a chance to test microcydin more thoroughly and to work with bacteromycin; it began not to matter which it was. All that field was opening up. He had a right to be working in it. Liz could understand that. Liz would do anything he wanted to do.

But that was just it. He had no right to go on letting her live on a pittance. It would mean taking a couple of rooms and keeping their living as cheap as they could. Liz was thirty-eight. It wouldn't be the lark it had been at twenty-two.

And if he did take this, then what? Next year the grant might not be continued, or be cut. He would have no safe berth, no capital. He would be a skilled laboratory worker, a research worker. There would be no security . . . except the security of his own mind.

The work didn't need him. He couldn't tell himself that. The work was safe; it would be done without him. He had offered his bit and that bit was interesting, not of great importance, to be sure, but interesting in the study of molds. And Nancy's recovery had indicated a possible method for treating brucellosis; it should work all the better with bacteromycin. That was all Science asked of him; now he could go back to running a sanitarium, and if he had learned the excitement of original investigative work, he could forget it now, the sooner the better.

"I don't think I could stand to have you start any more research," Liz had said.

Henry wrote on the telephone pad, "Obligated to take sanitarium superintendency. Greatly appreciate your offer and deeply regret inability to accept." It was awkward, but it would have to do. He took the receiver off the hook, but he held the hook down with his finger a minute. Then he replaced the receiver and put the wire he had copied and his answer in his pocket. He could just as well send it tonight from the office at the sanitarium when he went over to see Carl. He went back into the dining room.

All four faces turned toward him. He saw each one separately: Hester's amused, a little patronizing now; Mr. Cooper's sharply curious; Mrs. Cooper's interested in this manifestation of a doctor's life; Liz's anxious.

"It's a good thing we have a cold dessert, Henry," Hester said. "A soufflé would have been a tragedy by now."

"I'm sorry. That was a lengthy conversation," he said.

Mrs. Plew's lips tightened. She knew different. He didn't do any talking hardly at all, mostly just stood there in the pantry, holding his head on his hand. He was sick if you asked her.

Liz felt better now that Henry was back in the room. She had begun to be uneasy when he stayed away so long. Just for a minute, as he came through the door, she had thought he was pale, but now he looked all right.

Mr. Cooper had been telling about his trip to Washington, and she had been free to sit back and try to think what it would be like when they lived here. She would sit in Hester's place, and they would have the Coopers to dinner sometime. She would have the whole Board as Hester did, once a year, with a ham on the sideboard and potato salad and ice cream and cake.

Hester pushed back her chair, and Caesar rose with her, fanning his tail slowly back and forth. Liz thought how different it had been last Wednesday night when they left this table. Then there had been the excitement of going away, of Henry's paper. She had felt so free from Hester's amused scorn. Now there was no excitement, and she could never live here without feeling Hester's presence.

"We'll have our coffee in the other room," Hester said. She seated herself in the Savonarola chair and Mrs. Plew brought the coffee tray. Caesar lay beside her chair, nose against the floor to catch some breath of air from under the crack of the door.

"Henry," Hester said, "would you stir up the fire? You might as well learn the ways of that draft, it will be all yours to struggle with."

"The fire's pretty well died out. I think I'll have to start from the ground up," Henry said.

Liz looked at Henry quickly, but he was busy with the fire. She noticed how few remarks Hester had addressed to Henry. Usually she appropriated him, but tonight she had a patronizing air toward him. Hester seemed amused and aloof from all of them. She was leaving this place to her, Liz felt, as a woman gives away an old hat, a dress that is too short. "I can't use it any longer, but it may do well enough for you," she seemed to be saying.

"How do you take your coffee, Mrs. Cooper?" Hester asked.

"Both, please, and Mr. Cooper takes plenty of sweetening in his," Mrs. Cooper answered.

"Liz, I wanted you to come over this afternoon so I could show you around the house. I'm leaving tomorrow, but maybe there'll be time in the morning. You and Henry will sleep here tonight, won't you?"

"Oh, Hester, I really think we better wait till tomorrow night anyway." Hester was rushing her into this. And why didn't she say no more firmly?

"The only thing is, I'm so nervous with Carl away that I don't sleep. Even with Caesar here. I had Mrs. Plew make up the beds for you."

So Hester was only a timid child after all, afraid of a cold wind too. "Of course, if you would feel better," Liz said.

Henry took his coffee from Hester and went over to sit in Carl's chair. Suddenly Liz didn't want Henry to settle down in that chair. It wasn't the place for Henry. The sanitarium wasn't the place for him unless he was working on something of his own. But she couldn't say that to him. She couldn't say, go on with your research, Henry; go on working harder than you have time or strength for, even though nobody thinks it's worth doing, even though you may be disappointed again. That's your very life; it's our life. She couldn't say it because a fear rose in her mind, the kind of fear she had never known before. Perhaps Henry *wanted* this kind of life now. Perhaps he wanted this place because of the security it offered; but it couldn't be that. They had managed on so little money all these years and been happy doing it. Perhaps he was tired of working and working and not having it amount to anything in the end. Perhaps he wasn't even interested any more. . . .

Henry sat back in Carl's chair as though he were entirely comfortable.

"Did you enjoy the Medical Meeting, Mrs. Baker?" Mr. Cooper asked, sitting down beside her.

"Yes, thank you, very much," Liz said.

"Well, I'll tell you something the Board of the sanitarium just did at their last meeting," Mr. Cooper said, as though he were divulging a piece of great news. "They voted to set aside a sum to pay the expenses of the superintendent to two meetings a year, one in the fall and one in the spring. Of course, one of those will be a meeting of heads of sanitariums. So your husband's expenses will all be paid. All you'll have to do is work on him to pay yours and you'll be stepping off to the Medical Meeting in the fall. Isn't that pretty nice?"

"Yes, that is nice of the Board," Liz said slowly. Then she sat up very straight. "Of course, Henry won't have anything to present that soon, but he will need to talk to the men who are doing the same kind of research that he is." She glanced over at Henry and met his eyes.

Mr. Cooper looked at her as though he were seeing her for the first time. His mouth compressed into a firm line. He might as well get this matter clear at the start. A man like Carl Dalton was more to his liking anyway; this young man had too many ideas, and his wife was a determined little piece.

"Did you and Dr. Dalton use to like going to those meetings?" Mrs. Cooper asked Hester quickly. She could tell that R.D. was upset.

"Oh, we were both crazy about them!" Hester said.

Henry left his chair and carried his coffee cup back to the tray. "The meetings serve a purpose," he said. "I want to stop over and see Carl before it gets any later, Hester, if you'll excuse me. I'll bring over the bags we took with us?" he said to Liz, but he made it a question.

"Yes. We'll sleep over here if Hester is timid about staying alone. It really doesn't make any difference," Liz said.

The threat of this house, of mediocrity, Hester's scorn, the Coopers' disapproval were only part of that wind that had frightened her long ago, when she was still a child.

Hester went to the door with Henry to talk with him about Carl.

"I think I'll move nearer to the fire," Liz said. She crossed the room and sat in the Savonarola chair.

"I always think that's such an odd-looking chair," Mrs. Cooper said nervously. She was glad that young man left before R.D. said anything to him. He was getting ready to.

"It's an interesting chair, isn't it? But I wouldn't want to settle down in it for any length of time," Liz said.